UNEXPECTED REWARDS

BY JANE MCGARRY

To Barbara, Jodi and Irene for being the light in my darkest time.

There must be some mistake. For a split second, I am sure my ears simply misheard what was said. In this fleeting moment filled with warmth and promise, life will still be fine. But then, my heart drops like a stone when the sinking realization dawns on me. I do not misunderstand.

Not. At. All.

Stupefied, I almost blurt out an obscenity. Not a good idea given where I currently stand. In front of me, King William sits with the rest of the royal family. Behind me, the full assemblage of the court, my family, and just about every citizen of Adelina, my home city watch expectantly. It takes all my self-control to keep the disappointment from erupting into a tirade of screams and protests.

Thankful. That is how I should feel. After all, not every citizen is fortunate enough to be honored by the king with a special reward; however, *thankful* is the last word I would use to describe my current state of mind. How did I end up so utterly blindsided?

Today had started with such promise. My family and I were scheduled to attend this very ceremony—one meant to honor my father and his men for the protection of the king during a recent attempt on his life by Lord Otto, the usurper of Lindenwood. The presentation of the men had gone off without a hitch only a few minutes ago. They had made quite a showing, marching in presentation past the king in all their splendor, armor shining and lances gleaming. King William had thoroughly praised them, then promoted the class of squires who partook in the mission to knighthood, noting their bravery and valor. All but two squires, I would like to point out—Puck and myself. Puck since he did not participate. How could he when I drugged him to take his place? And me, well, because I am a girl, of course. Even though I *did* participate in the mission, and arguably played the most pivotal role in King William's rescue, apparently it was not enough to overcome the bias against my gender. Men, as always, control my fate.

My mother and sisters have been in quite the tizz these past few weeks over the excitement of attending this ceremony. Planning of dresses, jewelry, and hair has been the topmost discussion among them. We made a special trip to the clothier to select the perfect outfit for everyone, right down to my four-year-old sister, Lydia. For once, extra special attention was paid to me, since I would be representing the family in front of the entire kingdom. Anne, my older sister, whose life seems to revolve around these trivialities, took over all the major decision making for me. And, I must say, she did a spectacular job.

This very morning she spent hours alone on my hair, a big concern since I had hacked most of it off a couple weeks ago to disguise myself as Puck. At the time, cutting neatly and carefully had not been my top priority, so I ended up with a choppy, uneven mess on the top of my head. Anne had wrapped the unruly mop into cloth curlers last night, and today had painstakingly coaxed the curls into a beautiful updo interwoven with baby's breath. Then, she set about dusting my face with various powders, balms, and kohls. Finally, it was time for the dress, the one she had deemed perfect for the occasion. Sky-blue satin soon engulfed me, pooling around my feet on the floor. After much tugging and arranging, Anne stepped back and let me look at her creation in the mirror.

I gasped at the person reflected back at me. Never in my life had I looked like this—so feminine and beautiful, so like a girl, or, more accurately, a woman. My eyes swept over the top half of my breasts popping out of the low-scooped bodice.

"Anne, I can't wear this. It is obscene," I complained, covering the cleavage with my hand, yet marveling a bit at the enhancement provided by the dress.

"I knew you were going to say that. It's the style now, Miss Modesty," Anne muttered, but she pulled a light, gauzy piece of fabric out of her bureau and draped it elegantly just inside the neckline to make it look appropriate. "Better?"

"Yes, much—thank you," I said and took her hands. "And thanks for all your help. I could never have looked this amazing without your help."

"Yes, well that goes without saying," she jokes, but warmly kisses me on the cheek before going to get herself ready.

I sauntered out into our sitting room to wait, but was afraid to do any actual sitting, lest I crumpled my skirt. While I wandered around restlessly, our governess, Lucy, walked into the room and immediately teared up at the sight of me. She, as always, wore her heart on her sleeve, but even our stoic cook, Grace, stopped to do a double take on the way to the kitchen, her eyes moist when she told me how lovely I was. Lucy sobbed so much; I didn't understand a word she said.

A door opened down the hall and my younger sisters appeared. Ellen, who is nine, was about as uncomfortable in her fancy dress as I normally would feel in one. After admiring me, she spent the rest of the time shifting around as if she had on an itch sack.

Lydia, on the other hand, was radiant. In a dress of pale pink with a full tulle skirt that extended to her ankles and her hair up in a crown of golden curls, she looked every bit the princess. When I tell her so, she beams and runs to check herself out in the mirror again. "I do look like a princess, Livy," she cried when she bounded back into the room. "But I still think *you* should be the one to marry Prince Liam. After all, you and he are friends now."

Friends.

I suppose this is one word for it, though it would not define our relationship correctly. Prince Liam and I had been thrown together on the Lindenwood mission after it became clear I was not Puck. He was tasked with escorting me home. However, on our return trip, we realized King William was walking into a trap. We decided to go back after the king's party, eventually hooking up with the notorious outlaw, Athos, who provided invaluable help. During the course of our adventure, we fell in love and professed our feelings to each other. Liam had promised when we got home, he would find a way for us to be together. But then, two weeks had passed without a word—the longest two weeks of my life. So consumed with his absence, I had thought of nothing else, and barely ate or slept. The separation from him had been a long burning ache. My father once told me of wounded men, who lose a leg or arm, yet still feel as if it were there—a phantom pain, the perfect description of my mindset. It felt as though, at any moment, Liam would be there to talk to me, encourage me, kiss me...

Finally today, I would get to see him. Yet, seeing him wouldn't be enough. I needed to speak with him. The thought of getting near him but not being allowed contact was the worst torment imaginable. I had to know one way or another if he meant all he said. Not knowing was eating me alive.

"I have something for you, Olivia," my mother interrupted my thoughts. She rushed in, her vibrant yellow dress swishing with each step. In her hand she held a necklace, a gold letter *D* on a bead-encrusted ribbon, which fastened as a choker. This Davenport family heirloom was only to be worn on important occasions. "You should wear this today."

"No, Mother," I protested, my hands nervously twisting the fabric on my full skirt. "As the matriarch of the family, you are the one who should wear it."

"Nonsense." She shook her head and the loose strands of hair that framed her face fluttered side to side. "You are representing the family today. You have earned the right to wear it."

Motioning for me to turn around, she looped the choker around my neck and tied it, then spun me back to make sure it was centered. Satisfied, she moved on to examining my younger sisters. "For goodness' sake, Ellen, stop itching, and Lydia, sit down before you tear your dress," she admonished.

It was the nicest gesture she made since my return. Largely, I had been ignored in every possible way by her. No doubt she worried about the nature of the reward promised by the king, fearing it would be a continuation of my training.

Her fear about today was my most earnest hope. Upon our return from Lindenwood, King William had singled me out at a banquet. He praised my bravery and promised to reward it in kind. It was my utmost wish that I may continue my training with the squires. Clearly, no one would ever let me be a knight, but maybe some special position could be created for me. After all, my father was the king's Master-of-

Arms. Perhaps I could be his personal assistant. My class of squires was so used to me, I hardly thought they would mind if I served with them in some capacity from now on. There were many assignments not involving direct combat. Of course, I have proved myself in battle, so maybe, eventually, they would let me serve on more dangerous missions as well. Mother would not be happy with any such arrangement, but she would need to adjust if it were decreed by the king.

Anne floated into the room, resembling a Greek goddess, a beautiful dress of forest green cascading down her body. The hue emphasized her gleaming chestnut hair that flowed loosely around her shoulders. Red lips contrasted with her pale skin, which surpassed the finest piece of white porcelain in existence. Her looks rivaled any of the eligible young ladies at court, and trumped most of them. Believe me, she knew this and used it to her every advantage.

The clock on the mantle struck noon and it was time to leave. We filed out to our carriage, everyone lost in their own excitement. My younger sisters, who could not wait to witness the spectacle of court, hung out the windows, their feet under their knees on the seat. Anne chided Lydia for dirtying her skirt. Father climbed into the vehicle in full dress uniform. Mother beamed with pride, adjusting a crooked medal on his chest.

I tried to calm my breathing when we entered the castle walls. In just a few moments, I would get to see Liam. Finally.

Once at the palace, Father marched in the procession with his knights, then joined us in seats right up front. Lydia sat next to me, her tiny feet swinging back and forth in excitement. Our seats faced the dais where the royal family sat in front of the audience. The king and queen were flanked by their two sons, Prince Harold and Prince Liam—my Liam. He was gorgeous in his own dress uniform, a black jacket with red sashing. We exchanged a few clandestine smiles during the ceremony, but when King William stood to speak, the monarch blocked my view of him.

After the king duly honored the men, he summoned me forward. On unsteady feet, I approached the dais and curtsied. Liam came back into sight behind them. Admittedly, I hoped for his trademark sly grin, but when I peeked in his direction, I saw his face held an unreadable expression.

Good or bad?

There was no time to ponder it over, because King William began his address. "My fellow citizens, by now you have heard the tale of young Miss Davenport's heroism on the Lindenwood Mission. She showed both honor and bravery befitting of any knight in the realm. As a reward for this service, I will bestow on her a special position. From this day forth, she shall be..."

The unexpected end to this sentence is what took me off guard, what took my mind several seconds to process, what has left me standing here in an utterly bewildered state before the entire court.

"...a lady-in-waiting to Her Highness, Queen Helen."

There is absolutely no way they can be serious. I mean these people know me, right? What would ever possess them to make such an offer? Yet, from the pleased look on King William's face, I know he deems this a fitting reward. All I can manage is a smile and a perfunctory curtsey, which seems to be taken as my assent to this arrangement.

"And may I say, the queen will be fortunate to have such a bright young lady in her service," King William continues magnanimously, with a gesture of his hand between myself and his wife.

She regards me with a look of keen interest, an expression reminiscent of Liam's. Slyly, I try to catch a glimpse of Liam, but his eyes are now trained on the floor. At his side, Prince Harold bears a contented smile, much like his father's. Clearly, the whole royal family knew of this offer and was not caught off guard. Why didn't Liam speak up in my defense? Why didn't he explain in excruciating detail why this is a terrible idea? Why won't he even meet my eyes now? Are all the feelings he professed to having for me gone? Has palace life returned him to his senses, and now he means to show me how I would not fit in with his life?

Suddenly, I feel an arm around my shoulder. My father says, "Thank you, King William and Queen Helen, for your most generous offer. As you see, Olivia is so thrilled, she is stunned into silence." Then, gently pulling me back down by my family, he adds, "We truly appreciate the honor you bestow on our family."

I suppose there is more pomp and spectacle to the close of the ceremony, but I make no note of it. My ears ring and my thoughts are jumbled. Eventually, we disperse into a large ballroom for dancing and refreshments. Father steers me into a remote corner, where I fold in on myself, arms crossed firmly over my chest. Lifting my face, he says sternly, "Olivia, I realize this is the last reward you expected or even wanted. But as servants of the king, it would be an insult for you to refuse. Do you understand?"

"Father, please," I beg, my voice sounding small and odd, "please don't make me go. Not only will it be torturous, but I will likely embarrass our family most grievously with my lack of decorum."

He sighs, but does not contradict me. "Olivia, the only way for you to get out of this would be for me to immediately arrange your marriage."

Only one man has my heart and he is quite out of reach where marriage is concerned. I have no counterargument. A tingling feeling of dread creeps into my bones—I am trapped. How I wish now that I had the foresight to run away with Athos and his band. A life with outlaws is far more appealing than a life at court. Perhaps it is not too late. After all, I still have the stone Athos gave me. He promised it would lead me to him. I could steal off in the night and never have to deal with Stewartsland again. But I would never see Liam again, either. The idea withers like an unwatered flower.

A page of the queen's, dressed in distinguished purple robes, clears his throat behind us. "All pardons, Sir Davenport, but Her Highness would like a private word with Miss Olivia. I am here to escort her thus."

Escort me thus? Is this what I am going to have to listen to from now on? Heaven help me!

"Of course, lad," my father replies, handing me off, but not without a tense squeeze on my upper arm that screams at me to behave.

The page leads the way across the outskirts of the ballroom, through a door, and down a mullioned hall. He stops in front of the entrance to a secluded terrace. Two guards stand sentry outside the door, staring ahead into nothingness. They make no discernible sign they even notice our presence.

"Her Highness awaits you out there." The page indicates with his head, then retreats down the hall.

Is it odd to be summoned here all alone? Goodness knows, I am not familiar with the protocol of ladies-in-waiting. Perhaps the queen meets with them all privately or...perhaps Liam has warned her about me and she wants to lay down the rules right away. The guards remain motionless while I muster the courage to enter the terrace. These men no doubt heard of my bravery on the king's mission, where I faced battle and death, and now watch how I am too afraid to face the queen. Not wanting them to think I am a coward, I stand up straight and arrange my gown. Silently, I thank Anne for making me look presentable for royal eyes. Then, with a deep breath, I walk through the door.

Queen Helen stands off to the side with an attendant, who scampers out the door at the sight of me. She nods her copper-haired head at me. The bodice of her maroon gown is woven with golden thread. Her only adornment is a circlet of gold around her brow. Quickly, I drop to a curtsey.

"You may rise, Olivia," she commands.

I stand back up and fold my hands demurely in front of me. Hopefully, I can convince her I will try to behave properly, despite what she may have heard about me. Certainly, she does not hand out lady-in-waiting positions lightly. The last thing I want to do is offend her, so I bite my lip and remind myself not to blurt; a trait I am most well known for. Her green eyes penetrate my being.

"I wanted to have a chance to speak with you privately before you take up your position in my household. From what I understand, you may not consider this offer the honor we intend it to be." My eyes fly open wide, but she continues, "His Highness and my son have explained to me your extensive military training and your penchant for practicing combat skills. My ladies-in-waiting, however, spend a fair amount of time weaving and embroidering. There is also voice and instrument training, classical studies and, most important, court protocol. Yet, even given all these occupations, there is still a small amount of free time the ladies may dedicate to an interest of their choice. Although I cannot allow you to leave the castle grounds to continue training with the squires, I will give you the option of practicing on our archery grounds and in any manner of horse training you see fit, *provided* I have a final say. If I feel the training starts to be in any way unbecoming of one of my ladies, I will put a stop to it. Could you live with such an arrangement?"

"Yes, Your Highness. It is most generous of you to consider my interests at all. I am most flattered," I say sincerely. A small glimmer of hope sparks in my soul. Archery and horse training are Liam's favorite activities. Perhaps he suggested them.

"Very well," she nods, "I have heard a great deal about you and am looking forward to getting to know you better. You may report in three days' time with your belongings to the head of my household. And, I might I say, you do look most lovely today. You will be another beautiful jewel to grace my reception room."

"Thank you, Your Highness. I must give credit to my sister Anne for my appearance. It is all her doing. I would be completely lost at how to pull myself together."

"Hmm…yes, Anne." The queen muses over something. "I have lost three ladies this past year alone—two to marriage and one to illness. I wonder if your father would be willing to part with your sister as well. She is already a popular young woman, and having your sister here may prove helpful for you as well." She pauses. "Only one way to find out. I will go check with him now." She briskly strides out the door, barely leaving me a moment to curtsey.

Well, one good thing will come from today. Anne will be positively beside herself when she hears the news. I exhale and roll my neck, trying to ease the tension of the last hour or two. The terrace overlooks perfectly manicured gardens, geometric patterns of paths crossing through the green lawn. In the center, a magnificent three-tiered fountain of Neptune surrounded by mermaids gurgles softly. I lean comfortably on the railing and slip jewel-encrusted shoes off my aching feet. No one will be looking for me just yet, so I may as well enjoy the peace and quiet for a few more moments. Closing my eyes, I let the faint heat of the late autumn sun warm me, hear the tinkling of the fountain, and relax into the moment.

A brush on my sleeve makes me start. Prince Liam leans on the railing next to me. For a second I wonder if he is real or merely an apparition, but then he takes my hand and, kissing it, pulls me close. There is no time for questions about his feelings or if he has forgotten me or realized he doesn't love me after all. He answers all my lingering doubts by leaning down and kissing me firmly on the mouth. After two weeks, the world spins back into place. His touch is so familiar and the moment so magical, perhaps I am dreaming, alone on the terrace after all. He pulls away slowly, and then with his trademark grin, utters the words that hurtle me back to reality, "So what did you think of my mother, Miss Lady-in-Waiting?"

"Liam, why on earth does anyone think this is a good idea?" I blurt.

"You get to see me every day. What's not good about that?" he says with a wink.

"I'm serious," I retort. "Of course I want to see you, but I won't fit in here. It will be a disaster."

A soft wind blows a host of fallen leaves around the terrace floor. They skitter along until a stronger current lifts them off into the open air. All around the garden, the trees lose their foliage, surrendering to the shorter days and colder temperatures. The flourishing green of summer is a fading memory, much like my dreams for the future.

Liam takes my hands in his. "Olivia, when we returned from Lindenwood, I told my parents I loved you and that you are the one I want to marry. My father was concerned you were not suited for royal life, so my mother suggested this arrangement. I need my father to see you here at the palace, to get accustomed to your presence, so he will condone our relationship. Please, my love, for me, let's make this work."

Knowing the king has misgivings about my suitability does little to allay my anxiety about the situation. But one look into Liam's pure blue eyes, and I know I will do anything to prove my worthiness.

"Well, I suppose if I get to see you every day, I could make it work," I tease.

"That's my girl," he says, before kissing me again.

Liam wants to be with me, wants me here. My heart fills with happiness, the sting of the unwanted reward alleviated. But, even as I rejoice, a nagging thought worms its way into my mind, embedding itself like a parasite—if I fail here at court, I could lose him forever.

We spend a few blissful moments alone before returning to the ballroom. The rest of the afternoon is pretty much a whirlwind of cocktails and introductions. A parade of courtiers, whose names I have no hope of remembering, come over to congratulate me. Anne, who has been officially offered a spot with the queen, is beside herself. She canvasses the room with Mother, spreading the news to all who will listen. Father stays glued to my side, no doubt worried I will say something disparaging about my own offer. There is no opportunity to be alone with Liam again. All we can manage are a few smiles from across the room. Finally, my family makes our gracious good-byes and mercifully returns home.

While the rest of the family regales Grace and Lucy in the kitchen, I retreat to the familiar confines of my bedroom. Smoothing out the coverlet on my bed, I sit down to reflect on the events of the day. This morning I never imagined I would be readying myself for life in the royal palace. In fact, I would have scoffed at the very idea. I thought this evening would be spent preparing for my new role as honorary knight, content in the knowledge that my talents and skills were not only recognized, but utile. Instead, my instructions are to report in three days' time to Her Majesty, the queen. I mean really, *me* a lady-in-waiting? It is like sending the ugly duckling to court, but I have no hope of turning into a swan. I flop back onto the bed, one arm covering my eyes, the other swinging limply off the side. The thought of living every moment just trying not to embarrass myself makes my head throb.

A gentle nudging taps at my hand. Lydia's cat, Midnight, crawls out from under her bed to console me. He hops up next to me. I stroke his soft fur. Staring up at the ceiling, I ponder if I should get out of this mess, despite the access to Liam. Perhaps my father could say he finds my counsel and help too valuable to give up. We will, of course, still send Anne, but parting with two daughters is just too much of a blow for the family. This thought comforts me, until I picture my father's reaction to this request. He was in awe of the honor bestowed by the king. Certainly, he would never renege on the agreement. Besides, I think my father has been a bit troubled about what to do with me since we returned. Father knew any offer to remain in training would not be met well by my mother.

Midnight curls up next to me, his purrs sending rumblings through my abdomen. At least someone is happy. Since the odds of getting out of this are nonexistent, I suppose I should concentrate on the one bright spot—Liam. Admittedly, were it not for him, I would be disputing the whole situation with my father, even downright refusing to comply with the king's order. Of course, the thought of being able to see Liam on a daily basis is thrilling…and also terrifying. All of our time together has been spent away from the court and its strict dictation of decorum. Then, there is the fact the king is not sure I am the right person for his son. Liam seems confident I can disprove this point; me, not so much. Maybe when the prince sees how unladylike I am, he will realize his father was right. Although, if being with me in the wilderness for several days did not dispel any indications I am no dainty debutante, then I don't know what will.

The door bursts open and my younger sisters come toppling in, a swirl of giggles and squealing. Midnight jumps up to quickly reposition himself on the corner of the bed by the wall. With an annoyed sigh to show his displeasure at being disturbed, he turns his back on our company and lies back down. Lydia and Ellen bounce onto the bed they share, their eyes filled with the look of overstimulation usually seen on Christmas morning. Anne follows in their wake, floating through the door still dressed in her beautiful green gown, and sinks down next to me on the bed. Needless to say her enthusiasm about joining me at the palace has been unbounded.

"Oh Livy," she sighs, "could you ever in your wildest dreams imagine something so wonderful?" Her countenance is dreamy while she conjures up magnificent images of palace life.

"I bet she was imagining something altogether different," Ellen says, her serious look back in its usual place. "Something more related to knights and service."

My bereft smile confirms this as truth. I sense this will be a divided room, Ellen and I with one school of thought and Anne and Lydia with another.

"Oh Ellen, who would not want to live in the castle?" Lydia gushes, but then to my surprise, adds, "Livy can do her training just as well from there."

My sweet little Lydia, everything is still so clear cut and simple for her. Gently I explain the queen's ladies-in-waiting do not participate in such activities, but are there, for the most part, to perform the will of the queen. Yes, the queen will allow a bare semblance of my old activities in my spare time, but I don't gather there is much of that. My training for all intents and purposes is likely at an end. The truth of this settles into Lydia's mind and she balks at the unfairness of it.

"Then I don't think you should go, Livy. You love training too much," she states matter-of-factly.

"Oh, like that could happen," Anne scoffs. "It is not exactly an offer Olivia has a choice about. When the queen tells you to come serve her, you do."

Lydia looks ready to argue, but I hold up my hand to stop her. "It will be all right, Lyd. I knew my training was nearing its end. I just wasn't sure when. So now, I know. Besides, think now how much fun you will have with not one, but two sisters to visit in the castle."

My diversion works. Lydia immediately begins planning her first visit. She distinctly remembers Liam promising her another ride on his horses and a trip into his garden maze. Her blond curls spring around her head while she bobs on the mattress. As she details the story of her first encounter with Liam to us for the nine millionth time, I glance up at Ellen. The look in her eyes shows she understands both my sorrow and my trepidation.

The rising sun peeps through a slit in the curtains, announcing the arrival of morning. Not ready to face the day, I roll over towards the wall and try to coax myself back into a doze. It doesn't work. Reluctantly, I stretch and sit up, swinging my feet onto the floor. Chilly air fills the room, belying the shaft of sunlight. We are now well into autumn. Leaves blow wildly in gusts of wind, scratching at the windows and piling into the sides of the house. Soon, the branches will be bare.

Ellen and Lydia still sleep, all tangled and snuggled in their bed. I am envious of the warmth they find with each other in the cold months. But then, I wonder if Anne and I will be sharing a bed in the palace or maybe even sharing a room and beds with many other girls. Suddenly, I feel nauseous at the thought of leaving this little bedroom I have shared with my sisters all these years. It is hard to imagine any other room, no matter how splendid, wrapping me in such a sense of security and self. The notion leaves me feeling hollow.

I pull on a plain shift, wrap a woolen shawl around my shoulders, and head for the kitchen. Grace busily prepares breakfast, her long lean arms able to reach all corners of the room at once. She wishes me a good morning when I plop down into a chair. Where will we eat in the palace? How could it ever compare to sitting down with my family? I think about the many meals we have eaten together. How could I never appreciate until now how special each time was? What will I do without Grace…and Lucy, for that matter?

"Livy, honey, did you hear me?" Grace's voice breaks my thoughts. "Could you please go fill this bucket with water for me? It would be a big help." A concerned pause, then, "Dear, are you all right?"

"Yes, I am fine, Grace. Sorry, I guess I am not quite awake yet. Of course I will get the water." I take the bucket from her outstretched hands.

The crisp air shakes the cobwebs from my brain while I cross our yard towards the pump. Another figure stands ahead of me, but I am so busy feeling sorry for myself, I hardly notice him until we are right on top of each other. He, too, is filling a bucket.

"Puck," I croak out. Since I have been home, my best friend has managed to meticulously avoid me despite my best efforts to find him. His anger at my tricking him to go on the mission has been evident since I first returned. Not that I blame him. I know I need to apologize for many things, yet the words *I'm sorry* seem inadequate. He, meanwhile, stands frozen, clearly as surprised as I am at our encounter. In my usual fashion under duress, I blurt, "Puck, I am so sorry. I know it is not nearly good enough to make up for what I did. Please tell me what to do or say to fix things! I miss you so much, Puck! You're my best friend. Please don't hate me."

My friend is silent for so long, I am sure he is ignoring me. Purposefully, he pulls on the pump's lever. Water sloshes into his bucket in thick squirts. He picks it up as though he plans to leave me standing alone in this uncomfortable silence. But then, he puts the bucket down and looks at me. After a moment's consideration, he says calmly, "I don't hate you, Olivia. I am angry at you. I am not sure how long I will be angry at you, or if I can ever trust you enough to be your friend again." I make to break in, but he continues, "You, of all people, know what a hard time I have had getting the others to take me seriously. Now I am the butt of even more jokes. More the laughingstock than ever." My eyes fill with tears. Puck's small stature always held him back with the squires. "I know this was not your intention. In fact, I daresay in your selfish anger, you did not stop to consider the consequences for me at all. But your plan worked, so congratulations. It was better than anything I ever could have come up with. Not that you asked…" he trails off.

His calmness is unnerving. I would much prefer having a knockdown, drag-out shouting match like we usually do. This stoic attitude makes me feel as though he has already processed his feelings and demoted me in his mind to someone of no importance whatsoever.

"Puck, I am so, so sorry," I sob. "Please, can't we just make a fresh start of things?"

"Maybe someday. I guess we will still be seeing each other around here. Maybe someday I will be ready."

"But don't you know?" By his bewildered expression, I know he has not heard. "I have been ordered to be a lady-in-waiting to Queen Helen. Anne and I will be moving to the castle the day after tomorrow. So you see, I won't be around here anymore."

Puck absorbs all this, then picks up his bucket. "Well then, I wish you all good luck and health in the service of the queen. Our lives now seem to be heading in much different directions, Livy. I will always look back fondly on our childhood friendship." He bows and walks back in the direction of the armory.

For a little while, I stand there totally numb, a chilly wind nipping at my face. I have lost my training, my best friend, and I am about to lose the only home I have ever known. Grace yells out to see what is keeping me. Quickly, I fill the bucket while tears flow freely down my cheeks.

The day of the move arrives. Again, I owe thanks to Anne, who has us packed in no time. Between my total ignorance of what to bring and my utter apathy for the process, I am fairly useless. My sister whips our belongings into trunks with such ease, you would think she had been packing for castle moves her entire life. Anne's trunk bursts at the seams with her gowns, jewels, hair accessories, shoes, and the like. I could fit myself in mine among the lack of items lying inside.

Watching me stare into my mostly empty trunk, Anne says, "Don't worry. Remember, Queen Helen told us one of our first duties would be to visit the royal tailors so they can make us each a wardrobe fit for ladies-in-waiting."

Should this make me feel better? Getting to stand like a pincushion for a bunch of fops? And if we are getting a new wardrobe, then why is Anne bringing everything she owns? I suppose I better accept things not making sense anymore.

My mother waits in the sitting room for the carriage to collect us. She anxiously wrings a handkerchief in her hands, dabbing tears from the corners of her eyes. Mother has been beside herself with the honor of having not one, but two daughters going to serve the queen. Ellen confided in me that Mother had nearly fainted away when the king made the announcement of my reward. Then she had badgered my father about the prudence of the appointment. That is, until she found out Anne was going along. This had put an entirely different complexion on things. From then on, Mother has gushed over how fortunate she is to have such wonderful daughters. Though I do catch her eying me with apprehension when she thinks I do not notice.

Father sticks his head in the door to tell us the carriage is loaded and ready. And suddenly, it is time. The time I have been dreading.

Grace and Lucy stand by the door with Lydia and Ellen at their sides. Anne hugs them, basking in the moment. "I will miss you all so very much. I promise to write you every day."

Write them? We will be less than a mile away for goodness' sake! Yet, the air definitely has the feel of a long journey with no return planned. All I can manage are hugs. My voice has abandoned me. Mechanically, I climb into the vehicle and take my seat.

Panic sets in. Surely, this cannot be the last time I leave my house. I will be back someday, right? This move is only temporary.

The carriage jerks to a start, just as it always has when we depart, yet so unlike any other time. I watch helplessly as the house, *my* house, recedes farther and farther away. Anne leans out the window, waving her handkerchief, yelling more good-byes. The carriage rounds the corner of the gate and the house is gone.

I look to my parents for some comfort, but Mother is too busy alternately dabbing her eyes and setting Anne's hair just right to notice me. My eyes turn to Father, hoping for reassurance that all will be fine. He is not looking at me, but stares out the window with an expression I have never seen before. Whether it is worry or sadness, I cannot tell.

We bounce along down the dirt road to the main gate of the city. Once through, we proceed to the castle entry. The carriage pulls up to the grand staircase outside the main entrance. It rolls to a halt before footmen, who wait to help guide us and our belongings out of the carriage. Over Anne's shoulder, I see a short, kindly-looking man and tall, stern woman also waiting on the steps.

The door opens and an arm comes in to help my mother out. She descends the steps and curtseys to the two people who step forward to introduce themselves. While Anne follows my mother out, Father takes my arms.

"Livy, I am so sorry to make you do this for the family. I have hardly slept since the announcement was made, upset by both your unhappiness and mine. I am not ready to lose you so quickly, my sweet girl. I would much prefer to have kept you with me, kept up all your lessons and such. But I do not know how I could possibly refuse the king in this generous offer." He stops, appears on the verge of tears.

I hug him as much as the cramped compartment allows. "Father, don't worry. It will be all right," I force out.

"Promise me if you are truly miserable, you will let me know. I will help you extricate yourself somehow. I love you so very much," he whispers in my ear.

"I love you too, Father."

As if I were not already worried enough about the prospect of leaving home for here, my father just made it sound like a death sentence. Sighing, I reach for the hand waiting to guide me out of the carriage.

I alight to the ground where an authoritative man waits with a self-important woman. He introduces himself as Bartholomew, the queen's secretary—a person in charge of all the scheduling and affairs of Her Highness. While he explains to my parents the details of our accommodations, I notice the woman apprising Anne and me as if we were cows at a county fair. She nods and smiles when looking Anne up and down, then her withering gaze settles on me. With all the dignity I can muster, I hold her gaze, trying my best to look unbothered by her scrutiny.

"Ladies, this is Madame Le Clare," the secretary says, his waistcoat so tight on his plump belly, the buttons strain dangerously. "She is the Headmistress in charge of all the ladies-in-waiting. After you have met with Her Highness, she will show you to your chamber and help you in any matter while you get settled."

Madame Le Clare nods brusquely, but does not utter one word. Her features are angular with a prominent hooked nose. She reminds me of an eagle.

"So then, if there is nothing else, Sir and Lady Davenport, we will send you on your way. Your daughters are in good hands."

My father and mother climb back into the carriage. Mother gushes her thanks and well-wishes to both the king and queen. No hugs, no words of encouragement for Anne or me, just a small nod in our direction from my father. Then they are gone.

Bartholomew and Madame Le Clare motion us to ascend the stairway. People mill about outside, some with actual business in the castle, others just watching the comings and goings. Many eyes observe our party, and there are more than a few whispers and points in our direction. Anne walks with the surety of a person who had done this a hundred times before. I envy her composure; my shaking knees make the act of walking daunting.

We cross through the entrance into a large square room with a ceiling so high it reminds me of the cathedral. Windows flank three walls in two levels, allowing natural light to reflect off the exquisite marble floors and pillars. Hallways branch off in all directions. Even when we finally start down one, more corridors break off it. This place is a maze. Soon, I have lost all sense of direction.

Finally, one hallway ends at a doorway where a guard stands at his post. The impressive wooden doors are open and the smell of a pleasant fire seeps out of the room along with the lilt of voices. We are led into the queen's reception room, which she occupies with about ten ladies. Most of them sit with Her Highness around a large cloth they embroider. In one corner, a few more work on some other types of sewing. One girl sits alone in a window seat reading. Upon our entrance, everyone stops and stares. Bartholomew walks forward and bows his balding head. I can almost hear the buttons on his vest groan with exertion.

"May I present Anne and Olivia Davenport for you service, Your Highness."

"Thank you, Bartholomew. Welcome. Madame Le Clare, will you please make sure the ladies' belongings have made it to their chamber?"

The mistress bows out of the room with the secretary on her heels. Queen Helen sets her needle and thread aside and gracefully rises. The other women all rise as well.

"Ladies, this is Anne and Olivia Davenport. I am confident you will make them feel welcome," Queen Helen says, her tone commanding.

Multiple sets of eyes bore into us, assessing, like when a new animal is placed in with the herd. Will it be assimilated or attacked?

Anne nods politely, unfazed by the appraisal. I try hard to maintain an air of composure, but can feel sweat beading on my brow. The predatory orbs fixated on us remind me of a pack of wolves. I only recognize Lady Emily, Prince Harold's betrothed. Her mouth is upturned in a smile that does not match the leer in her eyes. A similar expression graces most other countenances in the room. Contrived welcome.

After we all drop into a curtsey, the Wolf Pack sits back onto benches set in a rectangle around a large ivory cloth. Intricate stitches in a vivid scarlet border the edges. Almost in unison, they retrieve their needles and resume their work.

"You may embroider with us if you like. We are working on an altar cloth," Queen Helen offers.

Emily slides over on her perch just enough for one of us to fit. Anne slides in readily. No one else moves a muscle or even looks at me. Self-conscious to be the only one in the room standing, I glance around. A smaller cluster of girls to my left stitch patterns on what look to be small napkins. They keep their heads down. Apparently, I am invisible to them as well.

Even though no one so much as peeks my way, my neck prickles as though I am being watched. Queen Helen has not glimpsed my way, yet I feel she still judges me carefully. Heat creeps into my cheeks, partly from shame and partly from anger at Anne for leaving me so exposed. She deftly guides her needle through the fabric, unconcerned with my plight. The prick and pull of the threads through the altar cloth is the only sound in the room.

A rap sounds on the door and I nearly leap out of my skin. A familiar voice says, "Good afternoon, Mother."

"Liam, my darling, to what do we owe the pleasure of this visit?" the queen asks, wryness in her tone.

"Just passing by and thought I would say welcome to your newest ladies."

The Wolf Pack, which nearly stumbled in its haste to rise when Liam entered, stares at him unabashedly. He strides over to Anne and kisses her hand, every eye measuring his movements. Then, he walks to me and does the same, though his lips linger for a moment longer on my flesh. Tremors run up my arm at the touch of his fingers on mine. A dizzy, almost drunken feeling fogs my already overstimulated brain.

"I hope the two of you are settling in well. I am so happy to have you here at home with us."

He stares right at me when he delivers this last line. The Wolf Pack's attention hurtles my way, full of annoyance and contempt. I look down to see Liam still has not released my hand, so I gently pull it away, then plant my eyes firmly on the floor.

Liam turns to the group. "I am sorry to have disturbed your work. I will take my leave now. Mother, until later." He blows her a kiss.

An attractive brunette standing near him taps his arm, and through her lashes coyly says, "Oh, Prince Liam, you simply must stay for a game of dice with us."

She *touched* him. I want to punch her.

The others echo in agreement. They form a circle around him, effectively blocking his path out of the room. Dice are produced out of nowhere and the small table with the Napkin Girls is cleared. Liam is railroaded over to one side, where he settles into a plush, tufted chair, his muscular form an imposing contrast to its feminine contours. Brunette takes the seat opposite him.

"Olivia, you must try to look interested. You have been standing like a dumb cow since we entered the room. Stop it. Try to act natural," Anne's voice whispers, her breath hot in my ear. With a firm hand in mine, she maneuvers me to Brunette's side of the table.

"Great roll, Elaine," one of the girls cheers.

Elaine. I will now hate the name forever. Elaine, who flirts with Liam and shows such familiarity. I almost want to follow Anne's advice and act natural. For me, this would mean clocking Elaine with the blunt end of my sparring sword.

Not that Elaine is alone in her actions. All the ladies circle the table, hovering over Liam like vultures scouting out a meal. They stroke his arm, whisper in his ear, and most upsetting, lean over strategically so their breasts practically spill out of their bodices. It is a scene I would normally find amusing…and pathetic. But the harsh lens of jealousy taints it. Other than Anne and me, only Blonde Girl, who was reading in the windowsill, does not maneuver for his lap. She remains on the fray of the crowd.

Liam finishes the game and rises. "Sorry, ladies, duty calls."

They fawn over him all the way to the door, where he has to duck around their human mass to say good-bye to his mother. He catches my eye, winks, then is gone.

The Wolf Pack stands like forgotten chess pieces scattered about a board, the root of their excitement removed. Bereft of their entertainment, they trudge back to their embroidery and sink back down on the benches.

Blonde Girl retreats back to the windowsill and picks up her book. She seems my safest bet, so I saunter over. A plush, burgundy cushion lies across the sill underneath her. The curtains drape across the edges, forming an almost private little nest.

"What are you reading?" I ask, praying she will answer.

"*The Iliad*," she replies. A moment of silence passes and I second-guess coming over here. Until she adds, "You would enjoy it. There are a lot of battles and adventure."

If one of the other girls had said this, I am sure there would have been ridicule in the tone, but she says it with sincerity in her voice. She knows my backstory and does not judge me for it.

"I'm Kat, well, Katherine, but my friends call me Kat." She holds out her hand to shake.

"Nice to meet you. I am Olivia."

"Yes, you have a rather…notorious reputation. Some think they already know all there is to know about you." She looks at her foot dangling a few inches above the floor.

"And you?" I ask in a tone that dares her to meet my eyes.

"I prefer to figure things out for myself." She smiles genuinely. "Care to join me?"

I have never had a close girl friend. Most of my time has been spent with the boys my age, but I find a kindred spirit in Kat. We spend the next few hours whispering in the window seat. Its heavy damask curtains enclose us in our own little world. While the other ladies gossip and discuss various social events, Kat and I cover topics such as reading, philosophy, and music with mutual agreement on most topics.

At length, Madame Le Clare comes to retrieve Anne and me. "Time to settle into your room and freshen up for dinner," she orders.

After a quick good-bye to Kat, we hurry after the mistress down another series of mazelike corridors, up a winding stairway, to a long hall with rooms set at intervals along its walls like notches in a belt. One large set of double doors makes up the end of the hall. Madame stops at a room midway down the hall, opens the door, and motions us in with her head.

Afternoon sun spills through windows against the far wall, shafts of sunlight dancing like water on the room's contents. One large canopied bed anchors the room. Two vanity tables sit between a pair of oaken wardrobes on the far wall. The fireplace, opposite the bed, is flanked by a large chair and a settee, and a writing desk stands on the near wall. A door on the right leads to our bathing room. It is a more than adequate space for my sister and me.

"This will be your room, ladies. I hope you find it suitable. My chamber is located at the end of this hallway if you require anything. Your servant, Sadie, will be here shortly to help you prepare for dinner."

"Thank you, Madame Le Clare. We are flattered by such generous accommodations," Anne says. She sounds as though this is the most natural exchange in the world. I, however, am still bewildered to be here.

Our trunks sit side by side at the foot of the bed, already opened and emptied. I don't know who this Sadie is, but she apparently has unpacked our belongings. Anne inspects the room. She looks in the wardrobes and under the bed, peeks in the bathing room, then glides over to one vanity and runs her finger over the countertop's contents. An ornate perfume bottle catches her eye and she can't resist spraying a squirt on her wrist. Finally, her eyes come to rest on me.

"Are you ever going to move from that spot?" she huffs.

"It's just all so new." Before I can help it, tears form in my eyes.

"Homesick?" she asks. I nod my head pathetically. She picks up a handkerchief, then gently dabs my eyes.

"Are you? Homesick at all?" My sister has shown no sign of distress or even mild discomfort at any point today. It strikes me how the palace has reversed our roles. I am usually the calm, cool-headed one, while she is the drama queen.

She sinks down on the plush bedding and pats the spot next to her. I ease down next to her, still fighting a losing battle with my tears.

"Livy, let me ask you something. When you went on the mission with Father, did you cry like this?"

"No, of course not. I was too excited by the adventure, by finally doing what I always dreamed of."

"Exactly. That is how I feel about this situation. Do I miss home? Yes. But it is overpowered by my excitement."

"Oh, that makes sense," I sniff out. "I wish I felt excited instead of terrified and out of place."

Anne takes one of my hands and wraps her other arm around my shoulder. Her head tilts to rest against mine. "You will never be out of place as long as I am around."

"But you left me standing there in the middle of the queen's chamber like a fool while you sat down to sew with your new friends!" I accuse, my hands tightening around the coverlet.

"Olivia, I will help you acclimate, and this is lesson one—in order to survive at court, you must learn to take charge. If memory serves, I believe this is a strong point of yours. Don't let them make you feel less than you are. If I had intervened on your behalf, they would have known you could not handle them yourself. Never, ever let them control you. Keep your eyes and ears open and be careful who you trust. Meanwhile, try to look at this experience as a new adventure."

"Thanks, Anne. I am glad you're here." Her words touch me, even though this is not an adventure I take voluntarily.

"Me too." She kisses my forehead just as there is a knock at the door.

Slowly it eases open. The top of a white servant's cap appears. "I am Sadie, your ladyships, here to help you prepare for dinner," a soft, murmuring voice informs us.

"Come in," Anne and I say in unison.

In pads a mulatto girl, two large almond-shaped eyes dominating her tiny face. She can be no more than fifteen. The girl lowers her gaze to the floor and awaits our orders. Her hair sticks out in braids from under her cap, and she folds her dainty hands.

Anne and I have been waited on only by Lucy and on the rare occasion, Grace. For the first time since we arrived, even my sister seems unsure how to proceed.

After a long moment of silence, I say, "Nice to meet you, Sadie. I am Olivia and this is Anne. Tonight is our first dinner in the royal dining hall, so we will appreciate anything you can do to help us prepare."

She smiles, a bright grin that lights up the room even while the sun quickly dips in the sky. Outfits are selected, hair is brushed and arranged, and makeup is applied. While Sadie puts the finishing touches on Anne's lips, I attempt to lace my shoes, but my bodice is so tight, I cannot bend to reach my foot.

"Let me," Sadie offers, her fingers deftly tying the lace.

The maid rises, then steps back to admire us. She brushes a stray strand of hair away from my eyes, the calloused fingertips belying her hand's delicate appearance.

"Perfect," she deems.

"I guess we should go now," I muse, chewing on my lip, which is slick from balm.

"Ready for your adventure to begin?" Anne asks, eyes dancing.

"Ready as I'll ever be."

My days pass in tedium. I am introduced to a world of corsets, embroidery, games, and the hovering presence of eligible (and not so eligible) men's flirtations. Never in my life have I had to sit and do nothing for so many hours at a time. Nothing productive, at least. You would be surprised how many alter cloths and handkerchiefs these people are convinced need to be made.

My sewing was atrocious, so the queen inquired about other tasks I could perform. It was decided I would do the least amount of harm copying scriptures onto small cards with pictures of various saints, marvelously painted by Kat, my fellow inadequate stitcher. These are routinely distributed to the poor, who I am quite sure cannot read anyway. After a week of this, my hand aches and my middle finger sports a nice blister.

The Wolf Pack pretty much ignores my existence, which is more than fine by me. They feign politeness, especially in front of Queen Helen, but cast knowing looks in my direction and whisper behind hands when she is not around. Our group of ladies runs into Liam several times in the hallways or the gardens. He always makes a grand gesture of kissing everyone's hand, and each time his kiss lingers on my hand just a fraction longer—a noticeable fraction. This is met with outright glares from my adversaries, particularly from Lady Emily, their alpha female. So far, they accept Anne into their cadre, but to my surprise she does not readily jump in and participate in the catty behavior that is their standard. She has also warned me they do not care for the extra attention our prince bestows on me.

Today after our morning chapel, we returned to the queen's room. Some young gentlemen join us and groups form around the room, playing different card and dice games. Emily and Elaine laugh coyly among a group of suitors at one table. Anne has attracted a few herself at another. Kat and I sit alone in the back of the room on our window seat. The men are nice, but it is more fun sharing private jokes and eye rolls with my friend.

A knock at the door is barely audible over the bustle of the room. In comes a page, who approaches the queen where she reads in her chair with a lute player strumming soft songs at her feet. Messengers come and go regularly, mostly from King William. Sometimes I wonder if he and his wife actually speak or if they only communicate on paper. Helen glances at the note then looks directly at me.

"Olivia, come here for a moment," she orders.

Kat and I exchange a quizzical glance. The loud din in the room has all but silenced. No one wants to miss any potential good gossip. Anne's face is set in a smile I recognize as forced. She worries this will embarrass her somehow. I walk to the dais and curtsey.

"Prince Liam asks me when you are free for archery. I shall tell him Friday afternoon." Her tone is pleasant enough, but her eyes are full of scrutiny.

"Thank you, Your Highness." I hear the strain in my voice, feel the burn of many eyes on my back.

"Of course, you must bring one of the girls with you. It would be inappropriate otherwise. The choice is yours."

Great. Not what I need right now.

I face the room behind me. The ladies all sit up straighter and give me their brightest smiles in hopes of being selected; all but Kat, who shakes her head ever so slightly.

This choice could be used to my advantage, could get me in good with the Wolf Pack. Luckily for me, I am not shallow enough to even consider this. Then, there is Anne. She would seem the obvious choice, but I fear if I chose her, it will hurt her standing in this social lion's den. Only one option is left.

"I will take Katherine, if it pleases you, Majesty." I know it will not please Kat.

"Very well. I will let him know to expect you Friday at two." She nods, effectively dismissing me.

While I walk back to my chair, I mentally calculate the number of hours I must endure until Friday at two when I can finally be with Liam.

⚜

"I am sorry for picking you."

Kat and I walk down a long corridor to the Great Hall for dinner. Servants rush past us with trays for those dining in their rooms. Courtiers stroll, gossiping about the latest juicy rumor. The aroma of food strengthens the closer we get to our destination.

"I just wanted to be with a friend, you know? Are you worried about backlash from Emily and crew?" I ask.

We skirt around a finely dressed group of ladies, their silk shoes caressing the floor. The sun is all but set, only a faint orange still visible low in the western sky. Servants light sconces set in intervals along the wall to counteract the dimness.

"Oh, heavens, no. And who cares what they think anyway? It's just that I become so self-conscious around the princes. They are so intimidating," she confides.

"Yes, I know. They can be."

"But you and Prince Liam already know each other so well. I would think you would be at perfect ease." When I think of Liam's *friendship*, heat creeps into my cheeks, but I make no reply.

The dining hall is bright and toasty. A series of long trestle tables are arranged around a large brazier in the center. On the far wall, one table sits on a dais perpendicular to its counterparts. This is where the royal family dines. They are not always here, and more often than not, only some combination of them is present rather than the entire family. Tonight, Queen Helen, Prince Harold and Lady Emily grace the special platform.

Kat and I take our places at the table reserved for the queen's ladies. Anne sits with Elaine and the other Wolf Pack members at the other end. She smiles and greets us. The other ladies merely look down their noses. *Typical.* A forgotten afterthought for them. We prefer this, of course, our private conversations not being judged by the lot of them.

Bread, warm from the oven, is placed in front of us, followed by several meat pies. The selection of food every night is sinful in its indulgence. Anne has already cautioned me about enjoying my meals too much or my corset won't lace. I eat my fill though; if the corset gets too small, maybe I can burn it. Nothing would give me more pleasure.

"I don't think he's coming," Kat states, when my eyes wander to the royal table for the millionth time.

"Who?" My puzzled tone doesn't even sound believable to me.

Kat does not dignify me with an answer, merely a "you know who and so do I" look. She leans back when a servant lowers a plate of roasted fowl for us to sample. I spear a nice hunk of meat, drop it on my plate and pour some more mead into my half-filled cup.

"Is it that obvious?" I whisper, when the man strides away.

"It's obvious to anyone paying attention, and here that is just about everyone. You and Prince Liam exchange more glances than most."

"No wonder they hate me," I gesture my head to the other end of the table.

"Well, it certainly adds to it, but let's be honest, they hate everyone," Kat teases. "And just think, on Friday, you will get to do more than just glance at him."

We chuckle and earn an exasperated stare from Madame Le Clare, who sits one table over. Impropriety attracts her awareness like a magnet. She holds our gazes until we lower our heads and demurely begin eating again. I wonder if the woman has ever smiled in her whole life. Likely not.

A movement catches my eye, a subtle rustling behind the royal table. My first night here, I noticed some large pillows piled on the floor in the corner obscured in the dimness. Their purpose eluded me, but tonight the space is occupied. From the nest of rectangular cushions, a figure wrapped in a cloak rises, casting an eerie shadow on the wall. Slowly, the hood falls down to reveal a bony woman with long gray hair. This must be the king's witch, of whom I have only heard rumor.

Her moves are wary, like a rabbit in a vegetable garden, ready to scamper off at the slightest noise. A full plate lies on a low bench nearby, left there for her by someone. She creeps over to retrieve it, bows over it as if someone may try to wrest it from her hands, and skitters back to her padded enclave.

Kat follows my gaze. "Is this the first time you have seen Niobe? She is a bit creepy to look at, I grant you, but totally harmless."

"I have only heard tell of her. I thought, perhaps, the tale was exaggerated. I see it was not."

I know from my father Niobe has been with King William since he was an orphaned boy. Kat confides how the king is almost deferential to her, which drives one cleric mad because he thinks her to be the incarnation of the Devil himself.

"The old priest who looks like a corpse?" I ask, recalling the frail man who had accompanied the king's party on the Lindenwood mission.

A platter full of pastries and cakes is laid before us. When I pick up a gooey-looking sweet cake, Anne shakes her head at me, then sighs when I take a big bite. Kat somehow ignores the delicious aroma emanating from the plate.

"Monsignor Lennon? No, he always looked the other way when it came to Niobe. Brother Alastair is new, sent to aid the aging priest. He was here briefly about a month ago, but had some unfinished business to tend to in Prescott. I understand he will be back soon."

"So he came from Prince Arthur's city?" I ask between bites of my treat. The king's brother rules with a fair amount of autonomy in the southern region of Stewartsland.

"No, originally he was from the Mainland. Then he served in Prescott for a few years. To say he is rabid in his beliefs is an understatement. The thought of a witch here is too much for him to bear, but good luck reasoning with King William on this point."

Niobe, who my father says is more a mystic and healer, was a help to King William when he was a young monarch. She saved his leg from a nasty injury and "predicted" some future events, such as the birth of his two sons during the course of his reign. He is extremely loyal to her.

In her dark nook, she cradles her plate possessively, picking a bite every minute or so, but never lets her guard down. There is something almost feral about her. Not in a frightening way, more like a weak, old dog. She belches loudly. Lady Emily looks over in distaste before her attention is again captivated by Prince Harold. Kat and I have to suppress another giggle.

"I am so glad you are here, Olivia. I finally have someone normal to talk to." She clasps my hands warmly and smiles. As much as I enjoy Kat's company, I still wish I were where things made sense, at my home table with Lydia, Ellen, even my mother. Wistfully, I smile back at my friend and try to ignore the heaviness in my heart.

The four days' wait is endless, a mind-numbing parade of card transcription, brisk afternoon walks, and dice games. How the other women do not go mad from the monotony is beyond me. As much as I love Liam, palace life is positively stifling my spirit. Friday finally arrives. After lunch, the queen suggests we all stroll with her in the garden. She is a big proponent of the benefits of fresh air.

"Olivia and Katherine, an escort will meet up with us to take you to Prince Liam," she advises. The Wolf Pack members do not even attempt to conceal their contempt, but eye me with malice. Kat sneaks me a wary smile; she must feel as uncomfortable as I do.

It is a sunny day, but the air holds a touch of briskness, a foreshadowing of the imminent winter. When we enter the gardens, Queen Helen glides along the path at a dignified gait, so smoothly, her feet appear to float just above the walkway. The ladies follow in clumps, like moons orbiting in Her Highness's atmosphere. Lady Emily stays in step with the queen. Elaine and Gretchen, a raven-haired beauty, follow in her wake. Anne strolls with Camille and Sarah, conversing amiably with them. Though these two are somewhat nicer than the other three, they still follow Emily's lead on behavior. At least their collective annoyance at my relationship with Liam has not been taken out on my sister.

In our room the other night, Anne confided to me her lack of trust for any of them. She has actually behaved more sensibly than I would have imagined since we got here. Her natural talents to compliment at the right moment, deflect attention when necessary, and flirt with just the right amount of coyness, fascinate me. While I can always be found sitting at the edge of the room like a mismatched piece of furniture, Anne could command the entire room if she wished. Yet she knows how to make the queen and Emily the center of attention. I envy her ability to act the part so well, and wonder if Queen Helen wishes her son had fallen for a different Davenport.

Now, she strides forward, arms linked with her two comrades, whispering companionably. Emily beckons them forward to whisper something and they all share a laugh. The entire group ambles ahead of Kat and me, who straggle along like forgotten ducklings. Queen Helen stops to speak with some older ladies, one a recent widow. They sit on a bench together and the queen holds her hands consolingly.

"Come here," Anne whispers in my ear and pulls me over behind a large bush. "When you come back from your excursion with the prince, be as close-lipped about it as possible."

"All right..." I falter, unsure why she is worried. No one speaks to me anyway.

"These girls are going to try to use anything they can find against you. They don't want you and Liam together. So don't give them any ammunition by bragging or whatever. Emily, Elaine, and Gretchen have the queen's ear. It is important they have nothing bad to say about you."

"Anne," I reply peevishly, "I am not interested in what Vapid, Vain and Vacuous have to say about me."

Before my sister can respond, a movement catches both our attention. Queen Helen looms over us. She, at the least, overheard my last remark.

"I would like to have a word with Olivia alone, Anne," she informs my sister, who scuttles away with a nervous curtsey.

My eyes fall to my feet. Well, where my feet would be if I were not wearing this ridiculously full skirt. Sweat rises on the back of my neck. It is like waiting to be scolded by my father. A brown leaf tumbles across the pavers, a brittle vestige of its once colorful form, exactly how my soul feels being trapped in the castle. I miss my home, my training, and my classmates acutely.

"Your escort is here. I just wanted to remind you that you are one of my ladies and I expect you to behave as such while you are out of my presence. And please, give my son my regards."

"Yes, Your Majesty. Thank you," I say, surprised to be let off so easily. I drop into a quick curtsey, hoping to make my escape, but she places her hand on my arm before I can pass.

"For the record, which one is Lady Emily, the future crown princess of Stewartsland, Vapid, Vain, or Vacuous?"

"I am truly sorry, Your Majesty, I did not mean to offend you," I reply humbly.

My mouth gets me into trouble quite often, but never before with the queen. She steps close to me and in a bare whisper says, "They are not the only ones who have my ear. Do not think me unaware of people's behavior or motives." I nod, now completely flustered. "Now go. Enjoy your time with Prince Liam."

We emerge from behind the bush to rejoin the ladies. The Wolf Pack wears looks of smugness, certain I was just admonished for something. Anne does not meet my eyes. Kat waits silently with our escort, a gangly, pimple-faced page, who vainly tries to look authoritative.

"Ladies, back to my room," the queen orders and they fall in tow behind her.

I stroll over to Kat and Pimple Boy leads us away. We wend our way through open paths and closed-off nooks until we finally end up in the archery yard. It is the same place Liam was practicing the day my sister Lydia trespassed on the castle grounds. Never could I have imagined then returning here under these circumstances.

Liam stands holding one of the targets while someone else ties it to the branch of a tree. Relief floods through me. Time with him will lift the burden of my incarceration in this castle. He turns, a broad smile lighting his face, and my heart swells so fast I almost feel dizzy. The man who had secured the target steps from behind the tree trunk.

"Adam!" I exclaim to the guard, who was with us on the Lindenwood mission. "What a wonderful surprise!"

"Hello, Miss Davenport." He strides over and kisses my hand. "So nice to see you again."

"Excuse me, fellow, but that's my lady," Liam says, jokingly shoving Adam aside.

I keep my hand extended, expecting him to take it as well. Instead, he uses it to pull me to him and proceeds to plant a long kiss on my lips. Somewhere through the haze this causes in my brain, I hear his mother's warning about behavior. Oh well, so much for that.

He finally pulls away. "And hello, Katherine, I am so glad you could join us."

To her credit, Kat acts as if this whole scene were perfectly normal. She merely curtsies and says, "It is my pleasure, Your Highness."

"Come now," he orders me and pulls us over towards a bench. "I want to monopolize every minute I have with you. Oh, Adam, you remember Katherine, right?" he calls over his shoulder. Hopefully, he does, since it appears they will now need to occupy each other's time.

We settle down, hands clasped. I just want to touch him—his arms, his neck, his hair, every single inch of him, because I am so happy he is real and right here next to me.

"So, how are things going so far?" he asks, genuine concern on his face.

"Well, not so good. I am a total…good gracious, what happened to your cheek?" My hand flies up to a black-and-blue welt on the side of his face, exposed when the breeze lifts his hair. It can't be more than a day old.

"Oh, it is my reward for trying to tame a stallion. And this too…" He pulls up his sleeve to produce his upper forearm. There is an angry, red gash with blood-crusted edges. "Needless to say, the creature won. I am usually pretty good with the wild ones, but this horse, well, he may be untamable."

"I bet Puck could tame him," I say, the words out of my mouth before I can stop them.

"Puck?"

"Yeah, my best fr…well, a person I was friends with. You know, the one I drugged to get on the mission?" Liam nods in remembrance. "He has an uncanny way with horses. I always tell him he must have been one in a former life. They seem to innately understand him." I sigh.

"You miss him, don't you?"

The thought of Puck guts me. There has been so much going on here, I had little time to think about our broken relationship. A crow caws overhead, its mournful wail piercing the sky.

"Yes. Him. Whatever our friendship was. I never appreciated it before—how much he was a part of my life. It would be nice to have him here while I adjust to all of this.

Anyway—" I shake Puck out of my head and redirect my attention to the matter at hand, "—has the doctor seen these injuries?"

"Yes. And luckily I live," he jokes, fixing his sleeve. His ebony locks ruffle softly in the breeze. "Now what about what you were saying—you are a total what?"

"Disaster. Total disaster. I wouldn't fit in here if I lived one hundred lifetimes."

"Well, we knew that would happen." Liam chuckles.

"So why am I here then?" The desperation in my tone surprises me.

"That's easy. For this," he leans in and kisses me again. His soft lips caress mine, sending shivers down my spine. All my anxiety and despair wash away. A pure feeling of contentment ignites, as though a flame is lit in me again.

"Oh yes, that," I whisper dreamily when we part. My hand remains on his cheek a moment longer, savoring the warmth of his skin.

"Don't worry. Just obey my mother and ignore anyone who is less than friendly. You are here for me whether they like it or not. Don't let them get the better of you. This is what they want, you know—to get a rise out of you and make my parents reconsider us. Once we can announce our engagement, you will be able to spend more time with me and less with them. Try to keep focused on us."

"All right, I will do my best," I promise.

My eyes wander over to Kat and Adam. They sit together on a bench in the sun. Their conversation looks relaxed. Kat even smiles and nods at something he says. Wispy clouds sail across the bright blue sky. It is truly a beautiful afternoon.

"Do you want to shoot some arrows?" Liam asks.

"Absolutely! I have been dying to get my hands on any weapon. Archery is not my strongest skill, but it is better than nothing." I jump from the bench.

Moments later, my fingers notch an arrow in a beautiful ebony bow. The assortment to choose from was overwhelming, but this one was the best fit for me. I stand about twenty-five feet away from the bull's-eye, but hesitate to release the arrow. My target sways front to back ever so slightly in the breeze, so I need to tweak my aim.

My first shot sails wide to the left, clattering onto some thick tree roots. The second does a bit better, but only manages to hit the white outer edge of the target. Hardly the skills of a marksman. I drop my hands in frustration.

"The movement makes it so much harder," I complain, pulling another arrow from a quiver lying on the ground by my feet. Stretching the bowstring back, I try to focus on the black center of the swaying circle.

Liam's hand slips around my waist from behind, his front hand grasps the bow and positions it a bit lower. "You have to compensate for the wind," he says, his mouth right against my ear. Warm breath tickles my skin and sends tingles shooting across my body in all directions. "Wait until just the right moment…now."

The arrow flies and embeds itself in the dead center of the target.

"Bull's-eye," he whispers, pressing his body against mine. His lips nuzzle my neck and for once I am glad for my short hair. His hands encircle my waist firmly, which is a good thing since my legs shake so much I would likely collapse without his support. For a moment, I lean into him, my eyes closed. The whole world melts away and it is just the two of us. His heart pounds against my back and my own answers in turn. Then Kat laughs at something and I remember myself.

"You know—" I disengage from his embrace and face him, "—your mother told me to behave. Next time I will have her remind you instead. I am having enough trouble around here without you causing a spectacle."

He just smiles and kisses my forehead. "Sorry. I wish I could just smuggle you away with me and forget all this protocol nonsense."

"Me too. We could always run away and join up with Athos and his band," I joke. The reference of our outlaw friend brings smiles to our faces.

We spend the rest of our time alternating between shooting and kissing. More on the latter, to be honest. Liam promises we will try to make this a weekly appointment, at least until it becomes too cold. Then, he will think of something else. Hopefully these few hours each week will sustain me through the rest of the time spent in other company.

"If you could think of some way I could get in some sword training, I would be most grateful," I say, while we discuss possible alternatives.

"How grateful?" he teases, holding me tightly.

"Excuse me, Your Highness—" Kat's voice breaks in, "—but it is time for us to go." She points to Pimple Boy, who has returned to escort us back to the palace.

The sun gradually sets, the shadows melting into the gathering dusk. Bare tree branches cast thick black lines across the darkening sky. We were given no exact time to leave, but dinnertime fast approaches.

"Of course, Katherine. I hope you enjoyed your time here this afternoon. We will plan to do it again next week."

While Kat assures him of her pleasant visit, I suddenly remember something. "Wait, I won't be here next Friday. I am going home for my birthday."

"Ah, yes. Your birthday. Don't worry then, I will think of something else." He seals this assurance with one more kiss before we reluctantly part. "I will see you two at dinner."

All too soon we are back on the path to the palace. My happiness is replaced by an agonizing emptiness. Even if Liam is at the royal table for dinner, I will not be able to talk to him, much less kiss him. And if the queen does not agree to our weekly meetings, then how will we be able to spend time together? Without these few precious hours together, life here will be unbearable.

Twilight descends and the flame in my heart is extinguished.

"I am sorry I did not have a chance to introduce you and Adam properly. Did you have a good time?" I ask Kat on the way to the dining hall.

"Not as good as you," she teases. When I don't answer, she continues, "Adam was quite nice. We had a pleasant conversation."

"Nice, huh?" I nudge her, my mind distracted from my self-pity.

"Whoa, slow down. He's married with a newborn baby. Don't get any ideas about us trysting like the two of you."

"We were not trysting," I huff. "We were…all right, yes, we were trysting."

Kat laughs and grabs my arm. "I think there is a story you need to tell me, Olivia. I knew you two had eyes for each other, but wow, it's beyond that, isn't it?"

"Yes, I will tell you over dinner," I promise. My heart lightens a bit. Liam and I have been through a lot together. Everything will work out in the end.

A merry mood full of loud chatter creates enough cover for me to spill my tale. Kat and I sit with heads bowed together while I recount my history with the prince, from the errant cat up until this afternoon. "And then you came over to tell me it was time to go."

"So you *are* here to see if you can adjust to palace life. I had wondered if it was just a rumor." Her eyes float to the other end of the table where Emily dominates the attention of the Wolf Pack.

"What exactly are the rumors?" I ask, not sure I want to hear the answer. A servant sets down a plate of meat pies, steam still rising from them.

"There are a few versions. In one, he had eyes for you and asked for you to be brought here for his parents to consider. In another, you had eyes for him and used your sway after helping the king to garner a position in the queen's household." I make a horrified face, but Kat says, "I pretty much ruled that one out the day I met you. But in neither version is the detail you two are already a couple."

The king and queen dine at the royal dais, random courtiers stopping to address them at intervals. Neither prince graces the table tonight; the reason Emily deigns to dine with us. In the shadows behind the monarch, Niobe hovers among her pillows, a sight I have finally grown accustomed to.

"Yes, Liam, umm, Prince Liam," I stammer, "told his parents about us and this was the compromise they offered to see if I would sink or swim here. He, of course, thought it was a great idea because we can see each other much more under these circumstances than if I were home, but I have found it…overwhelming."

"I can see that. But I also saw your metamorphosis when you were with him. It is like you came alive. And him, too. He is usually much more surly." She wrinkles her nose.

"Yes. Things are different when we are alone. This public lifestyle is so smothering and we are not even declared as a couple yet." The scrutiny will no doubt increase one hundred-fold when this juicy news comes out.

"Oh, I imagine the reaction from them—" Kat motions with her head to the other end of the table, "—will be less than complimentary."

A piercing shriek interrupts our conversation, followed by absolute silence. Every head turns in the direction of the outburst. It is Niobe. She rises from her pillows and steps slowly towards the king, though her eyes appear to see nothing. The room is entranced, the only movement the two guards rushing to either side of the royal table, their hands on the hilts of their swords. King William halts them with a raised hand.

In a raspy, clipped voice, she moans:

"The Great Boar will meet his fate in the spring
when the trees are in bud and the new birds sing.
Treachery will come to invade his den
an attempt once failed, to be tried again.
His downfall wrought not by disease or wraith,
But brought to bear by a vessel of faith."

Her words are stilted as though recited by an invisible force. She shudders violently at the end, then collapses in a heap at the foot of the king's table. The guards sprint over to her prone form, followed by the monarch himself. He whispers to them while Queen Helen hurries to his side. When she places a hand on his arm, they exchange a worried look. One guard gently lifts Niobe's birdlike body up and carries her out of the room with the royal couple in tow.

The moment the door shuts behind them, the room erupts into chaos. Women wail. Men dash into clusters and whisper excitedly. Our table remains silent, even the Wolf Pack too thrown to react. Anne and I exchange a nervous glance from across the table.

"Does that happen a lot?" I whisper to Kat. Her blood-drained face is answer enough.

Before she can reply, Madame Le Clare hurries over and orders us all to our rooms. We quickly follow her out of the hall. Our mistress is shaken and whispers something about *that woman* to herself.

At the top of the stairs, Kat whispers, "I'll try to sneak in later to talk about this." With a squeeze of my hand, she is gone.

I follow my sister into our room. While I am confused, Anne's eyes are lit with excitement. "That was certainly interesting. More exciting than a boring dinner at the Davenport table!"

"Well, I suppose that is one way of looking at it," I mumble.

"Oh, Olivia, you can't tell me the whole episode wasn't intriguing," Anne counters, dropping into her vanity chair.

Sadie enters and helps us undress. My corset removed, I breathe an entire lung's worth of air. Donning my comfortable nightgown is pure bliss. Our handmaid excuses herself to fetch us a tray of food. I flop down on the bed and Anne follows.

"So," she asks eagerly, "what do you make of the whole incident?"

Before I can open my mouth, there is a soft tap on the door and Kat's golden head peeks in. In her own bedclothes, she joins us on the bed.

"What news have you heard?" Anne asks. The three of us sit cross-legged in a circle on the mattress.

"Not much. But I am sure the members of the royal family are most distressed by the prophecy."

"Prophecy?" my sister and I say in unison.

"Yes. Niobe has been known to enter a trancelike state and 'predict' coming events," Kat informs us.

"So the Great Boar is King William?" I muse. Not a big leap—Stewartsland's crest is an oak with two boars on it. Besides, my father has discussed Niobe's occasional trances before.

"Yes," Kat confirms. "It sounds as though she foretold his death this coming spring."

The door opens again and Sadie enters. A tray laden with dark bread, cheese, meat, and some warm mead is set down on the bed for us. We are silent until she scurries out of the room, though I am sure similar conversations occur all over the palace right now, even among the servants.

"So how accurate have her past predictions been?" Anne takes the question from my mouth. She pours us each a glass of mead.

"It has been years since she had one this dramatic. She makes smaller ones about the sex of babies, harvests, or great storms approaching. And she has been uncannily accurate. King William keeps her despite the opposition of his advisors and many subjects."

"Is she all right?" I ask, cutting off a large slab of cheese. "She looked near death when they carried her out."

"I think so. Hannah, my handmaid, is old enough to remember her last major prophecy. She said Niobe remained unconscious for several days. While she did make a full recovery, her hair turned all white overnight," Kat informs us, before taking a bite of bread.

"Well, no worries of that happening again," Anne mumbles.

"Her lesser predictions, the ones she has routinely, only give her a bad headache."

"Does Hannah remember what the last prophecy was?" I ask, though I think I already know from previous discussions with my father.

"Yes. It was some twenty-five years ago. She foretold a man would show up and claim to be the brother of King William. Less than two months later, John Linden arrived," Kat discloses.

This foretelling was true, and the young King William even fought a war over it. Eventually, he had conceded territory in the north, which became Lindenwood. The man had ruled there until a few months ago, when his half brother, Lord Otto, had tried to kidnap our king. John Linden, then King John, died of illness during this time.

We all slowly digest what it could mean if Niobe's current prediction is accurate. I wish I had it written down word for word so I could show it to my father, especially if the king's life is truly in danger. My quiet contemplation is interrupted by a commotion in the hallway. Doors open and shut. A stifled sob is heard.

"Now what?" I groan. Goodness, I miss my quiet house.

Anne leaps off the bed and peeks out into the hallway. Madame le Clare marches past her into our room. At first, I am certain she will scold Kat for being in here after hours, but then I see her stricken expression. "Ladies, I come bearing terrible news. We have just been informed King William's brother, Prince Arthur of Prescott, is dead."

At least half of the ladies are gathered in the queen's reception room when Anne and I enter the next morning.

"...was ill for some time now, so not completely unexpected," Lady Emily says in a hushed voice. She stands with Gretchen, Camille, and Sarah. They glance up at us upon our arrival.

"Prince Arthur has been ill?" Anne asks the question I dared not.

"Yes," Emily confides, drawing us into her circle to my surprise, "a sickness of the lungs. He had been sporadically coughing up blood for a few years now. It has worsened of late."

Emily is originally from the city of Prescott, where the king's brother oversees the southern regions of the country. Her family is of high standing in Prince Arthur's court, but even so, I suspect she did not hear the news from them. I know from studies with my father that royalty does not usually advertise their bad health; it could be a political detriment. Likely, she knows this from her fiancé, Prince Harold, who would probably not appreciate her speaking about it among us.

"Maybe the prophecy was about Prince Arthur and not King William at all. I mean think about it. Niobe predicts a death and just hours later, Prince Arthur turns up dead," Gretchen speculates.

"Yes, exactly what I thought," Emily agrees, her blond curls bobbing in assent. Gretchen beams with pleasure, pleased our alpha female agrees with her theory.

I am unconvinced. The prophecy said the person would "meet his fate in spring" and it is currently the height of autumn. And how exactly does dying from a lung sickness fit in with "brought to be by a vessel of the faith?" I keep my opinions to myself.

Queen Helen enters dressed in mourning clothes, a somber look on her face. After our obligatory curtsies, most of the ladies rush to her side, alternately consoling and questioning her. Unable to answer everyone at once, she sits and gestures for quiet. We form a semicircle around her seat, anticipation hanging heavy in the air. Lady Emily dabs tears out of her eyes with a handkerchief. Funny, she was not so broken up a moment ago when she was gossiping like a washerwoman.

"Ladies, I am sure you all share my grief over the death of my dear brother-in-law, Prince Arthur. The royal family will be leaving tomorrow for Prescott in order to pay our respects."

Leaving? Liam will be leaving? Of course, it makes perfect sense when I think about it. He would have to attend his uncle's funeral.

"A small number of you will be attending me on the journey. Ladies Emily, Sarah, and Katherine, you will accompany me and join with your families in mourning. And Anne, you will come along as well."

Anne nods demurely. At first, I am not sure if I am happy or upset to not be included. Yes, I would get to see Liam, but probably not get to interact with him in any manner. It will be a long, tiresome excursion, jammed in a carriage for hours. In the end, I am content to remain right here.

"Very well," Queen Helen says, "you four ladies are excused to go pack your things. You will need enough for about two weeks' time."

Kat gives me a baleful look while she and the others file out of the room. The remaining unchosen women stand quietly. Elaine and Gretchen look peeved to have been left out. Camille looks despondently at her feet.

Great. Two weeks with them in a bad mood. Should be fun. Better start planning ways to avoid them now.

The queen addresses us. "Ladies, while I am away, I expect you to behave appropriately. Madam le Clare will be here to supervise any activities that involve the young men of court. Please bear in mind Stewartsland is currently in mourning. It is not a time for merrymaking and frivolity."

These comments are aimed at Elaine and Gretchen specifically. They are already put out. Now any ideas of "while the cat's away, the mice will play" have been extinguished too. This is shaping up to be one of the longest fortnights of my life.

"Now, if you will excuse me, I must prepare for my travels." We curtsey when she rises to leave. She is almost to the door when she adds, "Olivia, please come with me."

Everyone's head pops up from their bows. Bewildered, I look around. Gretchen's mouth hangs agape, while Elaine's eyes burn with hatred. Camille, as baffled as I am, simply shrugs at me. But there is no time to analyze the request; Queen Helen has already left the room.

"Yes, Your Highness," I stutter and hurry to catch up to her.

She says nothing more while I keep a few paces behind her. We turn a corner and head in the direction of her private chambers. Am I in trouble for something? I rack my brain to figure out what may have offended her. Maybe she will scold me for being too intimate with Liam at archery. Or…maybe she has made her decision about me already and plans to tell now just how unsuitable a match I am for her son after all. My heart pounds steadily against my ribs, which are squeezed tight inside my corset. Sweat forms on my brow.

The queen stops near the open door of a small salon, gestures with her hand for me to go in and then, oddly enough, turns and continues down the hall without me. Confused, I step through the doorway and things finally make some sense. Adam and Liam stand together by a tall window. Light streams in, setting Liam's ebony hair aglow. They look up when I enter.

"Olivia, you're here." In three quick strides, Liam is by my side, his arms wrapping me in a warm embrace.

"Your Highness, I will be just outside," Adam says. He passes us with a nod and closes the door behind him.

Finally alone, we kiss. Oh, how we kiss—warm, dizzying kisses that melt the world away. Our bodies merge together as one, like the moment a wave pulls back off shore and one cannot tell where sand begins and water ends. He holds my face in his hands, his fingers tangled in my hair. My senses all hone into a single point of longing for him. If only we could stay in this room alone forever without the worries of others' approval weighing us down. Reluctantly, I pull my lips away.

"I asked my mother to bring you here," he starts, lips still dreamily moist from our kisses. "I am surprised she complied."

"You asked her to bring me here so you could kiss me?" I say, only half teasing.

"Well, not only kiss you, although that is the best part." He pulls me in for another round.

When we part, he rests his head on mine and murmurs, "What am I going to do without you for two weeks?"

The statement knocks me back into reality.

"Oh, Liam, I am so sorry about your uncle."

"Yes, it is a blow. Sadly, we knew it was only a matter of time. He has been affected with a sickness of the lungs for quite some time now."

So Emily was correct. I do not tell Liam about her publicizing it among the ladies. On our time alone during the Lindenwood mission, he had confided he was not overly fond of Emily. I don't want to introduce any more strain into their relationship, especially since I am not her favorite. If Liam were to confront her about this, I am sure I would feel her wrath.

"And what of Niobe and the prophecy?" I ask. "Do you put any stock in her predictions?"

"I don't know. Normally, I do not, but this one was different than any she has had in a long time—the last one of this type was before my birth." The worry in his voice surprises me. I expected him to laugh it off. "My parents are most concerned with what she said, particularly with Lord Otto still out there. His motives were not clear when he tried to usurp Lindenwood and took my father captive—I mean our fathers. What did Sir Jack have to say about Otto when you spoke of it with him?'

This is one of the things I love most about Liam. He treats me as an equal. There was never a doubt in his mind my father and I discussed Lord Otto. My being a girl does not lessen his interest in my input on important matters. The only other man who ever treats me this way is my father…and, to be fair, Puck—at least back when Puck was my friend.

"Father basically has the same concerns about Otto's escape. Whatever he was up to, it appears he left it unfinished. Thoughts he will return to complete his business are certainly on the table. The oddest part to both my father and myself was how utterly unprepared he was when our army marched on him. He must have known they were coming, yet it proved his undoing. It doesn't add up. What about Niobe? Can she be of more help?"

I think of her frail form being borne away. Her outburst had not seemed an act just to garner attention. Perhaps I will use some of the next two weeks to learn more about her.

"No. She woke up weakened and confused. She does not remember anything beyond coming to the Great Hall for dinner. We had written down her words to show her, but she could not provide any additional clues to its meaning," he replies, frustration dripping from his voice.

"Well, you and I must sit down with my father on your return and puzzle it out," I say, hoping this will reassure him.

An hour or so together is all we can steal before Adam sticks his head in the room to tell Liam the king awaits him. We linger another minute, hands clasped with entwined fingers. I am loath to release them. The moments we spend with each other are the only ones where time flies past and I forget my lost life, lost training, and lost friend.

"I will miss you, my love," he whispers, his breath warm in my ear.

"I will miss you too. Promise you will be careful—keep your eyes and ears open." I stare earnestly into his eyes.

"You as well. I love you, Olivia."

"I love you too." We kiss one last time and he is gone.

He loves me. Of course, I know this already, but to hear the words stated makes my soul fill up with joy. I float weightlessly back toward my room, my feet barely touching the floor. A courtier passes, hands full of books and ledgers. He is an older gentleman, his steps unsteady, who catches his foot on a loose flagstone. Papers scatter like seeds on the wind, some landing right at my feet. I bend to help collect his belongings.

"Miss Davenport, my every apology! Please do not trouble yourself," he says, snatching his errant property.

"No trouble whatsoever," I reply. Nothing would trouble me in my current bliss.

"My most gracious thanks," he says when I hand him back the last of his papers. "And if I may be so bold, you look just lovely today."

"Thank you, sir, and good day." I nod and we continue on our separate paths. Never have I had a compliment from anyone here on my looks. My encounter with Liam has left me positively glowing. It is a feeling I could get used to.

In our room, Sadie and Anne debate which ensembles should make the journey to Prescott. Garments are scattered across the bed, and hang from the open wardrobe, a kaleidoscope of colors and fabrics. My sister's trunk stands open and is stuffed to the brim already.

"I think the dark blue one and the burgundy with the cream trim," Anne says. Sadie nods and removes the blue one from its hanger, then begins the arduous task of fitting the voluminous dress in the trunk.

"Where were you?" Anne asks, suspicion lacing her voice. She holds an emerald-colored garment up for inspection.

"Um…nowhere." I look at every inch of the room except where she stands. My sister has made little mention of

Liam and has asked no questions thus far. I am unsure if she has heard the gossip that circles the court.

In truth, I am afraid of what she will say if I tell her. The idea of me as a princess is laughable, I know this, but it will hurt to have someone else, someone I am close to, point it out. And if there is one thing Anne loves, it is to point out everything I do wrong in life.

"So, Queen Helen called you out of the room and took you *nowhere*?"

"How did you know about that? You had already left the reception room when she summoned me." Boy, I will never get over how fast news travels in this place.

"Never mind how I know. Where were you?" she presses and places the dress down, so her hands can sit on her hips in an accusatory manner.

My silence is her only answer. Sadie, having tamed the blue dress, retrieves the burgundy one and tries to wrestle it into the bursting chest. Her breaths of exertion are the only sounds in the room. Anne waits expectantly, while I stare at the floor.

"Sadie, Olivia and I will eat lunch in the room. Could you please bring some food up here and then go eat lunch yourself. We will resume packing later," Anne instructs.

Sadie smiles, happy for a break, and scurries out of the room. I saunter over to the window to stare out into the gardens. The tree branches are all almost bare, most of their colorful adornment littering the ground. Soon they will be just naked limbs, like empty arms outstretched to the sky.

"Olivia, do you think I am stupid?" She has come to stand right next to me.

"Stupid? Of course not...why?" I ask, confused by the sudden turn in the conversation.

"Do you think I do not see how you two look at each other? Do you not think I know how unusual it is to be summoned for an afternoon alone with him? Do you not think I recognize lips swollen from too many kisses this very moment?"

My hand flies to my mouth where the feel of his lips still lingers. Still, I say nothing. It should have occurred to me anything involving love and intrigue would not escape Anne's notice. She lives for these things.

"Look, I don't know exactly what is going on. I have heard some rumors from the other ladies-in-waiting, whose words I know not to take at face value. What I want to hear is something from my sister...if she would only trust me enough."

I look up into her earnest face. We were close once, Anne and I. Inseparable for a span of years in our childhood. Somehow, over the years, this connection was broken, but I see now in her eyes, the sparkle of the secrets we shared under the covers at night. Our own hidden world existed there.

"Of course I trust you. Honestly, I was just scared you would laugh at me if I told you. That's all."

Instead of brushing off my statement, as I was sure she would, Anne takes both my hands in hers. "I am sorry if I have ever given you reason to think that. I am your sister and I want to help you if you will let me. Will you please tell me what is going on with you and the prince?"

I tell her. We spend the next hour sitting cross-legged on the bed. I stop only once, when Sadie enters and sets down our lunch tray. Anne does not interrupt with comments or advice; she simply lets me tell her the whole story, along with all of my hopes and fears.

"And that is pretty much all of it," I finish up, putting one last hunk of cheese in my mouth. "What do you think?"

"Oh, Olivia, I am so happy for you. You just glow when you talk about him." She sets her glass on a nightstand and gives me a hug. Anne, as always, is in love with the idea of love.

"You mean, you don't think it's unrealistic?" I pull back, surprised. "I mean, me—a princess?"

"No. I don't see why it should be. If the king and queen have you here, they definitely are considering it. Prince Harold will be well married to Lady Emily. I am sure they can be a bit more lenient with Prince Liam—he is, after all, not the crown prince. We will just make them see how it will work out just fine." It is so like my sister to state things this matter-of-factly. She will enjoy nothing more than overseeing this amorous project.

"I am flattered by your confidence," I quip, then a question leaps to mind. "Do you think Father and Mother know?"

"I think Mother suspected something strange was afoot on the night of the banquet when Liam spoke to us." I remember the moment well. My mother was stupefied into silence for once. "But then, I think she decided she was imagining things. Father, well, I don't know. You are his favorite, so I am not sure he thinks about you in romantic terms."

"Do you think they will be upset?" I ask between bites of a meat pie.

"If King William accepts you, and Father knows it is what you want, I think he will be happy for you."

"Hopefully, I can convince the king and queen and the rest will fall into place," I say, with more optimism than I feel.

"Of course, there are other problems we will need to contend with," Anne warns. "We must be careful of the other ladies, particularly Emily, Elaine, and Gretchen. They have convinced themselves Liam could not possibly be considering you, and here he actually loves you already. This detail we should keep under wraps as long as possible. If they have wind of it, they will try to make sure all does *not* work out."

"Don't worry, I will avoid the Wolf Pack at all costs," I assure her.

"Wolf Pack? Is that what you call them?" She throws back her head and laughs. "How apt! I will just have to feed them some untrue information to throw them off the scent for a while."

"Thanks, Anne." I wrap my arms around her in a giant bear hug. "I am happy you are here for me."

Confiding in my sister lifts a weight off my shoulders. She will be a formidable ally dedicated to my cause. It is also gratifying to feel close to my sister again. Finally.

The royal entourage leaves the next morning. Members of the court staying behind amass on the central staircase to see them off. In the courtyard, dozens of carriages wait in line, bursting with trunks and satchels. King William and Queen Helen each have their own carriage, larger and more luxurious than the rest, which sit like mother hens in the center of the smaller transports. Flag bearers and a contingent of knights mill about, while their horses stomp, impatient for the journey to begin.

My father, the Master-of-Arms, will lead the way. He stands near his horse at the front of the train, discussing last-minute details with some of his knights. Sir Michael, an unwitting player in my Lindenwood adventure, nods in agreement with some point Father makes. David and Francis, my fellow squires just recently knighted, listen attentively to their superiors. Spotting my face over the heads in the crowd, he motions me over. I fly down the stairs into his embrace and bury my head in his shoulder. This is the first time I have seen him since moving to the palace. The others back away to let us have some time with each other.

"Oh, my dear Livy, how are you faring so far?"

"I'm all right," I begin, "Anne is helping me acclimate. It's a very, um, different lifestyle." Now is not the time to tell him anything more.

He pulls me close and whispers, "When I return, we will speak more of this prophecy. I understand you and your sister witnessed it firsthand."

"Yes, we did. I am anxious to discuss it with you." He smells so familiar, so like home. My heart aches.

"Until I return then, sweetheart," he says, bending to kiss my forehead.

The travelers now pour out of the castle, down the steps to their vehicles. Prince Harold escorts Lady Emily, who slips into one of the larger coaches right near me. Servants trail behind with baskets of food, carafes of wine, pillows, and other such amenities for the long journey. Anne, Kat, and Sarah follow closely behind.

My sister steps over, her face aglow with excitement. "I'll miss you." Then, her tone changes to one of warning. "Remember to be careful what you say and do around the other ladies—especially Elaine and Gretchen. They won't play nice when the queen is not around."

"I will. Safe trip, Anne." I kiss her cheek and give a quick nod to Sarah, who climbs into the rig behind my sister.

Kat embraces me. "I will miss you, and though I am sorry for the reason we must go, I am excited to see my family again. It has been almost a year."

"May your travels be safe," I bid, feeling lucky to still live near my family. To go months or years without seeing them would be miserable.

When I make to remount the stairs, two figures step into my path.

"Hello, Olivia," Francis says. He and David stand before me. Normally, we would slap each other on the backs, but they seem unsure how to handle me in my poufy dress. We settle for awkward handshakes.

"Hi guys, or should I say, greetings, Sir Francis and Sir David. How are you? Pretty exciting, huh? Your first mission as full-fledge knights!"'

"Yes, this is what it's all about," David remarks, glancing around at the excitement. "You aren't going to try to sneak along on this one, are you?"

"No, I'm not dressed for it," I tease back, flouncing my skirt. "Or else I would give it some consideration."

"You two, saddle up *now*!" barks Sir Michael. His scowl in my direction tells me I have not yet earned any forgiveness for deceiving him on the last mission.

"It was great seeing you, Olivia. It's not the same without you," Francis says.

After a moment of uneasy silence, they make for their horses. When I climb the steps to join the remaining ladies-in-waiting, a sad, empty feeling fills my gut. What I would give to hop on Pepper and ride out on this journey, or any one for that matter.

At length, King William and Queen Helen descend the staircase. He strides over to confer with my father, before mounting the steps to his conveyance. She swishes by us with a nod and enters her carriage. Bartholomew, her secretary, discusses last-minute details with other staff members, before joining Her Highness inside.

A hand falls on my shoulder. There, before me, is Liam. All the ladies around me drop into deep curtsies, so I swiftly follow. We rise and the others try to pretend they are not listening to us.

"I just wanted to say good-bye. It will be a long two weeks without you." Then he leans in and kisses me. One quick simple kiss, but enough of a gesture to cause the ladies to gape openly at us.

I stand dumbly, before I manage to mumble, "Be safe."

He squeezes my hand, then mounts his waiting steed. Afraid to meet anyone's eyes, I stand stock still and rivet my attention on the scene in front of me. Still, I can feel resentment and annoyance dripping off of Elaine and Gretchen in large, envious drops. So much for my sister's warning.

A trumpeter blows the signal to begin, bringing the train to life. Carriages groan to a start, horses pull anxiously against their reins, and the party parades out the front palace gate. Liam's stallion trots down a city street where he turns a corner, vanishing out of sight. He takes a piece of me with him. I won't be whole again until he returns.

With a sigh, I make to head back inside, only to find Elaine and Gretchen blocking my way. They do not say a word, but the contempt on their faces is like a slap across my cheek. The last thing I need right now is drama from the Wolf Pack.

"Excuse me, ladies." I skirt around them. For a moment, I think they will try to stop me, so when they don't, I hurry to the safety of my room. To be on the safe side, I ask Sadie to have my dinner sent up tonight.

The first week passes far more bearably than I imagined. With the queen away, there is plenty of free time available. I am able to ride out on horses a number of days. Though we are well into autumn's chill, I relish the freshness and the freedom of the journeys. I even sneak a wooden sword with me and shadow spar in the open meadows. No one says much to me, too afraid of the backlash from my adversaries, no doubt. To counteract my loneliness, I take to wandering around parts of the palace I have not yet had a chance to explore.

One chilly afternoon, I walk along a columned path where the kitchens open out onto the large herb gardens. A sturdy breeze brings the scent of rosemary and mint from the neatly ordered rows of plantings. There amidst the greenery, a small figure works, long white hair trailing down her back like a waterfall—Niobe. I position myself behind a column to watch her, my cloak pulled tightly around me. At first, it seems strange to come upon her here, but she certainly must not spend all her time in her chamber. As a healer, the garden is a likely haunt. She rifles through some of the plants, stuffing handfuls of leaves into a sack. A basket of trimmings sits at her feet.

Some children scamper around a corner up ahead. Their plain garments, some with stains and patches, mark them as the offspring of servants. They play a raucous game of tag, faces alight with joy, as they dart in and out of each other's reach. How I miss those carefree days.

Suddenly, one little boy trips and tumbles to the ground. Wails of pain pierce the air and he grabs his knee, a thin line of blood trickling down his tiny leg. I am about to go to his aid, when Niobe, who had seemed oblivious to their presence a moment ago, shuffles over. She kneels down, pats his head, then holds up a finger to wait a moment. The healer disappears into a door off the interior castle wall. A minute passes and she emerges with a cloth and a small bowl.

Niobe bends down to wipe the boy's wound with the cloth, then she dips her fingers into the bowl. Thick brown paste is transferred from her hand to his knee, while she whispers reassurances to him. He rises and takes a ginger step, then another. A broad smile breaks out across his face and he throws his arms around her in thanks. She pulls away, pats him on the cheek, and slowly shuffles back to resume her picking.

I watch the entire event as if suspended in a dream. This caring healer does not reconcile with the crazy witch who hides in the pillows at dinnertime. As if she can sense my gaze, she looks right to the spot where I stand partially concealed. When our eyes meet, I duck fully behind the column before rushing away, surprised by the guilt that courses through my body.

Friday arrives. My seventeenth birthday. The sun shines brightly through the drapes while I linger in bed for a few moments longer. This is the birthday I had been dreading because it would have meant an end to my training, but this issue was resolved (and not in the manner I would have liked) by moving to the castle. At least I will get to see my family today. It feels as though it has been forever.

A gentle knock on the door announces Sadie's arrival. She balances a large tray in her hands, which she sets down on the small table by the fireplace. It contains several dishes of food, a carafe of juice, and a candle.

"Happy Birthday, Miss Olivia," she says and marches across the room to open the curtains. A rectangular patch of light falls across the bed while I squirm out from under the covers.

"Thank you, Sadie." I wrap a robe around my shoulders, then step into my waiting slippers.

"October twenty-eighth. You are a Scorpio. Full of deep passion and drive for success, but with a strong outer reserve. That is what your sign says about you," she proclaims. Her fingers work some kindling into a small pile, which she lights with the candle.

"My mother doesn't appreciate the 'strong outer reserve' part," I joke.

I plop into the armchair, hungrily surveying the contents of the tray. A sweet roll bursting with raisins and dates is my choice. Still warm from the oven, it melts in my mouth. After much cajoling, I convince my handmaid to taste a bite before she bustles to the wardrobe.

"Any special outfit you would prefer to wear?"

"Nothing too fancy. I will be seeing my younger sisters, and with Lydia…let's just say she has a knack for dirtying things," I answer. My heart warmed at the thought of my littlest sibling.

Sadie selects a garment of dark blue, free of lace and ruffles, but with some delicate stitching throughout the fabric. Thankfully, it can be worn without a corset, which would have been a tight squeeze after my breakfast indulgence. Once she has me installed in the dress, she goes to work on my hair. Over the past month, it has grown in much better than I would have expected. She sets it in a small bun at my nape and adorns it with some seed pearls. After a thorough examination, Sadie deems her work acceptable and bids me good day.

I throw a satin cape lined with soft gray fur over my shoulders and head for the stables. Kendrick, the Master-of-Horse, is there, but instead of grooming coats or checking shoes, he stands in a fine suit. In his middle fifties now, he still strikes a good figure. My mother always notes how handsome he was in his youth.

"Ah, Miss Davenport, your horse is all saddled up and ready for your trip home." He points to a brown gelding tethered just outside the back doors.

"Thank you, Kendrick. And might I say, you look most dapper today."

"Yes, I am meeting my new assistant today. I have found this outfit intimidates a bit more than my work cloths and apron. Shows who's boss, if you get my drift," he confides, while we stroll to my waiting animal.

"A new assistant? What happened to Harry?" I ask, climbing the steps to mount the saddle. Kendrick offers a steadying hand while I adjust myself sidesaddle. Why do women consent to sitting in this blasted position?

"Oh, Harry. Well, his wife's uncle up and dies and leaves them with a great estate over to the west. So they have moved on to bigger and better pastures as it were. Bless them both."

"How nice for Harry then. And thanks for your help. Good luck with your new assistant. Hope you intimidate him." I kick my horse to a trot.

The ride through the city streets to the main gate is slow going. Stalls and merchants clog the streets, shoppers walk unheedingly, and children dart in and out of alleyways. When at last I am out into more open space, I finally urge the horse into a gallop. Wind whips across my face and I feel all Sadie's meticulous pinning come loose. Though side-saddle is restrictive, I still manage to get to a run. Nothing beats the feeling of a good, hard ride.

I pull back to a trot when I enter the gate to my home. My younger sisters await my arrival in the courtyard. Lydia bounces up and down like a spring, and even the reserved Ellen claps her hands in delight. It has only been a month, but they seem so much bigger to me.

"Hello." I wave and pull to a stop. Before I can fully dismount, Lydia has her arms flung around me. Amidst the cloud of dust the hooves kicked up, I can only make out the top of her golden head.

"Happy Birthday, Olivia. I miss you so, so, so, so much!" She squeezes me so hard my ribs hurt.

"I miss you too, little Lyd, and you as well, Ellen." I step over to embrace my other sister. "How is everything here?"

"Quiet with Father away," Ellen answers in her usual stoic tone.

We walk over to a hitching post and I tie up my horse. My mother, Lucy, and Grace meet us at the front door and I am hustled inside, a million questions and comments sounding from all directions. Mother, my sisters, and I settle into the sitting room with Lucy. Our housekeeper hasn't let go of my hand since I came in, afraid I may disappear again. A fire burns merrily in the hearth surrounded by all the familiar sights and sounds of home, and yet, when I look around, there is something off in how it all feels.

The next hour or so is spent describing every detail of palace life. Anne would most likely have done a better job than I, but my audience still hangs on every word. They interrupt me multiple times with any number of rumors they have heard. Most are either gross exaggerations or simply false, but the subject of Niobe's prophecy is more or less correct. I fill in the blanks for them about her outburst and the strange words she had spoken. Mother, superstitious as always, crosses herself repeatedly.

Grace comes out and announces dinner will be ready in an hour. It is one of her famous roasts—I would recognize the smell no matter how long I had been away. Everyone heads into the kitchen to help lay the table, but Lucy shoos me out. "No, no, birthday girl. You go relax. We will take care of this."

I saunter down the hall to my bedroom—well, my old bedroom, the door of which stands open in the fading afternoon sun. On hesitant feet, I cross the floor and sit on my old bed. Here, like the sitting room, the unfamiliar has crept in. The room seems smaller and different in a way I cannot quite pinpoint. Somewhere along the line, my bedroom in the palace became my room—my place of security. This room is just four walls that belong to someone who does not exist anymore. A hollow feeling fills my body at this insight.

The bedskirt rustles and a furry, black head peeks out. Midnight hops up and walks cross my legs, purring. "Hello, you," I say, stroking his glossy fur. But even he does not dispel the sense I am out of place in this room. With a last pat on the cat's head, I forlornly walk out.

Back down the hallway, I enter my father's office, our special sanctuary for so many years. Here the pull of belonging is stronger, the room less foreign, which brings me some comfort. I run my fingers over the shelved books and the organized desk. The smell of Father's pipe brings a nostalgic wave of relief. Through the window, I hear voices in the courtyard, so I go outside and walk around the house. Two men wash their hands at the pump, shirt sleeves rolled up over their forearms. My old classmates, Albert and Seth, chat amiably as they clean off.

"Olivia," Albert calls when he notices my approach. "What are you doing here?" He wipes his sweaty brow.

"I am visiting my family for my birthday." The word *visiting* sounds strange since I am talking about my own house.

"Oh, so is that why you are dressed like a girl," Seth jokes, rubbing his wet hand across the back of his neck.

"Ha-ha," I jest.

Three boys stroll over and nod deferentially to my friends. I do not recognize their faces. They must be from the newest group of squires. They are hesitant to even meet my eye.

"Ben, Aaron, Caleb, this is Olivia." Albert handles the introduction.

They gape a moment, then one of them remembers himself and says, "How do you do?"

"Fine, thank you." They nod as if embarrassed, then hurry away.

"I think they are scared of you," Albert confides. "Sir Michael likes to use your name as an example of what kind of trouble disobedience causes."

Great. Nice to know I can supply such a lesson.

"What are you all up to?" I ask.

"Just equipment inventory and maintenance. Figured it was a good enough time for it since half of us went to Prescott with the king," Seth answers.

"Is Puck around?"

"No, he had some sort of appointment today. You can see him next time…whenever that is."

There is uncomfortable silence. No one seems to know what to say. I grope around my brain for some topic. Albert, Seth, and I have known each other for years. There was always *something* to say. We are like brothers—except for me and the boy part—but being with them was always easy, comfortable.

Until now.

"Well…uh…I hope you enjoy your birthday and your time with your family," Albert says, shifting from one foot to another.

"Yes, it was good to see you, Olivia," Seth says. "So, uh, I guess we should get back to work."

We exchange awkward good-byes and they head back to the armory.

I wander into our back yard, where the scent of mint and oregano fill the air. On an empty bench, I sit to ponder my encounter. What just happened? The squires were my people, where I fit in with the world. Yes, they are knights now, but still, we have been friends and classmates forever. I am part of their group.

But I am not anymore, am I?

The realization hits me hard. They always acted as if I were one of them, included me as if I were one of them, spoke to me as if I were one of them. Does it just stop? One day I am in, the next out? Or maybe I was deceived the whole time. Maybe I never truly was one of them to begin with. I am not sure which thought is more hurtful. All I do know is it will never be the same again.

The sun has almost set, bathing the garden in a soft, orange glow. Brown, shriveled leaves blow around the pavers, their heyday over, forgotten. Like me. I don't fit in with my old life, and I don't fit in with my new life. Where do I fit in? With Liam? Yes. But I need something of my own. I cannot look to him to make me whole.

A chill creeps into the air devoid of the sun's warmth. I should go inside, yet my legs will not rise. Twilight deepens, casting the yard into dark silhouettes—shadows. An apt metaphor for how I feel—a shadow with no real purpose. Fairy tales make it sound as if love is the answer to fulfillment. And I do love Liam, but even with his heart, I am incomplete. Darkness wins out over light as I sit unmoving.

"Olivia," my mother calls some time later.

"Out here."

"Come on in, darling. Dinner is ready."

Darling? My mother just called me darling? The world truly is off its axis.

The meal is lovely. My favorite roast with gravy, fresh biscuits, creamy mashed potatoes, and sweetened carrots are served on the usual china, but it is not the same as it used to be—the recurring theme of my day. When they bring out a cake and sing, Lydia beams with a happiness I cannot mirror. I insist Grace and Lucy join us for a slice, one tradition I will not break.

Finally, after the last morsel of food is consumed, Mother says, "Ellen and Lydia, please help Grace and Lucy with the cleanup in the kitchen, so I may speak alone with your sister."

They all grab handfuls of plates and utensils, and disappear through the swinging door. My mother rises and motions me to follow her into the sitting room. We settle across from each other in the chairs that flank the hearth. The fire crackles soothingly at our feet.

"So how are things truly, Olivia?" she asks, hands clasped, face full of concern.

"They are tolerable. Anne is doing extremely well. She has been a tremendous support to me."

"Yes, well, we all knew Anne would thrive in the palace environment, but you? Well, I am surprised you are not begging to come home." Despite her words, her tone does not sound at all surprised.

"Yes, um, I guess I didn't want to insult the queen or anything," I say, hoping to derail this topic of conversation.

"It makes me wonder if, perhaps, there is something there that makes you wish to stay." I am silent, unsure what to say to the knowing gleam in her eyes. She continues, "A rumor has reached my ears about this being a trial period for you, to allow courtship with the young prince."

"And is this so unbelievable? That the prince might actually want to court me?" I huff. Mother has never deemed me an ideal daughter.

"No. In fact, when your father heard, he started to recall some things from the Lindenwood mission and said he believed it could be plausible."

My head drops into my hands. Father knows? I am not sure why, but I find this terribly embarrassing. Mother is quiet while she waits for me to deny or confirm. She will hear the truth sooner or later. It might as well be from me. Hopefully, she will not devolve into hysterics.

Hesitantly, I recount the entire story for her from my unmasking on the mission until the present. When the story is done, she says nothing, merely taps her index finger on the arm of the chair, the noise magnified in the quiet room.

"So you two really do love each other?" she says at last.

"Yes."

"Well, you must love him very much if you are willing to consider living his lifestyle," she muses.

"I do, Mother." I sound surer than I feel.

Her eyes brim with tears. "You have changed so much, Olivia, matured so much in just this month alone. And I am happy for you, but it is tempered with worry. Life as Prince Liam's wife will bring you no small amount of scrutiny. I am not saying you should forget about him, just please, don't forget what you will give up by marrying him."

Wow. Mother suggests I do not jump at an offer to marry a prince? I am not sure I can handle any more strange developments today.

"I promise, I will not make the decision lightly." My heart is too torn and fragile right now to say anything more.

Ellen and Lydia burst back into the room giggling. They stop at the sight of our serious faces.

"Should we go back in the kitchen?" Ellen asks.

"No," I say. "I want to spend my last few minutes with all of you."

All too soon, I am back on the road to the palace. The ride passes unnoticed. There is too much to contemplate. I leave my horse with a stable boy, then head back to my room. Home does not feel like home, and the palace is an unwelcome place of no purpose.

Sadie helps me out of my dress. She asks a hundred questions about my family and my visit. When she finishes brushing out my hair, she checks the fire one last time, then grabs her shawl.

"Good night, miss." She freezes in her tracks. "Oh, wait. There is one more thing."

She darts to the wardrobe and removes something. She approaches with a beautifully wrapped box cradled in her hand. "This is for you. He told me to give it to you tonight."

Before I can question her, she leaves the box on the vanity and scurries out with a sly smile.

I stare at the box for a moment, then pick it up and untie the red satin bow. It is wrapped in heavy paper embellished with an intricate floral design. A small wooden box emerges and I lift the hinged lid. There on a cushion of blue velvet sits a delicate necklace with a charm in the shape of a sword. In the center of the hilt is a small diamond.

A folded-up square of paper falls from inside the lid. It reads:

Happy Birthday, my Olivia.
Since you gave up your real sword for me,
I wanted you to have this one, along with my heart.

Yours always,
Liam

For a few moments I simply gaze at the pendant, afraid to even touch it. Then, slowly, I run my finger over it. I have never seen anything like it before. He must have had it made especially for me.

When my head finally hits the pillow, I am happy to know one thing remained true today—our love.

When I wake, only a hint of pink dawn edges the leaden sky. The bed feels empty without my sister in it. I have gotten used to her comforting, solid presence at night, to our confidences and stories at the end of the day. It reminds me so much of the closeness we shared when we were younger. Reconnecting with Anne has been one of the bright parts of my exile in this palace.

Once out of bed, I throw the curtains open just as Sadie patters in. She places the usual tray of sweet rolls and juice on the side table for my breakfast.

"Sleep well?" she asks brightly. She is always so chipper whether it is morning, afternoon, or night. I would love to know her secret, since I can barely manage human in the morning.

"All right, I suppose. I miss Anne," I admit, dropping unladylike into the vanity chair, a sweet roll in hand.

My handmaid goes to work on my hair, her magic fingers deftly coiffing my tresses. She uses a little scissor to shape some of the unevenness caused by my pre-mission styling. It looks better every day thanks to the extra attention Sadie bestows on it.

"Any plans for the day?" she queries.

"I have to transcribe some more prayer cards for the queen." I have been ignoring this work and now is as good a day as any to dedicate some time to it. A sigh escapes my lips when I imagine the next few hours of tedium. "How about you, Sadie? Any plans more exciting than mine?"

Our maidservant always becomes embarrassed when we ask her anything personal. "Well, after my duties here, I am going on a picnic with my beau." She smiles broadly at his mention. "It is a bit chilly, yes, but warm enough in the sun. Franklin likes to fish and it is a good time for it with the queen away and all. After that, we both have more duties to attend."

How I envy her life of simple pleasures, but Sadie works hard, as does Franklin, a farrier's apprentice in the royal stables. Their simple pleasures come at the cost of a lifetime of servitude. Yet still, a picnic with just Liam and no prying eyes—not even Adam's—would be exquisite.

With the last of my tresses pinned into place, she helps me slip into my dress. While Sadie goes to work on the linens, I excuse myself, then walk at a leisurely pace to the queen's reception room. The halls are fairly empty, both servants and courtiers not needed when there is no royalty to attend. A lone scullery maid washes the floor, water sloshing out of her bucket into small pools.

Shrill giggles drift out of the reception room up ahead, more abrasive than the maid's scrubbing. Unfortunately, they belong to Elaine and Gretchen, who barely spare me a glance when I enter. Camille, who sits with them, gives me an almost imperceptible nod of greeting. They are ostensibly working on an altar cloth, but perform far more work with their tongues than their fingers. Madame le Clare sits in the rear of the room, a pile of yarn at her side, needles clicking in the same efficient manner one would expect from her.

Strolling to a small desk on the side of the room, I gather up my supplies from the drawers, then pick up where I left off many days ago, copying a scripture onto a card of Saint Francis.

"So, according to Emily, her sister will be joining us here. She will return with them from Prescott," Elaine says loudly enough and with her head tilted in such a way it is obvious she wants me to hear.

Great. Another Wolf Pack member. Just what this room needs.

"That should change some things around here," Gretchen adds, and they share a conspiratorial chuckle.

A few gentlemen enter the room with raucous greeting and the ladies fall all over themselves welcoming them, until Madame le Clare clears her throat in warning. This subdues them somewhat, but the altar cloth is forgotten, stuffed into a trunk, while the dice come out. They all gather around a gaming table. All but me, of course. The only man I recognize is Lord Montgomery, who hangs behind. He usually spends most of his time talking to my sister. She has confided in me her interest in him. When our eyes meet, he gives me a forlorn look. It seems someone misses Anne as much as I do.

A cheer rings up from the men at the table. "Already you ladies fall behind. I guess it is not a day for feminine luck," an unctuous fool of a courtier quips. What his name is, I have no idea, but he has the air of one who has never worked a day in his miserable life.

"Well, since we cannot have one of you play on our side, maybe Olivia will join us," Elaine's voice drips with malice. "Maybe she will bring us luck since she likes pretending to be a man."

Every head spins in my direction, the room so quiet you could hear a pin fall. I merely grace her with a nasty smirk, then turn back to my work as if disinterested in their entire existence.

"No really, Olivia," Elaine continues, unwilling to let it go. "You are no good at anything else around here. Why not give it a try? Afraid you will see you were better use to the world as a boy?"

I have no answer for her because, in truth, she is right. My life was better when I was a squire.

"Elaine, let it go," Camille says, surprising me almost as much as the fact that Madame le Clare has remained silent throughout this exchange. She sits, needles still clacking crisply, feigning obliviousness. I knew she disliked me; now I know just how much.

"Let what go? It's not as if it's a secret she prefers acting and dressing like a boy. And goodness knows, she is built like one too," Gretchen pipes in. The men guffaw, all except Lord Montgomery, who stares with pure disdain at the two ladies.

It takes every ounce of discipline not to lunge across the room and show her how a "boy" fights by knocking her on her rear. But I know this is what she wants—to antagonize me until I break, to prove I am unfit for palace life. She has been waiting for her chance.

Slowly, I place the quill back into the inkwell and rise. With as much dignity as I can muster, I head for the door. The force of every eye bores into my very core. Anger rises in me like the tide ready to pound onto the shore, but I will not succumb to it. Not here. Not in front of them.

"Leaving so soon, Olivia? Too hard to hear what a disgrace you are to this court?" Gretchen calls after me.

Unshed tears of rage scald the back of my eyes. I finally see myself as they see me, as they will always see me. To them, I will always be a caricature, a one-dimensional paper figure. Not only do they not have an interest in any other side of me, they have contempt for the one part they acknowledge. I will always be the girl who trained with the squires, who now tries unsuccessfully to masquerade as a lady. This is all I will ever be to them, and unless I move elsewhere, it is all I will ever be in this kingdom.

It is funny how the peak of the societal hierarchy assigns slots for people to fill. Tiny, cramped boxes some shove their lessers into in order to keep themselves on top, then make these people the subject of ridicule, make seeing any other side of them impossible. Is it because they, themselves, are so one-dimensional that they refuse to recognize diversity of character in others? Better to simply pigeon-hole everyone into convenient categories where they will stay.

Tears now fill my eyes in earnest while imagining the glow of triumph on their faces. I race down the hall, ignoring the chastisement of Madame le Clare, who orders me back immediately. A startled servant presses against the wall to avoid me when I barrel past, his load of linens clutched to his chest.

Suddenly, I am bone-tired of being here. Exhaustion weighs me down like an anchor around my neck, pulling me deeper and deeper to unescapable depths. A wild thought of riding home and never coming back forms in my mind. My legs act of their own accord. They carry me down a staircase, two steps at a time, through a hallway and out the nearest door. I emerge into the gardens, almost knocking over a couple locked in a passionate embrace. The man shouts something crude at my fleeing form, but I barely process it.

I need to run to outpace the truth of the words Elaine and Gretchen just spoke. My lungs burn with each ragged breath I draw. They are right—I am a disgrace to the court, to Liam. Even if the king and queen miraculously approve of us, the court would treat me with a level of disdain I could not live with, and, more importantly, could not make Liam live with. It is the truth I have been refusing to admit to myself.

The stables loom ahead, beckoning me to leave now, before I lose my nerve.

I hurtle into the stall area, furious at life for allowing me to experience love that is doomed to fail. The horses perk up their ears when I storm past. A lone bucket sits in the middle of the floor and I give it a good, swift kick. It clatters across the cobblestones, where it rolls to a stop.

"Wow, what did that bucket ever do to you?" says a voice so achingly familiar, yet so incredibly out of place, I can only stare dumbfounded at the speaker. "Although, what do I know? Maybe the bucket had it coming."

"Puck?" Before I can think, my arms are flung around his neck and I start to sob, in fatigue, anger, and relief all at once.

"Oh, Livy, it's all right," he murmurs, rubbing my back soothingly. No questions, no demands, just the unwavering support of a true friend.

He consoles me until my tears have run dry, and finally, through my sobs, I manage to ask, "What…are…you…d-d-doing here?"

"Well, now that is a good story, so why don't we have a seat and I will tell you."

My old friend takes my hand, leads me to a hay bale and pats for me to join him. I keep our fingers entwined, his grip too reassuring to release. He looks older with a less carefree aspect to his face, but still my Puck, my best friend. There is no trace of anger or hurt in his eyes anymore. Hopefully, he can forgive my terrible treatment of him.

"So it seems there was an opening here at the stables," he begins, and I remember Harry and his wife's rich uncle, "and somehow Prince Liam knew I had a way with horses and recommended me for the position. How do you suppose that happened?" he asks knowingly.

"Oh my goodness, I told him the day we played archery," I whisper in disbelief. I also told him how much I missed Puck. My lips quiver again at the thought of Liam bringing him here for me.

"Well, I can't thank you enough, Livy. This is a dream come true. I never quite fit in with the squires. Let's face it, I wouldn't have made a great knight. But this, this is exactly where I fit in."

"I am so happy for you and so thankful you are here." I embrace him and try to keep from bursting into tears again.

"But what about you? I think it is safe to say *you* are not happy here—at least not at the moment. Tell me what is going on."

And so, Puck learns every detail from the moment I arrived at the palace until present. The burden that has weighed me down since I first stepped out of my parents' carriage starts to ease. Just being able to tell my friend lessens it more than I ever imagined.

"So do your parents know this is a test for you? That you and Liam are together?"

"Mother knows. She has heard rumors. I confirmed it yesterday."

"Interesting…"

"You aren't angry or hurt, are you? I mean, we never officially said anything, but I know you and I both assumed we would marry each other one day." I don't want to lose my friend again when I just got him back, but I have to know.

"No, Livy, I am not mad." He looks at our clasped hands. "You are my friend and I love you, but only as a friend. I am happy you found someone you love so much, even if the relationship has its…challenges."

"Well, knowing you are here will make things significantly more bearable." All thoughts of leaving flew out of my head at the announcement of his new position. "And Puck, I hope you know how truly sorry I am for making you miss the Lindenwood mission. I've said it before and I will say it now; I was wrong. I betrayed your trust and all I can do now is beg for your forgiveness."

At first he is quiet and I steel myself for his refusal. This is a hurdle we must surpass to have our friendship work. If he cannot find it in his heart to forgive me, it will be an invisible, yet impenetrable wall between us. I stare at my foot, drawing small circles with my toe in the dirt floor of the stables. When I am finally brave enough to meet his eyes, I see they are full of mercy.

"I was angry, Livy. Angry at you, at myself, at life in general. But now, looking back, I see my training to be a knight was like trying to stuff a square peg in a round hole. I wanted it to work so badly, but it never quite did. If you had not gone on the mission and met Liam, I would not be here right now. And I am content with where I am. So you see, everything happens for a reason."

Relief flows through me like a gentle gust of summer air. This is why I love Puck so much, why we balance each other out so well. He has the ability to see the bigger picture and the ability to let bygones be bygones far sooner than I could ever muster. Such wonderful qualities to have in a friend…a best friend.

"Well, since you seem free at the moment, how about a nice ride together?" he suggests, rising from the bale and pulling me up with him.

"Are you allowed to? I don't want to get the new worker in trouble."

"The stables are quiet with so many people away. More than half the horses are gone, either with the royal party or the courtiers who have left in the King's absence. Things will be different when they return next Friday, but for now, let's take advantage of it."

Puck and I ride out that day and every afternoon leading up to Friday. In fact, after the first day, I discard my dresses for trousers, which I have Sadie "borrow" from her brother. The wind streaming through my hair, the feel of the mount beneath me, and the easy banter with my friend slowly ease my spirit out of the corner to which it felt banished. I remember who I am and what I want—to be with Liam badly enough to figure out a way to fit into his world.

My maid remarks on the healthy glow in my face. It makes her happy enough to forget how scandalous she finds my pants and her part in obtaining them. Elaine tries to agitate me a few more times to no success. I merely smile blithely, going about my business until she decides I am not a fun target anymore. The saint card transcription, the fawning reception room games, even the corsets no longer bothers me. Liam is my sole focus. He is what I am here for.

Finally, on Friday, while I paint the final stroke on a Saint Peter card, a page bounds into our presence to announce the imminent arrival of the king and his party. Once again, the court crowds the main staircase, all those who left for the comforts of their own homes made sure to return by this day. The royal train pulls through the palace gate. My father leads the way, alert and imposing as always. Carriages roll in an orderly procession to the steps and slow to a stop. After the cloud of dust settles back to the ground, footmen open the doors and the travel-weary passengers emerge. Pockets of exuberance erupt where families are reunited.

Liam rode in with the knights, who were at the front of the procession. I crane my neck to spot him, but cannot push through the horde of bodies. Jostled down some steps, I regain my footing in front of a rig, just as my sister steps out.

"Anne," I exclaim, wrapping her in an embrace.

Kat climbs out on her heels and hugs me tightly. They both look wary, afraid to say anything, and exchange a glance that sends uneasy waves through my body. Before I can ask what is wrong, Emily descends the vehicle's stairs, another girl on her arm.

"Oh, Olivia, how wonderful to see you," she croons in a tone so phony I want to stab her. "Allow me to introduce my sister, Jocelyn."

A stunning lady with lavish blond hair, a porcelain complexion, and clear blue eyes extends her hand to me. When I place mine in hers, she grips it a bit too tightly, leans into my ear and whispers in a too-sweet voice, "Hello, Olivia. Pleasure to meet you. Just to warn you, I am here for one reason and one reason only. To marry Prince Liam."

It is a good thing Anne is by my side for Jocelyn's words almost cause my legs to buckle. She cannot be serious. Has Liam forgotten all about me in a mere two weeks? But then, if anyone could make him forget, it is this goddess of a woman who stands in front of me, a gloating smile on her lips. My hand flexes, wishing I had my sword to knock the look clean off of her face.

Gently, Anne pulls me away. She and Kat guide me up the stairs and through the labyrinth of corridors to our room. They maneuver me inside, my steps wooden, my thoughts incoherent. The click of the shutting door brings me back to my senses.

"Is it true?" I demand in an accusatory tone.

"Only half true. Emily and Jocelyn have concocted this scheme together, but to the best of my knowledge, Prince Liam knows nothing of it," Anne offers.

"To the best of your knowledge?" I huff.

"I'm sorry, Olivia. I...we—" She gestures to Kat, "— don't have the personal access to him that you do. There was no way to ask him outright. You will have to do it yourself."

"Oh, you bet I will." I lunge for the door, but two firm sets of arms hold me back.

"Not until you calm down," Kat says. She rubs my back in an effort to soothe, her eyes alight with worry.

"Seriously, Olivia," Anne begins, barely able to keep the frustration out of her voice. "What are you going to do?

Stomp over to the royal quarters and have a temper tantrum? Think how that would look."

Good point.

I rub the heels of my hands into my eyes.

Calm down. Take deep breaths.

I find no place of serenity, only terror at the thought of losing Liam. My heart feels as though a vice squeezes it, wringing out every last drop of life. I pace across the small chamber. Reason has been swallowed up by fear—fear that slowly simmers into a seething anger.

They watch me nervously. Anne blocks the door with her body, lest I try to make an escape. Various thoughts of how to torture and maim this Jocelyn parade through my head. Yet, nothing I can come up with would inflict the torment she has just delivered to me. Then, a horrible thought hits me—I didn't even stay in the courtyard long enough to greet Liam myself. What if he thinks I have forgotten him? This sets off a whole new round of paranoia in my brain. When I start murmuring half sentences to myself, my sister takes charge.

"Kat, go see if you can find Sadie and have her bring Olivia some tea." Anne opens the door a crack so my friend can slip out. Then, she regards me skeptically.

"You know, for a girl who rescued a king and associated with outlaws, you sure don't appear prepared for this battle," she muses.

"What?" My addled mind takes a moment to register her remark.

"That's all this is, Livy. A battle. She is here to get something you want. Don't let her. What would you do if this was an actual battle?"

"I would devise a strategy to win," I reply, wondering when Anne became a proponent of my training.

"Well then," she asks with a shrewd grin, "what are we waiting for?"

Dinner is not for another couple of hours, so there is plenty of time to discuss how to deal with Jocelyn. Kat returns with Sadie on her heels. My sister, my friend, and I sit on the bed where Sadie deposits a tray of tea and warm scones. The comfort of having them both back here with me quells my anger and leaves me in a much better state of mind to tackle the subject at hand.

"The funny thing is," Anne starts, crumbs tumbling to her lap, "I don't even remember Jocelyn in Prescott. If she was at any of the ceremonies or dinners, her appearance wasn't noted. I was surprised when all of a sudden we were told she was returning to Adelina with us. I truly don't think she poses any actual threat to you. I never even saw her and Liam speak to one another."

"She seemed pretty confident," I state. My feet dangle off the side of the bed where Sadie skirts around them.

"That girl is just as overbearing as her sister. Try being stuck in a carriage with them for two days. I don't know which one of them is more egotistical," Kat moans and my maid suppresses a smile.

"Yes, but she is beautiful," I complain. "And worse yet, I didn't even wait to greet Liam. I just left. What must he be thinking about me right now?"

"I think he knows what happened," Kat volunteers.

"You do? How?"

"I saw him surveying the crowd from his horse, searching for you. Then he dismounted and approached, but it was too late. Jocelyn had already spewed her venom. He watched Anne and I lead you away. I'm sure he felt it was best not to create a spectacle in public."

This news gives me some relief. At least he knows I was there to meet him. I drain the last sip of tea, then recline on the mattress, mulling all aspects of this new problem. The first thing I need to clarify is what Liam's take on the situation is. Yet even if he is unaware of her plan, she still has him in her sights. A more important piece of the puzzle is what Jocelyn and Emily have up their sleeves. They are much too seasoned courtiers not to have their own strategy.

"So I think it would be best, Olivia—" Anne interrupts my thoughts, "—if you keep a low profile right now. I will try to feel out the situation by speaking with all the queen's ladies."

"All right. And speaking of the other ladies, there were some interesting times in the reception room while you were away."

I spend the next few minutes filling them in on Elaine's antics. No one is surprised, not even Sadie, who shakes her head, annoyed I was treated so cruelly. Anne is happy to hear about Puck and his new position with the Master-of-Horse, which amuses me since she never gave him the time of day all those years he hung around with me. She also wants to hear every detail of my birthday visit home, apparently a bit more homesick than I would have thought.

We agree our best chance for finding out what is going on will be for Anne to subtly probe the other ladies for information. Kat also may be able to speak with a few of the gentlemen she has known since childhood to see what they have heard. My friend excuses herself to prepare for dinner. I remain on the bed, absently twirling a ribbon through my fingers.

"Speaking of your birthday," Anne rifles through her unpacked trunk.

She pulls out a package and hands it to me. A small journal emerges from the wrapping, its cover decorated with a painting of our house. Every little detail—the bright floral wreath on the door, the ivy climbing up the drainpipe, the crooked hitching post off to the side—is captured perfectly. Inside the creamy, lined pages await the swirl and flourish of the written word.

"Oh, Anne, it is so lovely. Thank you."

"You're welcome. One of the squires on the trip painted all sorts of decorative items. He has been on our property enough to render such an exact likeness. Now you can write all your secret love desires down." She puckers her lips to make kissing sounds.

I toss her a sour look, before leaping off the bed to hug her tightly.

Anne seats herself at her vanity and unbounds her hair from the stiff braid she wore for traveling. While Sadie prepares our dresses, I set about combing my sister's hair, a thick cascade of rich chestnut. The comb sails through the glossy locks with ease, unlike my mousy hair that knots if you look at it wrong.

"You may very well need one of those love journals yourself. Lord Montgomery will be ecstatic to see you again. He seemed at loose ends without you to fawn over these past weeks," I tease.

"Really?" she asks, a pleased smile filling her face. Whatever feelings are there, they are clearly mutual.

"I have to admit," I tell her, "I like him. He doesn't buy into the drama and scheming like all the other gentlemen do."

"No, he doesn't. You are right. He is almost too nice for his own good. It is a wonder he hasn't been eaten alive in this court."

Anne stands and lets Sadie re-lace her corset, then slips on a fresh dress. I am next and remember exactly how much I loathe corsets when the strings are pulled tight. Wistfully, I think of my contraband trousers hidden in a box in the closet. Seated again, my sister waits while our maid pins up her hair.

"I have to say, Anne, I am shocked you find someone so utterly uninterested in playing the court games attractive. Didn't you always lecture me about how participating in such nonsense is what brought one standing and status? I would think you would find Lord Montgomery boring."

"I once thought this way, but not anymore. Playing power games, demeaning others for pleasure, trying to push others down so you can feel more important, well, it's exhausting. Once we got here, I took a good look at the ladies who are ten years older than us and still acting this way. Even though many of them are the wives of dukes and earls, they are the most spiteful, unhappy people you would ever want to encounter. It made me realize how I don't want to end up."

For a moment, I am stunned into silence and almost want to check my sister's forehead for a temperature. But my views on life and love have shifted immensely over the past few months. It is reasonable to think hers could too.

Sadie moves over to work on my hair. Anne smiles to herself. A smile I know well. The one I get when I think of Liam. It is an expression of contentment and love, which only fractionally mirrors the warmth in my heart. Perhaps we have both found "the one."

"So what do you think of him, you know…romantically?" I pry while the maid weaves a ribbon through my braid.

"Don't you have enough trouble worrying about your own love life, Olivia?" Anne chides, but the scarlet rising in her cheeks betrays her.

"Ooh. An evasive answer. Must mean you like him a lot," I tease and make some kissing noises of my own.

When I dodge the hairbrush she tosses at me, we erupt into a fit of giggles. Even Sadie can't help but to laugh outright.

The dining hall is filled to capacity, all the courtiers anxious to show their faces to the returned monarch, who sits on the dais with his entire family. Liam's eyes find mine and his expression is one of tender concern. All I can manage is a stiff smile. How I wish for five minutes of privacy.

I slide down the bench next to Kat. Anne, meanwhile, takes a seat down at the Wolf Pack end of the table, their newly ensconced member holding a court of her own. Admittedly, it is hard to not stare at Jocelyn, changed from her travel attire to a fine green silk gown. Her golden tresses sail unbound on her shoulders. She has the same charismatic magnetism my youngest sister, Lydia, possesses. People are drawn to her like a moth to flame. In Jocelyn's case, I suspect one ends up like the moth—burned.

A tap on my shoulder startles me out of my musings. The bright scarlet livery of a royal page hovers over me with a small folded paper in hand. Once I take it, he disappears as silently as he arrived. Kat shrugs at my quizzical glance. I unfold the letter and read:

Dearest Olivia,

I looked for you in the courtyard, but you were already being escorted away. Please do not believe any rumors you hear about me. I will arrange a private meeting for us tomorrow. Until then…

All my love,
Liam

Without thinking, my eyes fly over to the dais where he sits. Of course, he watched me read his message and now smiles, lifting his glass with a nod. I smile and nod back. It is the only gesture we can share in a public place, but it is enough to ease the choke hold around my heart.

The Wolf Pack stare daggers at me from their end of the table before whispering amongst each other. Anne will not meet my eyes. She lowers her head and murmurs with them, an indignant expression on her face. It is important they think she is their ally, not mine.

"So how was the trip?" I ask Kat in an effort to look unbothered by my enemies.

"Long. But it was nice to see my parents. Well, my father at least. My mother just badgered me about possible suitors here at court. She is rather single-minded on that subject."

"Aren't they all," I mumble.

"Then there was all the uproar over Brother Alastair and the convicts." She nods in the direction of a table across the room where a large, bald, rather imposing-looking friar sits. "He was sent here to help out the monsignor. Prince Arthur recommended him to King William prior to his death. He has worked closely with Prince Stephan in the past."

Kat mentioned Brother Alastair was expected back when I first arrived. Seated next to the ancient priest, the newcomer eats heartily, his plate overflowing. The aging monsignor's head almost nods into the dish of pudding in front of him. At this point, solid foods are a thing of his past. They should make an interesting pairing.

"Yes, I remember about the friar, but what convicts?"

"Apparently, he helps rehabilitate criminals to do the church's work—tending the poor and elderly and such. A group of ten men accompanied him to Adelina to minister under his guidance here and provide manual labor as penance for their sins. There were some in the traveling party who thought they should make the journey here separately, but the king allowed it."

A servant proffers a platter of meats, smoke still rising off the juicy cuts when we put some on our plates. I take a hot roll from a basket which follows soon after. Dish after dish stream out of the kitchen to welcome the king home. No one will leave their table wanting, especially Brother Alastair, who seems unable to fill his plate high enough.

"And did the convicts cause any trouble on the return trip?" I ask, knowing my father would have put a quick end to any unrest.

"No, not at all," Kat replies between bites of her meal. "They are a sad group. They resemble staving beggars and were shackled in pairs at the ankle. I am not sure they could have even mustered the energy to escape, let alone thieve in the presence of so many armed royal guards."

"So where are they being housed?" The royal dungeon would be a cold, damp end to such a long journey. If they are in as bad a shape as Kat says, they may not last long.

"I heard they were going to be kept in some huts in the fields beyond the kitchens. Who knows how reliable this information is." She shrugs and goes to work on a meat pie.

For reasons I cannot identify, I get an uneasy feeling about this friar. When I sneak another glance, he stares with unabashed disdain at something. I follow his gaze to the dim corner where Niobe nests amidst her pillows. Kat had said Brother Alastair disapproved of the king's witch. He certainly makes no secret of this with his contemptuous glare.

"If he wants to get rid of her," my friend says, watching along with me, "I hope he is ready for a fight with the king."

"Yes, a big one," I agree.

A dish is placed in front of Niobe. She snatches it and hunkers down farther into the shadows, as if she, too, shares our misgivings.

Morning's bright glow fills the hallway on the way to the reception room. Since Queen Helen has returned, my afternoon rides will likely be curtailed. Her Majesty has not arrived yet, so the ladies flock around Emily and Jocelyn. The younger sister wastes no time establishing her place in the pecking order. Upon entering, no one so much as glances my way.

I take my usual seat and pull out the quills and saint cards to ready for another dull morning of transcription. Jocelyn laughs gaily at something, tossing her head in the air. She is so beautiful; it is hard to believe she is real.

Madame le Clare strides purposefully into our midst and claps her hands for attention. She has not acknowledged me in any way since the day I tore off to the stables against her direct order. I am not sure she had ever been disobeyed prior to that, and the breech of propriety was more than she could process. Better to just ignore me. I can't say I have a problem with this arrangement.

"Queen Helen orders all her ladies to accompany me to the dressmakers' rooms. It is time to select the fabric for the gowns to be worn at the Holiday Ball—Her Highness' gift to each of you."

Another dress? No one here is short on clothing. Is there no end to the wastefulness of court life?

The rest of the ladies obviously do not share my sentiments and jump up and down in delight. They excuse themselves from the few gentlemen in the room at this early hour and file out the door past Madame le Clare, an excited cloud of satin and laughter.

Not particularly eager for this excursion. I hang back, the last one to exit, but our keeper throws up her arm in front of my exit. "Olivia. Please remain here. Her Highness would like a word." With an ominous look, she heads off down the hall, herding the ladies together and pleading for decorum.

Great.

Singled out again. This will just add to the fun this afternoon when I am reunited with the Wolf Pack. Emily and Jocelyn received the rundown on the afternoon they chased me from the room. It will be more fuel for the fire from Gretchen and Elaine.

I stroll over to the window and press my forehead against the chilly glass. The grounds are cold and hard amidst the bare trees, belying the bright sunlight. Statuary stands lonely and unwelcoming without blooms to adorn them. Even the evergreens seem less vibrant at this time of year, no snow yet to decorate their boughs.

Queen Helen's soft footsteps sound behind me. I face her and drop into a curtsey. She nods, so I rise and stand, hands folded in front of me. If I am in trouble, I need to stay focused and apologize appropriately.

"Olivia, dear, how are you?"

Not the start I expected.

"I am well, Your Highness. I hope your travels were comfortable."

"As comfortable as can be expected. Please sit." She gestures to a chair near her raised seat and we both settle down, adjusting our skirts accordingly. Then I silently wait my scolding.

"I understand one or two of the ladies were less than kind to you in my absence."

At least she was correctly informed by someone, goodness knows who.

"It was nothing I couldn't handle," I assure. It is important she knows I can survive here; showing weakness and tattling on enemies are not options.

"Yes, I have no doubt of that," she replies. Her brow knits and she mulls something over. I remain quiet, unsure where exactly this conversation is going. My stomach clinches into a tight knot. Is she going to dismiss me? Crush all hope I have of a life with Liam?

After a long moment of deliberation, she says, "Olivia, I am going to be frank with you, and I am sure I can trust you to treat this discussion with all discretion."

"Most certainly, Your Highness."

"I think we both agree your time spent here in my rooms has not been particularly pleasing," I make to disagree, to let her know I can belong here, but she holds up her hand and continues, "which is why I will ask you a favor."

A favor?

She must want to ask me to leave willingly, to let her son go without any trouble. No training I had would have ever prepared me for this.

"I would like to appoint you as an assistant to Niobe." My utter disbelief leaves me at a loss for words. "She is skilled in the art of healing and infection prevention. Her service to our staff is invaluable, but her latest episode has left her slower, more unsteady than she was. I trust this will be acceptable to you."

"Of course, Your Highness. Whatever you ask of me." I think of the old lady helping the boy with the scraped knee versus the strange crone from the dining hall. Who knows which one I will have to deal with.

"There is a bit more," Queen Helen continues. "I will not lie, the prophecy about the king has me concerned. Both my husband and my son have boasted of your acumen. It would make me feel better to have a trained eye on Niobe in case any more details or evidence presents itself."

"So you want me to spy on her for you?" I blurt without thinking, then bite my tongue.

"Yes, if you want to word it that way. However, I feel we will each get something out of this arrangement. I will feel better with a direct link to Niobe's actions in light of her unsettling prediction, and you will no longer have to suffer around my ladies."

I bow my head in agreement. Whatever side of Niobe I encounter, it cannot be as spiteful as the women who grace this room.

"I want you to know, Olivia, I do not approve of how Elaine and Gretchen treated you." It comes as no surprise the queen knows exactly what went on in this room, but it amazes me when she names the ladies outright.

"Thank you, Your Highness, for that and for your generous offer."

"Very well. I will have someone escort you to Niobe in the morning. Now you are excused to the archery yard. Someone is most anxious to see you," she states, a knowing gleam in her eyes.

"Thank you, Your Highness. I am anxious to see him as well," I admit.

"You make him happier than I have ever seen. Who knew my sullen boy had such white teeth under his perpetual grimace?"

We share a soft laugh, then I practically skip from the room with excitement. Queen Helen's smile fades, though, and she places her hand to her forehead as if she tries to push an ominous worry away.

The same pimple-faced page escorts me to the archery yard. We stop at a doorway and Kat emerges to join us. *Figures a chaperone would be included.* I had hoped for some true alone time with Liam, but this seems next to impossible here. Oh well. At least it is my friend and not one of my enemies who will witness our reunion.

"How was the dress selection?" I ask, not sorry to have missed it.

"A bit uncivilized, actually. Those girls lived up to their Wolf Pack name when the silks and baubles were presented for selection—claws out, teeth bared. Madame le Clare was most aggrieved. I was happy to get out of there in one piece," she jokes. "With all the chaos, they didn't even have a chance to measure me before I was summoned. You and I will have to go back tomorrow."

"Wonderful. Looking forward to it." Sarcasm drips from my voice like venom.

"What did Her Highness want?"

I am unsure what to say. Queen Helen never said assisting Niobe should be kept quiet, and if I am no longer to be in her reception room, everyone will wonder where I am. Even if it is supposed to be kept secret, it will not take long for the truth to come out. Gossip travels faster than light in this place.

"She wants me to assist Niobe. After her last episode, she requires some help."

Kat mulls this over for a moment. "Well, it gets you away from Emily and company, so that is good."

We arrive in the archery yard and the page bows to us, before trotting back to retrieve his next command. Liam awaits, but Adam is not his usual second. Instead it is Puck. They stand together chatting amiably, as if they have been friends for years. It is a bit unnerving. Puck knows things about me I would be embarrassed for him to share with my beau.

After an embrace for Liam, I give one to Puck. "What are you doing here?"

Liam answers for him. "Adam's new infant is ill. I gave him leave for the day. Puck was kind enough to come along with me."

Quick introductions are made between my old friend and my new one. Then my prince hurries me over to a bench in the corner. Kat and Puck stand where we left them, like the awkward strangers they are. I will have to apologize to them both later for the inconvenience of babysitting Liam and me.

"Will Adam's baby be all right?" I ask.

"Yes. He had a high fever all night, but Niobe gave him an herbal mixture and the temperature broke early this morning. His poor parents were up all night tending to him. Adam looked like walking death this morning."

It is a relief to know the infant is out of the woods. I never considered how much the king's healer played a part in the everyday lives of the palace staff. Perhaps she can teach me some skills that are actually useful and not merely a way of passing the day. Healing one baby would make me feel more constructive than transcribing a hundred prayer cards.

"Speaking of Niobe, your mother has asked me to assist her during the week."

"Yes. She told me of her objective. My mother knows how astute you are. It will give my whole family peace of mind to know there is a set of keen eyes on her. Especially with Brother Alastair here," Liam remarks, hardness creeping into his tone.

"What does the friar have to do with her?"

"He thinks her very presence here is heretical. Already he has tried to convince my father to exile her from the kingdom." Liam's fists clench at his side.

"Surely King William would never do such a thing."

"The friar strikes me as a man who finds a way to get what he wants no matter what. And the monsignor is too frail to challenge him in any way."

Very true. The poor head priest has looked as if he died and they forgot to bury him for a few years now.

"You think a man of the cloth would intentionally harm Niobe?" In her outburst, the healer had mentioned a vessel of faith. Could she have meant the friar?

"I don't know what to think—about Brother Alastair, the prophecy, any of it. Promise me you will keep your eyes and ears open."

"Of course," I reassure.

"Look at me." He sighs. "I finally have you here and I am wasting all this time talking." He leans in for a kiss, so comforting and familiar I never want it to stop. But a thought worms into my head. I pull back.

"What's wrong?" he asks, eyes still closed, lips still distractingly close to mine.

"Um…I met Jocelyn Crawford. Apparently, she is here to win your hand," I say, wariness coiling around my insides like a snake.

Liam shakes his head in disgust. "That girl was a thorn in my side the entire trip. Her and her sister concocted this scheme to get my attention. And believe me, it worked—just not in the way they hoped. I spent a good deal of time avoiding them like the plague."

Actual confirmation he is not part of this game makes me feel better for a moment. I glance across to where Kat and Puck hang archery targets from the tree branches. The latter says something and they both giggle like schoolchildren. A picture of Jocelyn and her haughtiness pops into my head. Annoyance rises in my chest that Liam paints himself as a helpless victim of their ploy. He is a prince for goodness' sake.

"Did you tell her you had no interest?" I challenge.

"Olivia." He sighs and takes my face in his hands. "Please do not, for one fraction of a second, think Jocelyn, or anyone else for that matter, will ever change what I feel for you." His eyes are filled with such tenderness, it would be impossible not to know he is genuine.

"She is just so beautiful and poised and, well, everything I am not." My hidden fear blurts from my mouth before I can stop it.

"My darling, don't you know our hearts are like two halves of one whole? There is no one else who would fit there. Just you." He kisses me in a soft, lingering manner, driving all sense out of my head.

I pull away again, but he continues to kiss my cheek, then down the side of my neck. Shivers shoot through my whole body. It would not surprise me if actual sparks shot out of my fingertips. Then he works his way back up to my lips again.

"Are you convinced?" he asks when he finally pulls away.

It takes a second for the world to steady again. I remember my friends who may have witnessed our display, but Kat and Puck now lean against a tree, so engaged in conversation that they are oblivious to us. A bird calls out a lonely cry and sweeps from one tree to another, the skeletal branches providing no cover.

"Yes. I am convinced for your part. But I think you may find Jocelyn Crawford is much like Brother Alastair—a person who finds a way to get what she wants no matter what."

"Perhaps you are right," he agrees. "She puts me in a difficult spot. I cannot be rude to her and cause friction in my brother's relationship with her sister. Not that I am any fan of Emily's. For now, I will keep avoiding and rebuffing, but if this is not enough to give her the message, then I will spell it out in terms that cannot be misunderstood. All right?"

He speaks with a raw honesty in his voice, which calms my frayed nerves. Instead of answering, I weave my fingers through his silky, black hair and pull him in for a long, passionate kiss.

"Remind me to thank Jocelyn for igniting your territorial instincts," he jokes and I punch him gently in the arm before continuing where we left off.

Somewhere in the haze of my preoccupation, my mind registers laughter. Not the sound my younger sisters make in the midst of spirited play, but the sound of two connected souls who are sharing a private moment. The way Liam and I laugh when we are together—like lovers.

Kat and Puck now sit on a bench, heads ducked down close together, knees touching, looking rather friendly with each other...more than friendly. Then, there it is again, the laughter rippling out of my friends' mouths like music. I stare at them, too confused to move. Liam follows my gaze.

"You know," he whispers, "I think if we exploded into a million pieces right now, they would not even notice."

"Yeah, it sure looks that way."

A jumble of conflicting emotions bounces around my heart. I mean, Kat and Puck together? It's not such a bad idea. But it's my Kat…and my Puck—my new world and my old world colliding.

"You would be all right with them being together, right?" Liam asks, his tone guarded.

"Yes, of course. It just caught me by surprise," I admit. "Looks as if there won't be much archery happening here today."

"No, not much," he agrees, smiling broadly just before our lips meet again.

Time passes. How long, I do not know…or care. Neither do any of my companions. Finally, we are interrupted by someone loudly clearing their throat. The page returns to escort Kat and me to our rooms. After drawn-out good-byes, my friend and I walk the cobblestone path back.

We dare not speak in front of the page, but Kat's eyes are lit up as if she stole a handful of sun for each of them. Our escort leaves us at the bottom of the stairwell leading to the ladies' chambers. The steps are ascended two at a time and we crash through the door of my room.

Sadie stands over Anne, framed against the setting sun visible through the window. A fistful of my sister's chestnut hair is twined in our maid's hand as she readies her for dinner. They jolt in surprise at our noisy entry. Kat and I say nothing, then plop on the bed in a fit of giggles.

"Fun afternoon?" Anne drolls while Sadie smiles at our merriment.

We sit up and try to compose ourselves. This lasts only a second before we burst out laughing again. It feels good, this carefree moment, like the ones I had so often with Ellen and Lydia at home. My life at the palace has been sadly lacking in such instances, so I take time to soak it all up.

"Oh, yes. A wonderful afternoon. Why did you never tell me how charming Peter is?" Kat exclaims.

"Who on earth is Peter?" my sister queries, more confused than ever.

"Puck. She means Puck," I clarify, trying to quell my laughter. My friend and I lie side by side on our stomachs. We look at each other and start tittering again.

"What was Puck, um, I mean Peter, doing with Prince Liam?" Anne asks, once we quiet down.

Sadie keeps styling, her fingers deftly weaving an intricate braid, while we explain the whole story to my sister in a series of chortles and interruptions only true friends can manage. Our maid finishes her work, pushing one last hairpin into place right as we finish up our tale.

"I just never met anyone I connected with so much," Kat gushes.

My smile for my friend's happiness is so wide, my face actually hurts.

"How about you, Anne? Did you pick out the materials for your dress?" I ask.

"Yes. It was dreadful. Like pigs set loose at the county fair. But you will never guess what happened in the reception room later." She hops on the bed between us, a girlish move so contrary to her usual sophistication. "Montgomery invited me to dine at his parents' residence this weekend. He wants his family to meet me."

Kat and I agree this is an important step in their progressing relationship and congratulate my obviously pleased sister. We lace hands, united in our feelings.

"It seems love is in the air here at the palace," Anne proclaims.

And all us, even Sadie, squeal in delight.

"Olivia, come here," Madame le Clare beckons me the moment Anne and I step out our door the next morning. She stands, ridged as a statue, at the end of the hall, just outside the door to her own chambers. I wonder if she ever lets the veneer crack while within the safety of its walls.

Anne gives my hand a squeeze, then continues down her intended path to the reception room. I trod down the hall to our waiting mistress. The corridor feels considerably colder than our bedroom with its crackling fire. I long to crawl back under my sheets, to be embraced by their comforting warmth.

Madame le Clare shows no indication of even noticing the chill. Maybe she is a reptile.

"You will report to Niobe in the herb gardens this morning as per the instruction of Her Highness. Do you know how to get there or should I summon a page?" The way she accentuates her S's sounds incredibly snakelike, further cementing my reptile theory.

"Yes. I know where to find it."

She seems relieved to not have to call for an escort. Speaking with me has clearly delayed her normal routine. Her shoulder brushes past me in her haste to return to the queen's presence, but she calls back, "You should retrieve your cloak before you go."

After ducking back in my room, I head down the stairs, my woolen wrap draped around me. Nippy air pierces my face when I exit to the outside grounds. A few turns later finds me in an outside corridor flanked by the kitchens on one side and the gardens on the other. Heat from the fire-stoked ovens hovers in the air in front of the open kitchen doors, a toasty blanket of space in the otherwise chilly world. I linger in there a moment while I scan the gardens.

Niobe hunches over a bush at the far end of the garden. Her fingers deftly examine each leaf before cutting those she deems satisfactory off the branch. Does she expect me? Did she request an assistant, or will my arrival be news to her? I'm not too keen to get off on the wrong foot with a supposed witch. Perhaps she will see through the ruse and know I am here to spy on her. My feet inch towards her in trepidation.

Before I am even halfway through my approach, a thin voice travels from her direction. "Please, dear, if you would be so kind, hand me my basket."

I look around, unsure if it is me she addresses. There is no one else in the vicinity, but how she knows I am here is a mystery.

"It's right there. By your feet, on the left."

Indeed, a partially filled basket lies less than six inches from my left toes. I scoop it up, then cross the remaining space between us, somewhat on edge with the whole transaction. When I hand it to her, she raises her eyes to meet mine, one blue, one green. They are surprisingly bright, keen little orbs against her withering face. And, apparently, they have the ability to see behind her back.

"I am Niobe, child. I appreciate your willingness to help me."

Good. At least I was expected.

"My pleasure. I am Olivia Davenport." I hold out my hand. She envelopes it in her own, the skin so paper-thin it is almost transparent, but her grip is firm. In fact, this strength, combined with the ageless wisdom in her eyes, puts my uneasiness to rest. "Her Highness, the queen, asked me to provide you with whatever assistance you need."

"Thank you, dear. It was good of Helen to be concerned for my welfare." She drops her handful of clippings into the basket while I digest the fact she is on a first-name basis with our queen. "Come, let us go inside where it is warmer."

Her gait is slow, yet purposeful along the uneven path through the herbs. She leads me to a door in the outer wall, just down from the kitchens. When I saw her enter it the day she helped the young boy, I mistook it for some type of shed or storage room for the gardens. Instead, we step into a well-lit room, heated nicely by a crackling fire. Beyond it, another door leads to a darkened chamber where I can just make out the outline of a low bed. These are the rooms where Niobe works and lives. Not the cave full of cobwebs and dankness I pictured for a witch.

Instantly, I am overwhelmed by the scent of the place. The fragrance of multiple flowers and herbs intermingle harmoniously, though I can still distinguish a bit of each fragrance's individuality—pine transports me to the woods, lavender to the meadow with Lydia twirling, mint to the back garden of my home. Eyes closed, I inhale one luxurious breath and feel as relaxed and limp as a ragdoll. Niobe simply watches me, a curious grin on her face.

"Have a seat, my dear." She guides me to a plush chair next to the fire.

I sink into the soft cushion and take a good look around. Dried herbs and flowers hang from every rafter at haphazard angles. A sturdy workbench with shelves above it dominates the wall to the right of the hearth. Bottles and vials in all imaginable sizes are strewn across every inch of available surface, a kaleidoscope of color and shape. Some are filled with brightly tinted liquids, some with salves. Brushes, scissors, and small tools are scattered amongst the glass containers. The bottom shelf is lined with mortars and pestles in various sizes and materials—wood, stone, and some type of metal. Jars on the upper shelves are trickier to identify, though I do recognize some chicken feet in one and dead (I hope) beetles in another. Two rickety stools provide seating for the workbench and a broom stands in the corner like a sentry. On the floor in front of the table lies a rectangular rug.

"So you are here to keep an eye on me, eh?" Niobe's words startle me out of my observations as she settles into a chair across from mine.

"No, um, just to help you, um…" I am the picture of eloquence, as always.

"And if I just happen to tell you more about the prophecy, well, it wouldn't hurt, right?" The gleam in her eye is knowing, but not malicious.

"No, ma'am," I admit. No sense in pretending. It will be better to start things off with the truth rather than a lie.

"It's Niobe, not ma'am, and I appreciate your honesty. Now let's get to work." She pats my hand. "You and I are going to get along just fine."

And we do.

Over the next few weeks, I learn details of the healer's vast knowledge. Niobe instructs how plants and herbs can be utilized to quell swelling, infection, and congestion, how to make poultices for an array of injuries and ailments, and what substances help a woman achieve pregnancy…or end one. Her cellar, accessed by a door underneath the rug, is carefully stocked and inventoried with various mixtures ready to grab when needed, along with stores of the dried herbs, leaves, and flowers for her remedies. A large bookshelf filled with reference tomes sits forgotten on a side wall. Why she keeps them tucked down here instead of in her main room, I cannot guess.

Niobe's healing skills are only some of the talents I discover about her. She is extremely well read, can write, play the lute, and knows the entire history of Stewartsland more thoroughly than even my father, which is saying a lot. There is also a gentle wisdom about her, tempered with an unspoken strength. The more time I spend with her, the more I understand why King William has relied upon her all these years. It puzzles me why she isn't more respected by the lords and ladies of court and chooses to remain solitary in their presence. When I ask her why she dines in the corner of the Hall instead of at a table, she replies, "For the mystique, my dear. It keeps me from having to deal with those snobby courtiers."

Each day, we make the short walk to the far edge of the palace grounds. There is a vast population of workers—cooks, maids, guards, footmen, and such—who live in a small cluster of homes with their families on the royal property. After two months of residing in my room, with meals to eat, a clean bathroom and fresh laundry, I am ashamed to say I never even thought about the lives of the people who provided these services. They treat the healer with a friendly reverence and she introduces them to me by name, familiar with every face. My heads spins with the sheer number of them. It will be a while before I can commit them all to memory.

We also tend to Brother Alastair's penitents, who currently tutly construct a new latrine for the servant village. For the most part, this group keeps to themselves, but a few of the men have chronic issues such as gout. The strict friar has instituted a penance where unnecessary talking is forbidden, but our help is met with grateful smiles. Niobe asks to see one man's feet and I am horrified to see they are bare, clad only in sandals that offer no protection in this raw weather. She lowers the man's robe, nodding perceptively.

On our walk back to her quarters, she says to me, "We must look into gathering extra woolen socks for those men before their friar has them losing toes."

My days fall into a nice rhythm, and for the first time, I am at peace with life at the palace. Mornings are spent assisting Niobe. I get to know many of the families who live in the servants' village. Doors are always opened to us, kindness and amity bestowed as naturally as the pie and cookies they offer us in thanks. They are people I connect with much more readily than the men and women who idle their days away in the queen's room. In the afternoons, when I return there, it is always feeling a bit deflated.

Today, my feet drag me slowly back to the stifling confines of the reception room. Niobe and I spent the morning with a maid's son, a boy of only two, who burned with fever. The healer did everything she could think of, but there was little improvement. When we left the family hovering at his bedside, I asked, "How long until Thomas starts to get better?"

Niobe stopped to face me, took my hands in hers. "That boy will not get better, Olivia. There are some sicknesses that are beyond anyone's skill to heal." The weight of these words may have unmoored me had it not been for her steady grip.

Now, with every step, my heart breaks a bit more at the thought of his tiny form never again rising to run and play, of the anguish his parents will endure, and tears threaten the back of my eyes. My body barely registers the transition when I pass from the chill outside back indoors, my spirit too heavy to sense the warmth. The trill of laughter spills out of the queen's room into the hall, a sound so discordant with my feelings, it makes me feel even more alone. I take a deep breath, ordering myself to hold it together until dinner, and enter.

Time stops.

For a second, the women seem frozen mid-giggle, their bright dresses like splotches of paint on canvas; the men immobilized around the gaming table, cards and dice suspended in air; the queen posed like a beautiful statue atop her throne, a book held in her hands. All I can concentrate on is Liam, sitting with his back to me, and Jocelyn Crawford on his lap. *His lap!* Jealousy hits me like a vicious slap and the world starts moving again. She tries to show him some small piece of embroidery, but he firmly stands, nearly knocking her down, and it takes some effort on her part to regain her balance.

"Excuse me, but I must be going," he sneers, not even bothering to mask his annoyance.

Liam turns to go. This is when he and everyone else in the room notice me. I manage to close my gaping jaw in time. A look of pure smugness crosses Jocelyn's face. I consider punching it off in one blow. My hands ball into fists at my side. It would be so easy to put her in her place. Out of the corner of my eye, I see Anne rise and step in my direction. She clearly anticipates my explosion. The other occupants of the room step forward a bit, hoping for some action as well.

But Liam's eyes stop me. His beautiful blue orbs are closed off, iced over—the indifferent expression of arrogance I remember from our first encounters. He is not my Liam right now. He is Prince Liam in a situation he hates, unable to speak his real feelings for fear of protocol. Jocelyn's behavior has him as mad as I am. The anger in me is extinguished like a snuffed candle flame.

"Good day, Mother," he manages through a clenched jaw, and with a nod, strides past me in all haste. The room drops into a combined curtsey at his exit.

Jocelyn still stares at me defiantly, the malice in her eyes evident. I simply smile at her, then cross over to where my sister stands by the window. Kat joins us, her reassuring touch on my arm. Queen Helen, who watches all this unfold, smiles to herself and returns to reading her prayer book. She approves of my behavior, it seems—one good point to focus on.

Anne makes a show of rolling her eyes at me and strolls away to the game table. She cannot afford to look as if she takes my side. Not if we want her to get information out of the Wolf Pack. Kat and I settle down on a window seat. Icy air permeates the thin glass, but it gives us some privacy.

"Don't worry," Kat whispers, "he came in here to talk to the queen. Jocelyn chased him around like a cat stalking prey. He could not have been any more dismissive to her."

"Thanks," I mumble and we sit in quiet contemplation until Madame le Clare instructs us all to prepare for dinner.

When Anne and I enter our room, Sadie awaits. Our gowns are laid out on the bed and our hairbrush is at the ready in her hand.

"Miss Olivia, how is Penelope's son?" she asks, her large green eyes awash with worry.

"Not well, I am afraid," I sigh, as an image of the small boy fills my mind.

She nods silently, a tear falling down her coffee-colored cheek. So much of what Niobe taught me these last few weeks about healing has seemed positively magical, I almost forgot she was not a miracle worker. Dealing with death and accepting its power, will prove the hardest part of this work for me.

The maid wipes her face on her apron, then points to my vanity. "This letter came for you this morning."

A thick, ivory-colored envelope lies amongst my ribbons, the name *Olivia* written across it in Liam's careful penmanship. It came this morning, so it cannot contain any words about our latest encounter. Not that he would write about hating Jocelyn in a letter, lest it was intercepted. I turn it over in my hands in wonder before breaking the wax seal.

Olivia,
Meet me tomorrow at two o'clock in the archery yard to discuss Niobe.
Your father will be joining us as well.

All my love,
Liam

This must be my first opportunity to give an account of what I have learned from my spying. Unfortunately, there is not much to tell. Nothing about the prophecy, or King William for that matter, has even come up in my time with Niobe. Though truthfully, I have so enjoyed her teachings, I never brought up anything about it. At least I will finally be able to discuss the prophecy with my father in detail. His opinion is always my guidepost.

My fingers run over Liam's signature. Silly, but it feels as though I hold a piece of him in my hand, something concrete, something he touched. I am loath to part with the letter, but written correspondence can too easily fall into the wrong hands. After a brief moment of wistfulness, I toss it into the fire. The crisp edges shrivel brown and disintegrate against the flames.

Anne watches me while Sadie arranges her hair, but says nothing. I cross to my vanity and plop into the chair to await my turn for styling.

Niobe bows her head low when I enter her chamber the next morning. A gust of cold air blows into the toasty room with me, flurries of snow swirling in my wake. Slowly, she raises her face to mine and the sadness in her eyes needs no explanation.

"Thomas is dead," I speculate.

The healer nods, the reluctant movement an effort against the news she would rather not deliver. We stand in silence a moment. What can one say about the loss of a young life? No words are adequate to describe the unfairness of an innocent soul ripped from this earth. The logs crackle on the fire, casting its heat around the room. But there is a cold place in my heart where no warmth can reach.

"This is the challenging part of healing others, Olivia. There are never any guarantees. We can only do what is within our power and nothing more," Niobe says, gently taking my hand. "Come. One of Brother Alastair's penitents needs more salve on his infected finger."

She hands me a small, circular jar off the workbench. A white, pearlescent cream fills it, thick peaks rising above the rim like miniature snow-capped mountains. The container has the word *Echinacea* scrawled across it in her coarse, slanted letters. Her writing has gradually become easier for me to decipher. Niobe is left-handed and her penmanship tilts at an awkward angle. It is a trait that only propagates the theory she is a witch, since someone in history decided it was a sign of wickedness. Personally, I think the whole debate about what hand someone uses as a judge of character is silly. But many people around here do not.

"Echinacea is most effective in preventing the spread of infection in flesh wounds," the healer instructs.

She takes her ragged cloak off a peg by the door. One quick motion of her spindly arms has it situated around her shoulders. A basket of supplies—bandages, string, various herbs—settles into the crook of her arms. I put a lid on the jar and lay it carefully among our provisions. The door creaks open and a cruel bite of raw air hits my face.

"Now, let us see to those we can help," she says and we venture out into the cold.

Thoughts of my afternoon plans are all I have to get me through the morning. The weather brightens nicely, though the morning chill cannot be entirely chased away by the rising sun. By the time two o'clock comes, it is somewhat more bearable out, but a frigid breeze still blows at intervals. My feet crunch on the frozen ground of the gardens on my way to the archery yard. On my right, the hedges forming the garden maze stand, a conspicuous green against its bare brown comrades.

Liam, Adam, and my father cluster in a tight pack, rubbing their hands together against the icy wind, which cuts through this space with a vicious preciseness. I run to my father's open arms and savor the warm, familiar embrace. Then I turn to Liam for an equally enthusiastic hug and kiss. When we part, I glance at Father. He and I have not had a chance to discuss my relationship with the prince or my trial period here at the palace. The day of the reward ceremony, he was as surprised as I at the order for me to move here. We both assumed I would be working with him after Lindenwood. Now he looks at the ground, uncomfortable that his daughter just kissed someone…but not surprised. Somewhere along the line the details were filled in for him.

"If I may suggest, perhaps we can move this meeting inside," Liam says.

Relieved to escape the cold, we follow him inside, through a hallway and into an empty salon. Adam quickly sets about lighting the sconces, then strides out of the room. There is no fire in the hearth, but it is still much warmer than outside.

"Sir Jack, we wanted to discuss Niobe's prophecy with you. My parents are most concerned. What are your thoughts?" the prince asks, directing us to seats by the window. Father settles into a large armchair, while Liam and I take the couch across from him. I am acutely aware of his hand on my leg and hesitate to meet my father's eyes.

"I was given a written copy by one of His Majesty's scribes as best as the wording could be remembered. You know, in general, I do not put much stock in the witch's words—" He gestures his hand dismissively, "—but I know the importance they carry for His Majesty."

Liam nods. He, too, has always been skeptical of Niobe's prediction abilities. Adam bustles back into the room, arms full of wood. Before long, a fire sparks to life with a cheery popping sound.

"In any case, all the palace guards and every knight have been put on alert to report any suspicious activity. Additionally, since the prophecy specifically mentions "a vessel of faith," we have taken steps to ensure the safety of the wine His Majesty consumes at Mass. The bottle is guarded from the moment it is opened and a taster samples it first."

"Yes, my father was relieved this precaution was instituted," Liam informs us.

"Other than that, there is not much to go on. We will remain vigilant, especially at all public events like the upcoming Holiday Ball." As always, Father's delivery is direct and to the point.

"But this should not be a worry," I interject. "The prophecy said his demise would be in spring."

"True, but I will take nothing for granted in the meantime," Father says sternly. "And what of Niobe, Olivia? What is your take after working with her these past few weeks? Have you learned anything more for us?"

Liam remains silent, waiting for my answer. Adam stands against the wall by the door, silent as a ghost.

"No. She insists she remembers nothing of the night she spoke. Neither has she made any other predictions around me in my time with her." For some reason, it feels like betrayal to speak of her in this manner and guilt gnaws at my gut. Niobe has been nothing but kind in my tenure so far.

"Well, keep your eyes and ears open around her," my father instructs, a keenly mistrustful edge in his tone.

"Do you suspect her to be somehow involved in a plot against the king?" I blurt out the thought that festers in my brain. The annoyance in my voice is apparent.

"I don't know what to think, so I leave all possibilities open. Otto is still out there, his motives unclear. Back at the time of John Linden's conflict with King William, Niobe was influential in convincing the king to cede him the land that became Lindenwood. Perhaps she has hidden allegiances we are unaware of."

This was a fact I did not know, or did not remember, from my earlier lessons on the subject. All the training and studying I have done with my father taught me to think exactly how he just said: to remain vigilant to all possible threats. Yet I cannot reconcile this with the Niobe I have come to know. Am I blinded by my personal feelings toward her?

"Just so you know, she has been extremely kind to me and I have learned a lot in my time with her." A self-righteous anger forces me to defend her. "I think concentrating on her is a waste of time."

Father takes my hand and says more gently, "You know I trust your judgment and your skills to recognize situations for what they are. Please just keep your eyes open."

A loud rap on the door interrupts the conversation. Adam opens the door and whispers with a page, then motions to Liam, who rises to join them.

My father, who still has my hand, leans close and says, "Are you all right here at the palace?" His voice is laden with concern.

"Yes, truly I am. And Anne is as well." I squeeze his hand reassuringly.

"Livy, I can see there are strong feelings between you and Prince Liam. I suppose I should have noticed them sooner, but at my age, one sometimes forgets about the blossoming of love." He says all this matter-of-factly, but I am so uncomfortable I wish the chair cushions would swallow me up. "It seems both of your feelings are genuine. Just please, promise me you will consider what a life with him would entail. What being a princess would entail."

"You mean you don't think a rule-breaking, sassy-mouthed blurter would make a good princess?" I ask with feigned offense, my attempt to lighten the mood. But Father remains serious.

"I think you must consider who you are and what you would be giving up." He cups my chin tenderly. "But indeed, Olivia, you have always been a princess in my mind."

"Thank you, Father," I say, my eyes misting up, "and you will always be my first true prince." I throw my arms around his neck.

At the sound of a throat clearing, we both look up at Liam. "Sir Jack, my father needs you at once. Raiders have attacked the mining villages of Lindenwood, now with little protection at its disposal. A contingent of men must be deployed with all haste."

Father's nostalgic expression transforms to his soldierly one. He rises and kisses me good-bye, before purposefully striding out of the room with Adam at his heels. A small part of me aches to run after him, to saddle up and ride off on this mission, but I know this is not possible. My hands smooth the skirt of my gown in resignation.

"I am not surprised to hear of the attack. Word would have spread to the Mainland that King John no longer rules. A perfect void raiders would be only too happy to step into," I say to Liam.

"Well, I hope my other news will not surprise you either."

"What?" I ask warily.

"My father has asked my brother and me to lead the mission. I leave at dawn."

My heart sinks further. Even Liam will be included while I am left to rot in this corset-wearing prison with a bunch of sycophants. Just imagining the excitement of combat versus the drudgery of the castle is maddening. Liam must sense my disappointment. He pulls me into his arms.

"I wish you could go too," he says, his breath tickling the top of my head.

"Well, you know, I am well-versed in sneaking on missions," I joke. "We know how flawlessly that went last time."

"Yes. If I recall, you saved my father's life. Perhaps people should pay better attention to that fact before they so easily dismiss your worth."

His indignation at my exclusion makes the stab of it hurt a little less. He takes my face in his hands and kisses me until I cannot tell up from down or left from right.

"I'll miss you," I whisper against his cheek when we come up for air. "Please be careful."

"I will miss you too. I should only be gone a couple of weeks. Make sure you keep an extra eye on my father while I am gone.

"Come, we only have a few hours." He whisks me over to the couch and we sink down on it as one.

"Whatever will we do to fill the time?" I ask, coyly batting my lashes.

"I think we are *both* well-versed in that." He winks, then pulls me into an embrace and all thoughts of prophecies and missions and anything but each other are forgotten.

A thousand thoughts weigh on my mind when I enter the dining hall. How quickly they resurface once I am back to reality. Liam and I spent every last moment together, so I had not even returned to my room for Sadie to make me presentable. Hopefully, the once-over I gave myself in a mirrored panel in the hallway served well enough.

Kat barely notices when I plunk down across from her. She is too busy watching for Puck, her green eyes scanning every entrance with anticipation. He always tries to position himself so they can moon over each other at mealtime. A smile engulfs her face at the sight of him sliding into a seat at the table next to ours, and he graces her with the goofy, lopsided grin of a love-starved puppy. It takes all my self-control to not roll my eyes. But truly, am I any better around Liam?

A laugh catches in my throat when I think of how the "old" Puck and Olivia would have ridiculed our newer versions. We both thought ourselves to be quite invincible in matters of the heart. Funny what only a few months' time has done to us. Speaking of which, the royal family will dine in private tonight, so there will be no Liam for me to stare at.

Anne scoots down closer to us and in an unprecedented move, as do the rest of the ladies. This startles Kat back to herself, her face transforming from pure joy to confusion. My friend and I regard them with distrust, as if an actual wolf pack had us surrounded. They all look to my sister expectantly, the cloying scent of their perfumes hovering like a cloud above them.

"Olivia, have you heard anything about raids on the coast?" Anne asks. Every face turns to mine in rapt attention. Jocelyn, who is right across from me, narrows her eyes.

"Yes, um, there were some raids on the mining communities, which were part of Lindenwood. Men will be dispatched to deal with it accordingly."

It is odd and unnerving to be the person dispensing the gossip. Not that this is confidential information. Clearly it has already made the rounds at court, and I did not exaggerate the facts in any manner. Yet, it is strange to be discussing military matters with a group of ladies who ridicule me for my training.

"Will the king be going?" Emily asks. Why she cares, I cannot imagine. Usually, she barely acknowledges my existence.

"No. Prince Harold and Prince Liam will lead the mission."

Can this conversation please be over?

"Oh," cries Jocelyn as if wounded, a hand fluttering to her heart, "my poor Prince Liam. May he be spared from harm."

Really?

The ladies pat her back and hold her hands in sympathy. Gretchen even goes so far as to fan Jocelyn's face with a napkin. It is a scene so theatrical, I am reminded of my mother's acts of drama. Yet while those mildly amuse me, this one just sets my teeth on edge. If she keeps behaving this way, I guarantee she will be the one who needs to be spared from harm.

Anne locks eyes with me and shakes her head, the movement hardly noticeable. Kat puts a steadying hand on my arm. I inhale a deep breath, trying to remind myself she instigates on purpose. I can't let it work. Too many other important matters vie for space in my mind right now. Let Jocelyn go on with her driveling.

"How was your day?" Anne asks brightly in an attempt to redirect the conversation.

"Not good, actually," I confess, the brutal hurt of the morning returning. "A small boy, Thomas was his name, died from fever. He was a maid's son, just two years old. I feel so helpless about it. I am going to ask Queen Helen if I can give a burial cloth to the family."

"For a *maid's* child?" Jocelyn sneers, her overwhelming concern of a moment ago replaced with utter disgust.

"Yes. For a maid's child," I answer firmly, then stare her down.

"Olivia, darling," she starts, and I swear my hatred is so intense, it must be visible, "let me give you some advice. If you want to survive in this court, you will need to reorganize your priorities. It's pretty simple really—some people matter and some people don't."

For a moment, I am silent, appalled that a human being spoke these words aloud. But when it settles in, I find I am not surprised. These spoiled, pampered courtiers truly believe they are more important than everyone else. They had the sheer luck to be born into these riches, this lifestyle, these opportunities, yet they see it as fairly granted, as though they somehow did something to deserve it and someone like Thomas did not. Liquid rage consumes every inch of my body, flooding through every pore with my powerlessness over this injustice.

Through clenched teeth, I spit, "Are you implying that the life of this innocent boy did not matter?" Kat's grip tightens on my arm, imploring me to keep my cool.

"Of course," she resumes, in a tone one uses to explain the obvious to a child. "In the end, his death will go unnoticed. As if he never existed."

In a flash, I am out of my seat. Cups topple over, sending streams of ale across the table. Dishes fly to the floor, a plate clatters there against the collective gasp that sails across the room. I grab the front of Jocelyn's dress and pull her across the table, well aware of the deafening silence that has fallen.

"What did you say?"

Jocelyn is pale, all traces of smugness melted off her face, replaced by a look of sheer fear. I want to hurt her, show her how it feels to not be in charge for once in her life. Anne grabs my extended arms and tries to pry them off of the beaded bodice, but they hold fast.

"Olivia, please don't." My sister's eyes plead with me as much as her tone.

Madame le Clare recovers herself enough to rush over. Out of the corner of my eye, her angular form comes into view, like a hawk marking its prey. I release Jocelyn, who crumples to her seat with a sob. Her entourage immediately descends on her, cooing and stroking all over again. Our mistress demands an explanation, but I turn on my heels and stomp out of the dining hall. When I am just out of the door, astonished murmurs fill the room.

Footsteps pursue me, so I break into as much of a run as my gown will allow. After several turns down random hallways, I burst out a door into night air so frosty, it makes me catch my breath. The royal gardens unfold before me, orderly shadows in the darkness. Thankfully, they are empty.

It takes my eyes a moment to adjust while I wend my way deeper into the grounds, my fury still raw enough to warm me against the chill. I skirt around a fountain and through a break in a thick hedgerow. The moon glints off the dusting of snow that covers every surface, casting the gardens in an otherworldly glow. Statues standing like lonely wraiths watch me with stony eyes while I wander aimlessly along the paths. My footfalls are almost silent, smothered by the soft fallen snow.

High walls of evergreens tower over my path, the garden maze arching up before me like a giant sentry in the night. I follow along its side, farther into the property. The back of the maze runs near Niobe's quarters. Perhaps I should drop in on her. She would not subject me to a million questions or a lecture about my behavior. My hand grazes the soft needles where I round the corner to the rear side, content with the thought of seeing my healer friend. But then I hear an unexpected sound—voices.

Surely, it cannot be someone searching for me, not yet at least. Still, the fact I am out here all alone at night is an unusual circumstance that I don't care to explain to anyone. When the sound of whoever it is comes closer, I slip into a space between two sparse bushes and stand just inside the first wall of the maze. Two voices speak in insistent whispers. A lover's quarrel? Hopefully they will pass by soon and I will remain undetected. They are far enough away, I can only hear every few words.

"…told me…the king…guarded…"

At the mention of the king, my ears perk up. Quietly, I edge my way down my row of bushes until the voices are almost directly on the other side. Although the evergreens should provide enough concealment in the dark, I instinctively crouch down and listen.

"This is a dangerous request you ask of me. It was not part of the original plan," the first voice, a raspy one with a

Mainland accent, says. "What will be done to guarantee my safety?"

"I merely deliver the messages, sir," the second person mumbles. "She gives her word the time she provides will be safe."

She?

"Tell her I will do it, but let her know I am not happy about it. I was to have until the spring when there would be more protection," Raspy Voice sneers.

"I will tell her," Mumbler replies. "She said to remind you not to worry. The king trusts her. There will be no danger for you."

Raspy Voice harrumphs before their footsteps move away in opposite directions. Knowing I need to see where they go, I attempt to quickly backtrack to the break in the maze wall. Unfortunately, this is not such an easy process in the pitch dark, on the slippery icy-coated grass. By the time I pop through to the other side of the bushes, there is no visible trace of anyone. One set of footsteps leads over to a covered cobblestone path where the trail ends in vain. I follow the other set a few yards along the evergreens, until they meet a dirt path. In the daylight, I have been able to track farther, but not in the inky dimness of night.

My toes lie like frozen little stones in my slippers and my breath forms a frosty cloud with each exhale. But this external chill does not hold a candle to the icy dread that creeps from my head right down to my feet. There is a plot against King William, and the conspirators are already operating from inside the castle.

A cacophony of thoughts explodes like fireworks inside my brain while I head for the palace. I replay the conversation over and over so when I repeat it to someone, there will be no detail missing. Indecision over who to tell first—Liam, my father, the king—is decided for me when I step inside the castle. Bartholomew spots me and hurries over.

"Miss Davenport, the queen would like to see you immediately."

My mind is so jumbled from what I just learned in the maze, it takes me a second to remember my ungracious exit from the dining hall. Whatever Queen Helen wants to say to me on that subject will likely be forgotten when she hears my information.

Bartholomew leads me through halls, the wet hem of my dress dragging behind me like a mop…an expensive mop. My fingers and toes tingle at the newfound warmth, a dull ache spreading through them. The secretary walks with leisurely strides, as though it is completely normal to escort a wayward lady-in-waiting to Queen Helen's side this late in the evening. He stops to relay some instructions to a servant about Her Highness' breakfast in the morning, and I am forced to stand and wait until he finishes.

It takes all my self-control to not push him out of the way and run with all haste to the queen's chambers. The sooner I can blurt this story out, the better. Knowing I have created one scene already today, I match my step with Bartholomew, though inwardly I curse his sluggishness. Finally, his glacial pace deposits us in front of the wide double doors to Queen Helen's chamber. I have never been inside her personal rooms before, but I have passed the gleaming wooden doors, carved with an exquisite forest scene full of fauns and nymphs. Her secretary opens them and ominously gestures for me to enter.

Warm air fills the room, an inviting fire dancing merrily in the hearth. Two large chairs flank the fireplace. A small dining table sits on one side of the room and an ornate desk balances out the other. On the far wall, a doorway leads to the queen's sleeping chamber. The room connects with the king's private chambers, or so I have been told by my father. The whole space is decorated in a fashionable, yet not ostentatious manner—the picture of refined elegance, much like Queen Helen, herself.

A chambermaid dips into a quick curtsey before scampering to announce my arrival to Her Highness, the round white hat resting on the back of her head disappearing into the sleeping chamber like a miniature moon. Queen Helen glides out and I drop into my own low curtsey, eyes cast on the floor.

"You may rise and join me by the fire, Olivia," she instructs, crossing the room to settle in one of the chairs.

She wears a long, forest-green robe and her hair, which I have only seen up, lies around her shoulders in thick copper waves. An imperial air still hangs about her, but she looks younger, less imposing than normal.

I creep over to the other seat and lower myself down, praying my skirt is dry enough to not leave a water stain on the cushion. Protocol dictates she must speak before I can say anything. She, however, sits in silence, stoically watching the fire. A large log tumbles off the top of the flaming pile, spitting sparks and ash onto the grate. The clock on the mantle ticks away each second, its sound magnified in the stillness.

Slowly, she turns her eyes to where I am perched on the seat, one leg jostling up and down like a mallet.

"Would you like to say something first?" she asks.

"Yes, Your Highness, but it is not for all ears."

Queen Helen looks confused, but says to the chambermaid, "Sally, please go fetch a warm blanket for Miss Davenport to wrap around her shoulders."

As soon as the servant scuttles out of the room, I tell the queen everything I overheard in the maze. When I finish, she stares at her hands for a long moment while digesting the news. A rustle from the corner draws my eye to where a golden cage hangs from the ceiling. In it sits a bright, yellow bird who shakes out his feathers, then nestles his head under a wing. I have read about canaries before, but never imagined I would get to see one.

A rap at the door and Sally steps back in, a blanket draped over one arm and a tray in her hands. She sets some hot tea and scones down on a small table between the chairs. Steam rises from the teapot spout, curling up in the air like a transparent ribbon. My stomach rumbles, the result of missing dinner.

"Here is a blanket from the Queen's laundry, Miss Davenport." She drapes it carefully around my shoulders.

"That will be all for now, Sally," Queen Helen says. Sally walks around the desk and exits through a small door, which must lead to her sleeping quarters. Her Highness always has someone at her beck and call.

The queen pours two cups of tea and hands me one, then nods for me to help myself to a scone. I select one from the plate; its buttery texture feels like heaven in my mouth.

Hopefully, I can restrain myself from stuffing in the rest of them.

"I will convey what you have told me to the king tomorrow. He may wish for you to repeat the story to him. For now, I would rather not tell your father or my sons. Let them embark on their coastal mission without this burden on their minds."

I nod and take a sip of the tea. The warm cup soothes my half-thawed fingers and I feel the blood returning.

"And what of this *she*?" the queen asks. "Any thoughts on who it may be?"

"You think it's Niobe, don't you?" My tone is more accusatory than I mean it to be. She does not answer, so in true fashion I blurt out exactly what I am thinking. "I just find it hard to believe. Why would she turn against the king after all this time? She has never shown any ill will toward him. It doesn't make any sense."

"Much of this doesn't make sense," she counters. "Just promise me you will keep a close eye on her."

"Of course, Your Highness."

She is quiet again, lost in contemplation. I would have thought it would feel awkward to sit alone with the queen, but I am oddly at ease, in the same way I am with Liam.

"On another subject..." she finally says.

Uh-oh. Time to talk about the dining hall.

"Did you know I originally came here from Trusole?"

"Yes, Father has mentioned this to me," I reply, remembering the name of another small island kingdom, though this turn in conversation catches me off guard.

"My father was king of that land. When I was fourteen, the alliance for my marriage with King William, who was only sixteen at the time, was forged. And so, I was packaged up like a prize horse and shipped to Stewartsland."

It never occurred to me how young both she and the king were, nor how hard it must have been to be sent away from one's family, one's home, and one's country at such an age. Naturally, I utter the first thing that comes to mind. "That must have been awful."

Queen Helen chuckles a bit at my tactless honesty, then resumes, "It was. I cried every minute of the seven-day journey. Along the way, I made all kinds of escape plans. My father told me nothing of William, so I was afraid I would be stuck with a fat, old drunkard."

We both laugh. It is nice to sit and talk with her, someone whose fate was determined by the rules of royal protocol. I feel less isolated.

"But when I arrived, I saw he was just as young and scared as I was. It created an instant bond." Her tone becomes more serious. "We were lucky, though, because in the end, we did fall in love with each other. Not all arranged marriages end up so well.

"I was happy when my babies were boys. I knew any daughter I bore would be parceled off like I was. It was such a desperate and helpless feeling to have no say in such a momentous part of life. This is why I am fighting so hard for you and Liam."

I am both startled and touched by her admission. "Thank you, Your Highness."

"Harold is different than my younger son. He took up the mantle of responsibility inherent with his station from the start. Fulfilling his duty to the throne is enough for him. But Liam, he was always more sensitive, more passionate about life...and fairness. As he grew older, he resented the constraints put on him, not just regarding marriage, but about every aspect of being a prince. Then he met you. It has changed him, brought back the light I once saw in him as a little boy. I want to know one of my sons gets the chance to marry for love."

For reasons I can't quite name, tears come to my eyes. I knew the queen was our ally in this matter, but I assumed it was just a mother doting on her son. To know she actually understands how I feel, understands the unfairness of the manmade rules keeping Liam and I apart, fills my heart with emotion.

"So knowing this," she continues, "I want to ask you, as a favor to me, to please try to control your temper. We can have no more scenes like the one at dinner. Agreed?"

"Yes, Your Highness. I truly apologize for letting my anger get the better of me. It will not happen again. Your support is more than I could have asked for. You will not see your trust in me misplaced."

"I am happy to hear that. The other ladies think you were brought before me to be reprimanded. Let us not enlighten them about our actual conversation."

"Of course, Your Highness."

"Very well. You may return to your room."

We rise and walk to the door.

"And Olivia, I heard about your request for Thomas, and yes, I will send a burial cloth to his family in the morning."

"Thank you very much, Your Highness," I say, overwhelmed at the thought of how much this simple gesture will mean to his family.

"I also heard what Jocelyn said to you." She leans closer, her eyes alight with the same mischievous glow I've seen in Liam's. "And between us, I would have wanted to punch her too."

"I would have liked to see that, Your Highness."

She opens the door to see me out and we smile to each other. To my surprise, when I rise from my curtsey, the queen takes my face in her hands and kisses my forehead before wishing me good-night. Then she is gone, the comforting warmth of her room merely a memory in the cold, dim hallway. I feel as though some of it still glows in me, buoyed by the kindness and understanding Queen Helen bestowed on me. My feet carry me back to my room, where I drop exhausted into bed next to my sleeping sister.

It is hard to follow Queen Helen's advice about the conversation I overheard last night. The moment I see my father next to his horse in the courtyard, I want to run and tell him everything. But Her Highness is right. These men should be allowed to leave this morning without additional worries on their shoulders. It feels like a betrayal to withhold information from him, but I cannot go against a direct command from the queen. This is new ground for me— having to put my father second.

Father talks briefly with a few men. When they leave, I make my way over to him. A nippy wind gusts across the air, blowing his neatly trimmed hair up in little tufts while he double-checks the buckle on his mount's saddle. His face breaks into a smile when he spots me.

"Looks good to me," I say, giving the strap a tug. My eyes fall on the assortment of knives sticking from a saddlebag. It reminds me of the dangers he will face, the dangers he will need his entire focus for. "Be careful."

"I will, though I don't think there is much to worry about. Likely the marauders will retreat when they see an armed contingent arriving to deal with them." A true statement. "Keep your eyes and ears open, Olivia. I expect a full report when I return."

"I will, Father." Guilt worms its way into my heart, but I keep my mouth shut.

I stand on my tiptoes and kiss his cheek. Anne, who just walked up, does the same. My sister and I step back with a few of the other ladies. Since the king is not participating in this mission, the crowd is much thinner. Jocelyn is there. She will not meet my eyes. Maybe I scared her enough that she will finally keep her mouth shut. One can hope, at least. The others eye me smugly, no doubt happy about my "reprimand" by the queen.

Liam strides down the palace steps. At the sight of him, Jocelyn elbows her way past me with Elaine and Gretchen hot on her tail. When he approaches, they crowd around him like bees to honeysuckle. After a group curtsey, they wish him a safe trip.

"Thank you, ladies," he drawls, the picture of boredom.

He squeezes through them. Jocelyn looks aggrieved for a split second before rearranging her countenance. Liam nods to Anne and Kat, who flank me. They drop into quick curtsies. I should too, but before I can, he grabs me around the waist and plants a long kiss on my lips. For once, I don't worry about the public display. In fact, I rather welcome it.

"Good-bye, my love," he whispers, his breath soft against my ear.

A trumpet blares and the men saddle up. Liam and I pull apart. Our fingers extend, touching tips until the last possible second. He walks to his waiting steed and climbs atop. Adam, who is already mounted, gives me a knowing smile. Kat and Anne stare at the ground, but wide grins grace both their faces as well.

The Wolf Pack? Not so much.

If anger could be bottled, one could extract a potent sample from Jocelyn right now. Her glare borders on downright evil. A chill goes through me. Though I should feel secure in my relationship with Liam, a nagging feeling takes hold. While the horses gallop out the gate, their tails swishing in unison, a thought claws its way to the surface—what if we have just woken a sleeping dragon?

17

The flurry of preparation for the Holiday Ball overshadows all other activity for the next week. Queen Helen heads the planning, selecting everything from the decorations, to the menu, to the guest list. Bartholomew scampers through the hallways at all hours of the day, a pile of notes clutched in his hands. Deliveries arrive daily and the courtiers speculate on the contents of the packages, a myriad of size, shape, and color. Large Christmas trees spring up at various points in the castle, each adorned in a special theme. My favorite is one with hundreds of different hand-painted angels hanging from the branches.

All the activity is almost enough to distract me from missing Liam. Almost. But there are quiet moments, when I wonder where he is and what he is doing. It is hard to know he is out there, on the same planet as I, yet I can't reach him. Amazing how you can feel so connected to a person that it physically hurts to imagine them existing outside of your presence.

Work with Niobe is busy. We dispense treatments for chilblains and chapped skin throughout the village every day. Brother Alastair's penitents are hit particularly hard, their clothing and accommodations not up to the challenge of the bitter winter air. So far, the friar has not allowed us to distribute the woolen socks we have collected. My healer friend asks me to beseech the queen to reason with the strict clergyman over this matter. Niobe has not been allowed access to the royal couple since I overheard the conversation in the maze. She is told they are too busy to meet with her. I pay close attention to every interaction she has when we are together, and I hint around for more information about the prophecy, but I have still not heard or seen anything even remotely suspicious.

Thankfully, Queen Helen persuades Brother Alastair to allow his convicts the socks to wear under their crude shoes. When I hear him begrudgingly acquiesce to Her Highness' request, it is hard to not notice him dressed in his warm, fur-lined robe. He would not last one afternoon in his men's clothing.

Icy air assaults our senses the morning we bring the approved footwear to the penitents. They work at the edge of the servant village, huddled in small groups for warmth. Once the new pit was finished, they began to construct the framework for the latrines. The sound of hammer to nail rings out, reverberating through the cold. There is usually little talk with us on our visits, but today a grateful tone soon spreads among the group. Our gifts are most eagerly accepted. An older man touches my hand in thanks when he takes a pair. His eyes crinkle with a smile so kind and gentle, I wonder what fate led him here.

These unspoken human connections are the most fulfilling part of my work with Niobe. But just as the warm feeling spreads across my heart, the next man snatches socks from my grip without even a glance in my direction. He is balding, with a jagged scar from his left ear to his chin, and clearly a far different disposition from his elderly comrade. After donning them, he stomps back over to nail two crossbeams together. The contentment slowly drains from me when I watch his angry strokes.

A few cold hours later, my rounds with Niobe are complete. When we reach her door, I hand her my basket of supplies and make to depart.

"You have a gift with people, child," she says. "They relate with you on a deep level. You invoke a sense or respect and love with them. This will serve you well when you are princess."

We have never spoken of my relationship with Liam. Yet somehow I am not surprised she knows. My grandmother, my father's mother, died when I was ten, but she always knew me better than anyone, as though someone had provided her with an inventory of my brain. There is a similar link between Niobe and me. This makes me long to believe in her innocence.

"Thank you," I reply and hug her frail shoulders.

"Now go get warm, little one."

"Little one? I'm six inches taller than you," I tease.

She winks and heads across her threshold. A brief shower of warmth wafts out, then is cut off when the door clicks shut.

There is one good thing about the upcoming Holiday Ball—my afternoon schedule is wide open. While the queen busily prepares, her ladies are given a degree of freedom. Happily, I spend a good number of hours sparring with Puck, who finds his work at the stable fairly idle this time of year.

Kat and I hurry down right after lunch, as we did every day last week. Bright sun from a cloudless sky is no match for the biting nip in the air. Kat does her best Madame le Clare impersonation for me and we stumble into the stalls laughing our heads off. Puck pops out from one, a grooming brush in hand. He blankets up the horse he was combing, then comes

154

to join us. The horse snorts loudly behind him, a cloud of breath spewing from his long nose.

"Ladies," he says with a bow. "How are you this fine day?"

"No small talk. Do you have time to fight? Yes or no?" I demand.

"Is she this bossy in the palace?" he jests to Kat, who now stands beside him. Puck's arms encircle her and they share a quick kiss.

Kat and Puck. My two best friends. In love with each other. I am truly happy for them, but it is still uncomfortable to listen to either one talk about the other. And I certainly don't want to watch any displays of devotion between them.

"Yes, she is quite bossy," Kat answers facetiously. "Always telling the king and queen what to do. And forget Prince Liam. She has him dancing like a trained bear."

She twirls around, waving her arms like the poor circus creatures. Then she and Puck dissolve into giggles.

"Ha-ha," I say sourly. "Do you have time to fight or no?"

"Yes, yes. Keep your pants on." He jokingly points at the commandeered trousers I wear. He walks down to the end of the stables before ducking into an empty stall.

"Have you heard anything about the party up north?" I call down to him. If Queen Helen has heard anything, she has been tight-lipped about it. Any hint of news would bring me comfort. Liam's absence leaves a hole in me.

"Just last night, the Master-of-Horse received word the raiding party was dealt with and the men should be home any day now." Puck reappears with two wooden swords. I hope it is tomorrow so Liam does not miss the ball.

He hands one to me. The hilt feels so good in my hand. A real one would be better, but this will do. In an instant, I assume my stance, ready to go. When I look up, my opponent is not in front of me. Instead, he methodically places a blanket on a bench, then makes sure Kat is settled before finally turning to me.

"Done plumping pillows?"

"Jealous?" he asks, taking position. Wind whips through the building, the open doors at each end creating an ideal tunnel for its play. Errant pieces of hay swirl around in the air.

"Yeah, I remember all those times you worried about my comfort. Oh wait, that was…never." We circle, neither initiating a blow. Yet.

"Well, you were never a lady like Kat," he quips, then winks over at my friend.

"Got that right. Take this!"

Our swords connect. Loud crashes ring across the stables as we parry and thrust from one end to the other. The horses barely glance our way. They had been spooked the first day and watched us warily, unsure what to make of the whole thing. Now the creatures stand, their tails slightly swishing, with a rather bored expression. I pin Puck to one of the stall doors, my sword pointed at his heart.

"Looks like I take the first round."

Over the next few hours we take a few breaks, but only to grab a quick drink. Sparring is such a natural part of us, and we have both missed it sorely. Kat is a patient onlooker. She cheers for us both equally, though there seems to be more vigor in her support of Puck. It is a rare person who would accept the friendship between Puck and me without envy or doubts. I am blessed to have someone as wonderful as Kat in my life.

Finally, when the sun moves lower, our long shadows fade into the grayness of dusk. These shortest days of the year darken unforgivingly early. The air chills noticeably and my fingers start to ache on the sword's hilt. When it becomes too hard to see, we call it a day, depositing the weapons in the back of a stall for easy access.

"Anything new with Niobe?" Puck asks, wiping the sweat from his brow.

"No. Everything is completely normal. Today we brought all the penitents woolen socks to help them make it through the winter," I reply and we saunter back towards the door.

"That must have made them happy," Puck muses, his eyes firmly on Kat. She stands at the front of the stables, a murky outline in the dimness, feeding a carrot to one of the horses.

"For the most part they were." I try to focus on the man who smiled rather than the man who scowled.

We reach my friend, who pats the steed gently on the head. She and Puck share a kiss good-bye, then say, "See you at dinner," in unison.

Outwardly, I roll my eyes at them, but inwardly I miss Liam so much it hurts. Puck said they should be home in a matter of days. Though not long, it stretches before me like a life sentence. A despondent sigh leaves my lips. Kat must know where my thoughts lie. She links arms with me reassuringly and we head back to the castle.

An hour later, we stroll into the dining hall. Dinners have been uneventful since Liam left, but for one interesting detail. Jocelyn has somehow managed to garner a seat at the royal table next to her sister the past few nights. She has enjoyed the privilege, preening and posing like a peacock on display. Anne and I do not know what led to this change in the seating arrangement. The Crawford girls and the rest of the Wolf Pack have been mum.

Tonight when we arrive, Jocelyn is actually seated next to the king. She is a pillar of attention, ready to interact with him whenever he spares her some notice. Queen Helen sits on the other side of His Majesty, a decidedly disinterested look on her face. King William makes a passing comment and Jocelyn's grating laugh carries through the air to where Kat and I sit.

"Any idea what she is up to yet?" my friend whispers. It is about the tenth time we have had this conversation.

"Not exactly. My best guess is she hopes to win the king's favor so he will arrange for her to marry Liam." I sneak a peek at the royal dais to find Jocelyn watching me smugly. This must be her new tactic after seeing Liam kiss me farewell.

"Well, don't worry," Kat assures. "Liam will not be swayed."

True, but these power games are disquieting to watch. Liam won't be swayed, but I need to have the king in my corner. His blessing will be crucial if I want any future with my prince.

A page hurries through the hall, each purposeful step clicking on the stone floor. On a tiny silver tray sits a note, as if it is too important for his hands to touch. The courier stops in front of the royal table and bows low, keeping the tray aloft in one arm. King William motions for the letter, reads it, then places it on the table. He nods dismissively at the messenger, who rushes out of the room as though his heels are on fire.

Our monarch confers quietly with Queen Helen. Jocelyn tilts her head in their direction, hoping to overhear the conversation. By the irritated look on her face, I gather she is unsuccessful. King William stands and silence falls instantly around the room, the last voices snuffed out the moment they see where all attention is directed.

"I just received word from Sir Davenport. The coastal mission was successful. The raiders have been driven out of Stewartsland. The party should be home tomorrow night."

A cheer erupts with a smattering of applause. The king sits down and converses happily with his wife. Jocelyn sits on his other side like a forgotten doll. People mill about the room to celebrate the news. Servants roll in several barrels of ale to tap and steins are passed around.

"It's wonderful they will be coming tomorrow. Prince Liam will be at the ball after all," Kat says, placing a hand on mine.

"The mission must have been trouble-free for them to be returning so soon. And it will be comforting to have him back here with me."

Puck plops down next to Kat, three frothy mugs of ale in his hands. He slides one to each of us and we toast before taking long swigs. While my two lovebird friends coo to each other, content washes over me at the thought of reuniting with Liam.

Then, suddenly, uneasiness seeps in, cracking the borders of my good mood. Before I even raise my eyes, I know she stares at me, my years of tracking coming into play. When our eyes meet, there is no denying the challenge written on Jocelyn's face. She is not done in her quest for Liam. In fact, she is only getting started.

The next morning dawns harshly, winter finally setting its full icy grip around us. A layer of slick frost coats the cobblestones on my walk to the healer's. She waits outside for me, two large baskets on her hips. Even wrapped in my fur-lined cloak, the cold air bites me with wicked teeth. Niobe stands, her own cloak draped haphazardly on her shoulders, not bothered by the barrage of frigidness.

"Ready for a bit of a walk?" she asks and hands me one of the baskets.

I nod my assent, though what I would prefer is the hot fire in Niobe's cozy front room. We trudge along the outskirts of the property, beyond where Brother Alastair's men dutifully continue constructing the framework for the new latrines. Hammer strokes ring crisply across the chill air, the men's breath puffing out in clouds of exertion. The friar is nowhere to be seen, of course—content in his warm rooms, no doubt.

My companion and I come to a crude door in the castle wall, where the structure seems in even worse shape than the area Lydia breached a few months back. This thought jolts me a bit. Has it only been a few months since I watched my sister's tiny form disappear to the other side? How did I live all those years prior without Liam? I cannot remember what it was like to not have him in my life.

Niobe draws back a rusty bolt. It squeals in protest before the door swings open.

Really? One pathetic bolt between the king and any number of intruders?

I need to speak to Father about addressing this issue.

The healer leads the way across a fallow field, where the frozen ground crunches under our steps. Out in the open land, we need to lower our heads against the bitter wind, the gusts assaulting us mercilessly. Niobe is unfazed and, unable to raise my eyes, I follow her feet along the unforgiving terrain. Finally, she stops in front of a clump of holly bushes, growing right at the edge of the forest.

"I need to get a bunch of these berries collected before they cut the boughs off for the ball."

Sometime today, these branches will be trimmed to provide decoration for the main ballroom. She sets to work picking the hard, red berries. Wordlessly, I follow her lead. With my basket balanced on one arm, I reach for a bunch of the scarlet fruit.

"Holly berries have a number of uses," she instructs, "such as inducing vomiting, as an astringent to staunch bleeding, and also for dyeing fabrics."

The ground around the bushes is uneven, pitted with stones and holes. Our work is slow going, but at least the surrounding trees provide cover from the wind. Little by little, the baskets fill up and I find myself enjoying the simplicity of the task. No drama, no gossip, no monitoring or judging like every moment in court, just a straightforward undertaking that will yield some beneficial results.

"That should be plenty," Niobe says, after examining our combined total. "Let's head back." And it is a good thing we are finished, because servants arrive with scythes to gather the holly for the ball.

The sun is high in the sky, its daily trip much protracted this time of the year. Bright rays fall all around us, yet they provide little warmth. We retrace our steps through the dilapidated door, the bolt once again pulled shut, and back across the outer grounds toward the palace. It is a relief to finally enter the healer's quarters and feel able to breathe again, like resurfacing into the air after a deep dive. Niobe clears a space on the workbench and we set down our baskets.

With my hood pushed back and my scarf loosened, I throw a new log onto the dying fire in the hearth. The wood crackles to life and I warm my frozen fingers in the heat.

"I will store about half of these in the cellar." She motions to the trapdoor. "They will keep well down there in this cold."

"What about the rest?" I ask, unwrapping my cloak and placing it over a chair.

"I will pulverize most of it for use in certain tinctures. They must be stringently prepared though. Too much holly juice can be poisonous if ingested. The rest I will use to make a good batch of dye."

Niobe's knowledge and skill never cease to amaze me. Time and time again, I've told her to write all her learning down. She has a rudimentary potions book, but her notes are difficult to understand. The idea of writing a book overwhelms her, but someday I hope we can work on one together.

"Let me get started pulverizing," I say, grabbing a mortar and pestle off the shelf.

"No, dear, the ball is tonight. You must have a lot of preparation to attend to."

"I suppose." I sigh, placing the tools down on the table. "Though it's not something I am looking forward to."

Niobe crosses to me and takes my hands—an unexpected, tender gesture. "Whyever not? You are young and in love. It is a magical time in your life. I can handle these berries myself. Go. Make yourself beautiful for that prince of yours."

A hesitant smile forms on my face while she gently puts my cloak on my shoulders, then ushers me to the door. Maybe she is right. Maybe I should be looking forward to tonight. After all, Liam will be back. Maybe it will be a magical night. Heartened, my steps quicken to a lively pace toward my room.

If only I knew how wrong I was.

The floral scent of Anne's perfume hangs in the air when I enter our room. Sadie puts the finishing touches on my sister's hair. Our handmaid coils a long braid in an elaborate pattern atop her head. Glossy chestnut locks glow in the beams of fading sunlight which streams through the window, coppery highlights shimmering with each move of her head.

"It's about time. Where have you been?" Exasperation tinges her voice as she rises. She looks like a woodland nymph in her dress of forest-green velvet with deep red accents. It reminds me of the holly bushes I just left.

"With Niobe," I answer, slumping onto the bed.

"Oh no you don't." My sister grabs my arm and pulls me to my feet. "No lounging. Sadie has her work cut out for her as it is, and you've left her little time to pull it off."

I am passed off to the maid, who helps me remove my plain day dress, then I step out of the shift underneath. Anne stands at the ready with my corset in hand. With a sigh of resignation, I lift my arms so she can wrap it around the front of me. Sadie grabs the laces from behind. She slowly encases me in its unforgiving grip. If men had to ever wear corsets, I feel certain they would have invented something far more comfortable by now.

My dress is lowered over my head. It is the same fabric and trimmings as Anne's, but in a different cut. In fact, all the ladies-in-waiting have a slightly different version of the same garment. We will resemble a litter of show puppies when we stand together. Heavy velvet settles around my shoulders like a dead weight and I wonder how my sister glides around with such perfect ease.

"Do you know if the royal party returned this afternoon?" I ask while the buttons are fastened up my back. If they did not, I will be sorry to have gone through all this trouble.

"Yes. They rode in about two hours ago," Anne confirms. "They will all be there for the ball, so don't worry."

The familiar sense of excitement swirls around my belly knowing I will see Liam soon. Though I hate being separated from him, the exhilaration of reuniting almost makes it worth it.

Sadie deftly applies my makeup, her face squished in concentration the entire time. While her hands whiz from kohl to balm, I try to remain still, but my foot taps an impatient rhythm on the floor. Then she begins the arduous task of my hair. She plaits several tiny braids on each side of my head, then joins them at the crown. The remaining tresses are teased and pinned in such a manner, my hair looks much fuller and longer than it actually is.

Finally, she adorns the coif with tiny porcelain beads, the shade of holly berries. My mind drifts to Niobe, who must be grinding up the real berries we collected this afternoon. Did she wish to be included in tonight's affair? Perhaps she was asked and declined. It is anyone's guess where the healer is concerned.

"There. Finished," Sadie proclaims, patting one last lock into place.

"Oh, Sadie, it looks amazing," I stammer, hardly able to believe the reflection that stares out at me from the mirror.

"Pretty as a princess," she says knowingly. "Both of you."

Anne smiles while she dabs some perfume on my neck, then hands me the jewel-encrusted *D* necklace.

"No, you wear it. I want to wear my sword necklace." I retrieve it from its box and fasten it around my neck, then take one last moment to examine myself in the mirror. Sadie may as well tell people she is a miracle worker from now on to have made me look this beautiful.

"Come," my sister says, opening the door, "time to go show off her stunning work to our men."

The main ballroom is alight with hundreds of candles. They fill the walls in multiple sconces, lie strewn across the windowsills, and rest in the three giant chandeliers. Tapers of assorted heights and thickness, with fat trails of wax trailing down the sides, are everywhere the eye can see. It must have taken hours just to light them all. Dancing flames reflect back in the mirrors that panel the two short ends of the room and sparkle off the gold-and-silver decorative balls, which hang along the ceiling, creating our own personal starscape. Large holly boughs line the walls and garland lines the tables, their woodsy scent floating across the air.

At the far end of the room, the royal family sits on a dais, a festive green-and-red silk canopy draped above it. One long wall is filled with a stage where the orchestra plays, the conductor's head sticking up like a solitary bloom. Across from the musicians, floor-to-ceiling windows form a wall, punctuated by several sets of French doors. Foggy panes conceal the view of a large courtyard. The near end of the room is anchored by a buffet featuring a large ice sculpture of trumpeting angels. Beneath the statue, the surface is covered in platters overflowing with fruits, breads, meats, and sweets. Servants drift around the room with flutes of champagne expertly balanced on trays; in and out they weave through the maze of elbows and shoulders with consummate grace. Tomorrow night, on Christmas Eve, everyone will solemnly attend Midnight Mass, but tonight is for revelry and celebration.

It takes a moment of jockeying through the sea of people to spot Liam where he sits next to Queen Helen. A dour expression clouds his face. Last year, I would have written this off to his arrogance—the aloof prince too good to associate with the rest of us. Now I see it for the mask it is and almost chuckle to myself. As if he senses me, he looks over, our eyes locking across the room. I smile, floating away on elation. But instead of lighting up with happiness or even glinting with a sense of mischief, his eyes are filled with concern, as if they hold a hidden plea. Uneasiness rises in my chest, a knotted ball of worry snuffing out my joy.

Something is wrong.

"Good evening, Miss Davenport." Lord Montgomery bows in front of me, my sister already on his arm. He effectively blocks my view of the royal family.

"Good evening," I mutter and try to position myself where I can see Liam again.

"You look lovely this evening." He takes my hand and kisses it.

"Thank you." I hear the distracted tone in my voice.

Anne's eyes narrow. She looks over her shoulder to the dais, but says nothing. Montgomery releases my hand, then takes both of my sister's, his eyes beaming with pleasure at the mere sight of her. Jealousy rears its ugly green head. I want that look from Liam. The orchestra starts a lively tune. Couples line up opposite each other to dance a galliard.

"Excuse us," says the lord and they bounce off to take their places on the floor.

Time to find out what is wrong.

The edge of the dance floor is swarming with people. I wedge my way through them, praying no one else interrupts me. No such luck. A figure steps in front of me.

"Miss Olivia, good evening. It is so nice to see you again." The music nearly drowns out his words.

It takes me a moment to shake off my preoccupation before I recognize the gentleman. Prince Stephan, Liam's cousin from Prescott, raises my hand to his lips. We originally met at the tail end of the Lindenwood mission. His toad-like demeanor has not changed since then. It is difficult not to compare him with his far more handsome cousins.

"Prince Stephan," I curtsey. Two dancers nearly spin right into us and he pulls me out of their path. "The pleasure is mine," I add, "And, might I say, I am so sorry about the passing of your father."

A glimmer of sadness passes over his face, but fades quickly. "Yes, it has been a rough month or so. I brought my mother up here for the holidays, hoping to cheer her spirits." He glances over to where Princess Beatrice speaks with some elder member of court. Though his words sound sincere, his sorrow somehow feels less than genuine to me, but perhaps this is his demeanor.

"How thoughtful of you. We are fortunate to have you here." I curtsey again, hoping to make my escape. I should be honored he even remembers me, let alone took the time to converse with me, but I just want to get to Liam. Although we have only been parted a week, the time seems far longer. I just want to be in his arms again.

"Yes, we will be here through New Year's. I am sure we will speak again." He bows, then strides away.

The dance comes to an end amid rousing cheers. A slower piece begins and couples pair off to dance. Space opens at last, which allows me to breach the distance to the dais and I hurry through. Liam stands just before it, his eyes scanning the crowd. Just as he spots me, my view is cut off by a twosome twirling past. He reappears, but moves away from me toward the dance floor. Confused, I stumble forward, following his receding form. It takes a moment for my mind to process the lean arms that encircle his body, for my heart to sink when it comprehends the betrayal. Liam dances with Jocelyn, who has pressed herself firmly against him while she whispers in his ear.

It is like the moment when you are scalded and your body reacts before your brain can. Every fiber in my body winces in pain at the sight of them even while my eyes stare, disbelieving. Blind rage consumes me. Who does she think she is? I will tear her limb from limb no matter who is here to see it. My lungs inhale one unsteady breath, then I take a step toward them. A firm grip enfolds my upper arm and pulls me in the other direction.

"Don't," a familiar voice rasps in my ear. Then Puck's face is in front of mine, Kat at his side. She touches my arm and whispers in a reassuring tone, but her words vanish unheard, dissolved in the simmering fury I am barely able to contain.

"Livy, don't react. That is what she wants. Look at me. Look. At. Me."

My anger disintegrates enough around the edges; I can finally focus on Puck.

"You will walk with me and Kat across the room as if you haven't a care in the world. Got it?" His arm guides my wooden steps across the ballroom, weaving among the crowd, and out one of the French doors onto a terrace.

"Calm down. Now." Puck's face is close to mine, his hands on my cheeks. I push them away petulantly.

"I want to kill her, slowly, painfully," I sneer through clenched teeth.

"Precisely the response she is hoping for, Livy."

Why does he always have to be right?

Kat wraps her arm around my shaking shoulder. "I am sure there is a reason…a good reason," she states.

A deep breath of the crisp, chill air clears my head. Of course, there has to be a reason. This is Liam after all. I know him well enough not to doubt him. He deserves the chance to explain.

"Now come back inside and act as if it doesn't bother you at all. Show King William you have the fortitude for royal life. Let her look like the interloper here," Puck insists.

He is right. Thank goodness my dear friend is here to act as the voice of reason. Things may have gone badly if he were not. I link arms with Kat, who watches me warily. She manages a small smile of encouragement and we stride back into the room, heads held high.

The first person I lock eyes with is Anne. She twirls around the dance floor in the arms of Montgomery, but her face is heavy with concern. I nod at her, let her see I am all right. Her partner glances at me and they exchange whispers.

Liam is now back on the dais seated between his father and Jocelyn, who converse pleasantly while his sits like a statue in the middle. His eyes search the crowd and come to rest on me. Again, a silent look of despair passes over his face.

"There is my girl," my father's voice rings out.

"Hello, Father." I wrap my arms around him.

"How about a dance?" He leads me onto the floor. Clad in his dress uniform, complete with all his medals of valor, Father is a commanding presence. People part to make room for us. The orchestra plays a basse, the flowing steps allowing us time to talk.

"Enjoying palace life?" he asks, a teasing gleam in his eyes.

"Not especially," I reply sullenly. He probably does not need to know I almost ripped a courtier apart by hand a few minutes ago. My gaze drifts to Jocelyn, who has her hand on Liam's leg. Reflexively, I want to grab my sword, but it lies useless in my family's armory, as impotent as I am at the moment.

"Well, I hope you are factoring this in when you consider a relationship with the prince." His tone is serious now, and though I know he only wants what is best for me, it hurts to have yet another person point out the problems a life with Liam will cause.

"And what of Niobe?" he continues. "Has she entered any trancelike states while you were with her?"

"No. Only the one in the dining hall. None since then that I have seen or heard of." In fact, it is hard for me to reconcile the dazed woman from that night with the healer I have come to know. "She is a bit eccentric, but very well learned in healing and herbs. Though I suppose you already know this. There has not been one word or action the least bit suspect. But I do have some new information about a conversation I overheard in the garden maze." I fill him in on the details. Talking with my father about this feels so natural. It almost takes my mind off my festering anger.

"Interesting. I am sure Queen Helen has filled in His Majesty. We will have to look into this further."

My mother spins past in the arms of her son-in-law, Lord Davis, her face aglow with excitement. His wife, my oldest sister Jayne, stands with Anne on the edge of the dance floor, their arms entwined, as the two catch up with each other. I wish my little Lydia had been allowed to attend, as does she, I am sure. Lydia has a way of anchoring me when I feel unmoored.

"Mother is enjoying herself," I note.

"Was there ever any doubt about that?" Father quips.

"No. Never one." I laugh.

On a series of crescendo notes, the dance ends. A slower one begins in its place, the dulcet tones filling the air. Lord Davis returns to Jayne and my mother approaches.

"Hello, dear," she greets me with a kiss on the cheek. "You look beautiful. Your hair looks as if nothing bad ever happened, thank goodness."

"You can thank our maid, Sadie, for that," I say. Her eyes glisten with pride at a dream she most likely thought she would never see…me resembling a lady. "And you look lovely as well, Mother."

She smoothes the front of her russet-colored gown and smiles. Knowing her, there were many hours of thought and energy put into her final look. I can't fault her, though; she is still more stunning than most of the women half her age. Father puts his arm around her shoulder and kisses the top of her head.

"Excuse me, Sir Davenport, Lady Davenport," says a voice, and suddenly Liam stands beside us. "But I would very much like to have a dance with your daughter."

"Of course, Your Highness," Mother replies in awe, dipping into a curtsey.

My acknowledgement is a much stiffer bow of the head. The moments with my family had briefly smothered my worry, but now it hurtles back full force. He takes my hand and I follow him onto the floor, silently praying my knees don't give out from the terror that rises in me like the tide. One hand fits on the small of my back, the other grasps mine. His palms are uncharacteristically sweaty.

Something is definitely wrong.

I look into his beautiful, blue eyes. They swim with misery. Now that I am going to find out the reason, I am not sure I want to anymore.

He clears his throat. "I didn't want to have to tell you in public, but I can't let the night pass and deceive you."

Not good.

At my silence, he continues, "Somehow Jocelyn has influenced my father. He wants me to court her, to give her a fair chance, because he considers her a more suitable match."

There she sits now, right next to King William, her usual smug expression in place. Our monarch absently surveys the room. The monarch I saved—who praised me for it—stabs me in the back without a second thought. I should have left him to die in that escape tunnel.

"And what do you think of that?" I ask pointedly.

"Naturally, I protested…abundantly, but…" He stops, won't meet my eyes.

But? But cannot be good. *But* can only be disastrous. I stop moving and we stand looking at each other like mannequins while couples rotate around us.

"But what?" I whisper, the cacophony of music and chatter turning into an otherworldly buzz while my senses brace for the impact of his answer.

"But…my father told me if I did not give Jocelyn a fair chance, he would not only send you from the palace, but ship you down to Prescott and arrange a marriage for you there. I don't know what to do, Olivia. I don't know how to fix this."

A barrage of thoughts leap to mind, none of them in any way accepting of this information. Send me away? Ship me to Prescott? As if I were livestock? And arrange a marriage? So many protests, I hardly know where to begin. The music ends and couples saunter off the floor. Liam and I stand alone in the center. Eyes will be upon us soon if we remain here like statues.

With every ounce of composure I can muster, I curtsey and hear my voice say, "Thank you for the dance, Your Highness. I hope you enjoy the rest of your evening."

Then, I walk away.

My feet stride past my sister, whose eyes I won't meet, and past my parents who motion me over. They move of their own accord out a side door into the garden, my steps shaky on the icy cobblestones, before reentering a hallway. Then they carry me up the stairs and a down corridor to my chamber. I owe them thanks for finding the way, because my mind ceased to function right after Liam's announcement.

The heavy wooden door of my room suddenly looms in front of me. I push it open, not even reacting when it slams against the inner wall with a loud bang. Sadie jumps up from her chair, a frame of needlework dangling from her hand. She looks at me expectantly, but I say nothing.

"Is everything all right, Miss Olivia?" she finally says.

A mute stare is her only answer. Her almond-shaped eyes narrow in concern. "Here, come sit down. I will fetch you some wine."

The maid places her needlework on the bed, a tiny house with the roof half stitched. She softly closes the door, then guides my arm towards a chair by the fireplace. Halfway there, the door bangs open again and we both turn with a start.

"Your Highness," Sadie gasps, dipping into a curtsey.

"Olivia, please talk to me," Liam says, shutting the door behind him. Sadie tries to disappear against the wall.

"What is there to talk about?" I huff, arms crossed over my chest. "It seems the decision has already been made."

"Don't you understand? I have to pretend to go along with this or he will take you away from me," the prince protests.

"No, I don't understand. Not for one minute. Why does Jocelyn have such sway over your father? What has she ever done for him? I saved his life, for Pete's sake," my rising voice trembles with anger.

"It's not that simple," he yells. Sadie keeps her eyes trained on the floor. I should dismiss her, but in my anger I neglect to.

"It is that simple," I shout, making the maid wince.

"Did you think this relationship would be free of complications? My entire life is full of complications!" He slams his hand down on our writing desk; pens and ink joggle and clatter.

"Well, then maybe I should just leave and not burden you with another one," I challenge.

His jaw sets, then he says pointedly, "The Olivia I know stands up for what she wants. She doesn't run away like a coward."

Rage explodes through me. I grab the closest object, which happens to be Sadie's needlework, and hurl it at him. The tiny house cartwheels across the space toward his head. Liam ducks. It hits the wall behind him, the frame smashing in two, then drops to the floor. My maid's hand flies to her mouth.

Anne bursts through the door.

"What on earth are you two doing? Do you realize the ruckus you are causing?" she scolds. "People are hanging out their doors to hear you."

Liam and I are mollified into silence. Sadie just stares at her toes.

"Now," she continues, "I don't know what happened here, and frankly, I don't care. If either of you has a shred of common sense, you will end this nonsense immediately."

"You—" She points at me, "—stay here until you cool off. Which knowing you, will be morning at the earliest.

"And you—" She actually pokes her finger into the prince's chest, "—give my sister time to calm down. Go back to the ball and, at the very least, make a less scandalous exit for the evening."

All three of us stare at her dumbfounded. Then, without words, Liam strides past her out the door.

"Now, if you will excuse me, I abruptly left my partner to deal with this…situation. I would like to rejoin him. Good evening." And she is gone, the door shut firmly behind her.

It takes a moment for my handmaid and me to come to our senses. When we do, I rush across the room to retrieve her handiwork. The wooden frame is cracked into two pieces, the house hanging in a warped fold between them.

"Oh, Sadie, I am so sorry." I hand the mangled remains to her.

"Not to worry. I'll have this fixed up in no time." She rolls it up as best she can and sets it on the desk. "Now, let's get you out of your corset so you will be more comfortable."

A short time later I sit in my toasty nightgown, a cup of warm wine in hand. Sadie brushes my hair in soothing strokes, carefully rooting out every last bead and hairpin. The gentle motions of her hands finally manage to calm me down somewhat. In fact, at this point, I am both emotionally and physically spent. To her credit, my maid has not made one comment or asked one question about what happened.

"Thank you," I murmur and take a bite of the muffin she wrangled up for me somehow. "I apologize you had to witness such a scene."

"I am sorry someone upset you so terribly, even if it were Prince Liam." At my silent nod, she adds, "I am sure tomorrow he will feel badly about it all."

"Yes, but he may be too afraid of Anne to come near me," I tease with the first hint of relief I have felt so far. Sadie tries to suppress a smile.

"Admit it," I goad, "it was pretty hilarious when she dressed him down like a naughty schoolboy." I facetiously poke my finger through the air.

Despite a valiant effort, my maid is unable to stifle a laugh. We dissolve into a fit of giggles. The fact that Anne continues to be the voice of reason here at the palace amazes me still. When Queen Helen invited her to join me, I thought my sister would be the one making the scenes, not quelling them. She is actually more fit for royal life than I am. Funny how life continues to surprise you, just when you think you had it all figured out.

Hours later, lying in bed, sleep does not find me. Fretful thoughts about a future with Liam torture my mind while I toss and turn. I have tried to shut off my emotions and use reason to work things out, but so far, no good solution has presented itself. Sadie dozes in a chair by the fire, a shawl wrapped around her shoulders. In slumber, she looks peaceful and content. How I envy her.

At last, the door quietly opens, then shuts. Anne has returned. Too worn out to deal with her lectures, I feign sleep. Our maid jolts awake and their muffled whispers fill the room. The fabric of my sister's gown rustles while she is helped out of it, followed by silence, then a long exhale, when I assume her corset is unlaced. Footsteps pad around and then the door opens and shuts again with Sadie's exit.

A few moments later, Anne slides between the sheets, nestling under the covers. Somehow her presence flips the last hinge off the container I have shoved my emotions into. Before I can help it, I weep, my shoulders shuddering with each breath. My sister inches closer and wraps her arms around me from behind.

"Was that your first fight?"

I nod.

"It will be all right, Olivia. You two are meant for each other. You will feel better about it in the morning. I promise. Try to get some sleep."

She snuggles against me. Soon, her breath rises and falls in such a steady, rhythmic way, I know she is asleep.

A restless doze is all I manage. The shadows in the room start to take form as the sun approaches the horizon. Niobe is an early riser. I may as well go down by her and do something useful. My feet feel like lead when I swing them over the edge of the bed. I slip into my simple day dress, then weave my hair into a stumpy braid. After a quick splash of water on my face, I wrap my cloak around me and step out of the room. Anne never even stirs a pinky.

This early, the hallways are nearly empty but for a few servants who bustle about their morning duties. I cut through the kitchens on the way to the healer's in the hopes of grabbing a hot roll for breakfast. To my surprise, the large room is almost deserted. Odd, since it should be a hive of activity at this hour. What few occupants it has all hang out the door to the herb garden. I pluck a roll out of a bread basket on someone's tray and savor a bite. The murmur of a crowd catches my attention. I reach the doors that open onto the garden and peer around two servants who stand blocking it.

A large contingent of people, mostly kitchen help, rings the herb garden. They whisper and point at something against the far wall. Elbowing my way through the onlookers,

I finally reach the front of the crowd. It takes a moment for my brain to comprehend the scene.

Niobe lies on the ground, her body twitching to and fro. A broken clay pot is by her feet, dark red liquid oozing from the shards. The same substance that stains the healer's outstretched hand—holly berry juice.

But the true horror is behind her, what makes the roll drop from my hand and tumble away forgotten. On the garden wall, scrawled in dark red letters, are the words:

THE DAY APPROACHES
DIE WILLIAM DIE

No one moves. They just stare, muttering and pointing. Niobe lies on her side, one cheek on the frosty ground. Her eyes are closed and she moans restlessly. I take a step towards her, but a burly man grabs my arm and warns me to wait for the royal guards. Before I can tell him where he can go, the crowd parts again, this time for Brother Alastair. He surveys the scene, his face curling into his usual self-righteous sneer.

The echo of booted feet on the cobblestones announces the arrival of two of the king's guards. Two stalwart soldiers pause, then creep toward Niobe as if she were a cornered snake. One nudges her with his foot. Her head tilts to the side to reveal a trickle of blood streaking down her face, a tiny red river against her pale, white skin. This sight spurs me to action. I run to kneel beside her and cradle her head in my lap.

"Step away, miss," one of the guards instructs. His tone, like the eyes that bore into me, is callous. He confers quietly with his comrade, who hurries off through the kitchen at breakneck speed.

I stand to meet his eyes. "I am one of Queen Helen's ladies-in-waiting. This is my instructor. She is injured and I am well within my right to tend to her."

He eyes me up and down, but does not stop me when I crouch back down to Niobe. The blood originates from a cut on her forehead and is only starting to dry, so the wound is not too old. A large bump on the back of her head greets my fingers upon further examination. I carefully note her position on the ground as a theory develops in my mind. Gently placing her head back on the ground, I rise to give the area a more thorough look. When I bend to touch the broken clay pot, a hand thrusts out and snags my arm mid-reach.

"Do not touch that, miss, until the area has been investigated," the guard snaps. The crowd watches our exchange intently, unbothered by the chilly breeze. This is just too intriguing of an event to be ignored. It seems breakfast will be served late today.

"Well, were you planning on investigating anytime soon? Or were you just going to stand here?" I huff. He merely tightens his grip on my arm.

"I am waiting for my superior, miss. It is his job, not mine." The crowd's collective heads rotate back and forth between us.

"There will be no need. I can already tell you what happened here." A joint gasp flutters through our witnesses.

He looks surprised, and dubious, but before he can respond, his companion returns with several more guards. One steps forward to survey the scene, frowning when he reads the words scrawled on the wall. Glancing through me as if I were meaningless, he addresses the sentinel, "Was this how you found things?"

"Yes, sir."

He turns to the hoard of onlookers and orders them to leave immediately. They disperse slowly, a disappointed murmur running through them like a wave. I am sure they will move just far enough to be out of sight, but not earshot.

"What is she—" He jerks his head at in my direction, "—doing here?"

"She is a lady in the service of the queen and claims to know this person." His voice is laced with disgust while he again toes Niobe's prone form. "She also claims to have figured this whole situation out already."

"Oh really," the superior answers in a tenor that makes me want to throat-punch him…again. He does not recognize me, but I clearly remember him as the guard who accosted Lydia and I when she accidentally trespassed in the royal gardens a few months back. If someone picks you up like a sack of flour and drops you at the feet of a prince, the memory tends to linger. "Do go on."

"My belief is that the victim was in the garden gathering herbs when she was attacked from behind. There is a substantial lump on the back of her head. After she was hit, she fell forward and cut her forehead, likely on a rock. Then she was dragged over here while someone dipped her hand in the berry juice to make it look as if she had written on the wall."

"Is that so? And just what do you base your little theory on, young lady?" The contempt in his voice is maddening.

"Look." I point a few feet away where a basket lies half full of mint leaves. "She was hit there, and fell, then dragged over here. The person responsible covered the track marks in the dirt, except here," I walk a step to where the mint plants meet the earth border. "These mint stalks are crushed and broken where her body passed through." Whoever had done this tried to make it less noticeable, but with my years of tracking experience, the signs were obvious.

"That proves nothing," the man says, a dismissive wave of his hand in my direction. "How do you know she didn't merely step on those plants before she wrote her message on the wall? How do you explain her fingers being covered with the exact substance the words were written in?"

"For one thing, footprints would have sporadically broken the mint. These are crushed and pulled as one in the same direction. For another, how did she hurt both sides of her head? If she fell either forward or backward, there would only be one injury. And lastly, it is her right fingers covered with the ink. I happen to know for a fact Niobe is left-handed."

Although I can tell he desperately wants to contradict me, the leader can find nothing to refute.

"You know a suspicious amount of information about what transpired here. We will escort you to a chamber for further questioning," he instructs.

"Only if you concede to my demand the healer be brought to the infirmary immediately. She needs medical attention."

He mulls this over for a moment, then whispers to one of his officers. A short time later, two men appear carrying a stretcher. They lift Niobe onto it as if she were a feather. I make sure to wrap a blanket tightly around her frail form, then they hoist her and are off. The only sounds she makes are some indistinct moans. It will likely be hours before we can get any details out of her.

Three men flank me down an outer corridor, servants and courtiers all stopping to gape. This incident will cause a firestorm of gossip, no doubt. We mount a short set of stairs, then enter inside and head down another hallway to a part of the castle completely unfamiliar to me. They direct me to a small rectangular room, empty but for a large table. I plop into a hard wooden chair on one side. The leader sits across from me, glowering.

For several minutes, we just regard one another with mutual contempt. Then the sound of voices approaches the room.

"My superior will question you now," he sneers, clearly awaiting my comeuppance.

I merely return his smile, knowing full well what is coming. The door opens.

"What in the blazes is going on, Commander Sparks?" a gruff voice barks.

"We have a person of interest to question." I want to smack the haughty expression right off his face, even though I know there is no need.

He points at me and I relish every moment of his face changing to a look of dread, when I glance at the man who entered and say, "Hello, Father."

An hour later, at the table with my father, Prince Harold, Prince Liam, Prince Stephan, the commander who brought me here, and a few high-ranking knights, I repeat my tale of the morning's events.

"So there was no one near her when you first saw her?" Father asks, his fingers pinching the bridge of his nose.

"No. There were a number of servants outside, but they were all afraid to get anywhere near her."

"And you saw no one suspicious in the area?" Prince Harold presses. His presence unnerves me a bit. My interactions with him have been minimal and I don't have a feel for what he thinks of me in regards to my training…and his brother. "Did you have a chance to check for any footprints or any additional clues that may have been in the area? Anything to indicate which way they came from or went?"

"No. The royal guard arrived shortly after I did. By what I was able to observe, I feel certain you will not find many clues. Whoever did this wanted to cover his tracks.

After I pointed out why I felt Niobe was attacked, I was immediately taken here by Commander Sparks." I can't help but smile at his angry face.

"With all due respect," he breaks in, "are we going to consider it a foregone conclusion the witch was attacked on this girl's word alone?"

"I think her record on matters such as this speaks for itself. Therefore, yes, we will consider her theory." To my surprise, this endorsement comes from Prince Harold, rather than my father or Liam. It effectively shuts Sparks up. Although, judging by his scowl, his contempt is not forgotten. "I trust you have left men on the scene to investigate the area. Unless they turn up something new, Miss Davenport's hypothesis seems plausible given Niobe's injuries and the fact she is left-handed." Sparks glowers at me, but remains silent.

"Yes, it would have been rather difficult for her to wound both sides of her head if she merely collapsed, as you suggest," Liam adds. This is the first time I have seen him since our argument last night. I push pictures of him dancing with Jocelyn out of my mind and try to remain focused on the topic at hand.

"However," Sir Michael comments, "she has been known to go into deep trances before. Perhaps she injured the front of her head earlier on, and banged the back of it when she fell. And who is to say which of her hands she would use while in one of her stupors?"

After fooling Sir Michael in my disguise as Puck on the Lindenwood trip, he will clearly never be a fan of mine. He must love noting the flaws in my theory. And I have to admit, he makes a good point. Though I still vote for my version of events.

Father rubs his temple with his thumb and forefinger, a familiar gesture when he puzzles something over. He looks weary, more so than I have noticed in a long time. This prophecy business is taking its toll. "You mentioned you and Niobe had picked the berries earlier in the day. Did anyone else know you had collected them?"

"I can't say. I mean, we were not secretive about where we went. There were dozens of people who might have seen us come and go. Anyone who had business being in the back fields. And the servants who came to collect the holly boughs."

"She didn't mention anyone having an interest in the berries?" Liam queries.

"Not at all. She told me she would be making some tinctures and dye from them. Nothing out of the ordinary."

"His Majesty, my father," Prince Harold begins with a reverent nod, "suffers from much uneasiness since Niobe's prophecy in the fall. He still trusts her, but I cannot claim the same. We know of no credible threat to the king, other than perhaps Lord Otto. His motives were unclear, yet our intelligence shows he fled Stewartsland the day we attacked Lindenwood, and has not returned to the best of our knowledge."

"If I may," Prince Stephan breaks in. "I have some information to share regarding Otto. My troops on the southern coast informed me he gained entry into one of our ports a few months ago. He was pursued and escaped again by boat. I only learned of this news shortly before I left to come here and was planning on sharing it with you all."

"Well, that would seem to rule him out as the perpetrator," Sir Michael says. "Which brings us back to the witch." I cringe at the term and picture the poor helpless healer lying injured in the snow.

"But why would Niobe have any motive for doing this?" My tone has more of an edge to it than I intended.

The elder prince looks at me, his eyes not filled with condescension or contempt, but with the same anxiety we all feel. "I do not know, Miss Davenport. All I do know is she has done some strange things while in these trances. While I do not think her waking self would harm my father, I cannot speak for her actions when she is under one of those spells."

Maybe I cannot be objective. Maybe working so closely with her has left me too emotionally attached to the situation. Maybe being trapped in this wretched castle has dulled my once keen instincts. But my belief in Niobe's innocence remains.

Silence falls, heavy and full of indecision. My father deliberates. We wait to hear his conclusion. Liam gives me a small smile of support, which nicely offsets the sneers of Sparks and Sir Michael.

After several moments, Father says, "I think the wisest course of action at the moment is to wait for the results of the investigation. It may help us decide once and for all Niobe's level of participation. She is either involved, perhaps while in a trance, or has been attacked. Either way, I feel she needs more eyes on her movements. I will not yet post a guard directly with her, but I will increase the number of patrols past her quarters and see what information, if any, turns up. Agreed?"

Murmurs of assent float around the table, some more enthusiastic than others. No one contradicts my father's directives, though.

"And Olivia, please see if you can get any details out of her."

"Yes, Father, I will," I answer, determined to get to the bottom of what is going on.

Everyone rises. The men excuse themselves. They bow to the princes and bid my father farewell, but walk past me as if I were air.

Figures.

On the way out, the crown prince puts a hand on my shoulder. "I have complete faith in your abilities to help keep my father safe." Before I can do more than curtsey quickly at the compliment, he heads out the door.

Father comes over and hugs me tightly. "Keep your eyes and ears open. Any information, even the smallest, most insignificant detail, and I am told at once. Understood?"

"Yes, sir." I squeeze back with all my might.

"Your mother sends her regards. And Lydia and Ellen are anxiously awaiting your presence at Christmas."

"Yes, I am as well."

"Well, I am off to collect information from the investigators." He bows to the younger prince and departs.

Liam and I are finally alone. No, not alone. Two men stand sentry right outside the door in the busy hallway. Even if we close the door, the men will hear us if we argue again. This would probably do little to help my cause…if my cause even matters anymore. If the king is adamant his son court Jocelyn, what chance do I have?

Liam takes my hand and leads me to the door. "Come. We need to talk."

"About what?" I huff, my indignation at last night finally surfacing.

He leans close so no one but me can hear his words. "About how I am not giving up on you…on us." Tears threaten to fill my eyes, the exhaustion and stress of the past twelve hours sinking in, when he adds, "So I would truly appreciate if you did not give up on us either."

Gently he guides me out of the room. We navigate down the hall, courtiers bowing on either side when he passes. Adam materializes and follows in our wake. I am so disoriented by all that has happened, it is not until we cross a threshold into the royal family's wing when I understand where he is taking me. Double doors of carved mahogany suddenly loom in front of us. He pushes them open, then nods to Adam to remain outside. The next thing I know, I am standing inside Prince Liam's own chamber.

It feels strange, overly personal in a way. I had given no thought to him being in my room, but standing here feels almost like trespassing. His room, which is easily five times the size of mine and Anne's, is decorated in dark shades of green and burgundy. Neatly stacked papers and books stand on the top of a desk, a dark blue plume rests in an ink jar at their side. Two oversized chairs flank the fireplace where a large stag head is mounted over the mantle. A large four-poster bed takes up one whole side of the room, its curtains and canopy a luxurious silk. The entire room has a musky, but not overpowering male scent in it. Overall, it is exactly how I would have imagined—classic and understated, just like Liam.

I walk slowly around, inspecting every corner. There are more books in shelves on either side of the fireplace. They are a nice mix, some about royal lineage and war strategies, but also some literature and poetry. We definitely have the same reading tastes. The mantle has a small likeness of Liam from when he was a boy, his head topped with the same unruly hair even back then. Next to a porcelain replica of the Stewart crest stand two small tin soldiers so worn with time, their faces are half faded. Playthings from his youth he has not parted with yet.

His closet door is ajar, revealing a massive amount of suits and uniforms lined along the walls. A dressing table and chaise sit in the middle of the narrow rectangle. I have to quell the urge to go inside and touch his clothes, picture how he would look in each garment.

Finally, I reach the bed. My hand runs across the smooth coverlet. Knowing this is where he sleeps every night, to actually have a visual image of it, stirs something deep inside of me. The thought of falling asleep right here, wrapped in his arms, is the most comforting sensation I have ever experienced. In this moment, I vow to battle for him with every ounce of strength I have. There is no way I will let Jocelyn ever be the one to share this bed with him. Liam was right—I fight for what I want.

The prince has stood silently, watching me take it all in with a bemused look on his face. Suddenly, he is behind me, arms encircling my waist. I lean back into his embrace. We stand this way for a long time and I absorb all the room has shown me about him. Seeing where he spends his time and the items he surrounds himself with makes me feel closer to him somehow, like a secret garden has been opened to me.

"Please don't be worried about Jocelyn. I will never agree to be with her. There is only you," he whispers, his breath warm on my neck. "We will figure this out together."

I turn and take his face in my hands, then pull him in for a passionate kiss.

⚜

An hour later, I walk into my chambers. Anne takes one look at my swollen lips and disheveled hair. "Made up then, did you?" she quips.

"What?" I answer, still too distracted by my time alone with Liam.

"Well, either you were kissing a certain prince or you have some explaining to do for your frightful appearance."

"Oh…yes, we, umm…talked it all out…"

"More than talked from the looks of it," she says knowingly.

"But that is not all that happened this morning." I sit on the bed crossed-leg, facing Anne who lolls in a chair by the fire, still in her robe. "Niobe was attacked. At least, I think she was attacked."

I give Anne an overview of what I found in the gardens and all the events that followed. My sister listens intently, then she is silent. The logs on the fire crackle, a warm protection against the cold wind hissing against the window. My stomach growls. In all the commotion of the morning, I only managed one bite of roll in the kitchen earlier.

"Why would Niobe do this? I mean, she is strange, obviously, but not dangerous. I agree, it sounds as though she is being framed," my sister states.

Sadie bustles into the room humming to herself, some clean towels hanging over her arms. She enters the bathing chamber to deposit them, her melody fading in her wake. There is a rap on the door and Kat sticks her head in.

"Oh good, you're here. I just wanted to chat." She tries to fake nonchalance, but I hear the unease in her tone.

"You heard about Niobe?"

"Yes," she whispers, hopping onto the bed beside me. "What happened?"

"It's a long story," I begin when Sadie emerges from the bathing chamber. I am unsure how much to divulge in her presence so I stop short.

"I am ready to dress you ladies for dinner whenever you are ready," our handmaid says.

Dinner? Where did today even go?

Then I remember it is Christmas Eve. Dinner will be served earlier this evening so people can prepare for Midnight Mass. My sister will clearly need the extra time since she hasn't managed to get dressed at all today after her late night. Frankly, I am so exhausted I hope I stay awake for it all.

"I think my sister and I will eat here tonight. Please arrange to have our meal sent up." Anne instructs. "Kat, you are welcome to join us."

Hesitation clouds my friend's face, so I add, "Sadie, when you go down to dine with the servants, please have Peter Cooper sent up to the room to join us. And please make sure there is plenty of extra food for him."

So rarely do I use Puck's given name, it sounds foreign on my lips. Kat's body relaxes though, and she accepts Anne's invitation. The thought of a cozy dinner with my closest companions comforts me. Our servant bustles out, no doubt happy to have the extra time not needing to dress us has afforded her. She promises to send Puck and the food, and to be back later to get us ready for Mass.

Puck and our meals arrive simultaneously. We drag the vanity chairs over by the fire and the four of us dig in to fowls so tender the meat falls from the bone, roasted vegetables, warm corn bread, and mince pies. Anne, Kat, and I are as ravenous as Puck. Only the sound of chewing is heard for the first few minutes. Then Kat and Puck listen with rapt attention to the story of my morning.

"It seems odd to me that someone would try to frame Niobe," Puck says. "Are you certain she wasn't under one of her spells?"

It irritates me that he so quickly looks to poke holes in my theory. "Weren't you listening to me?" I huff.

"Yes. But you must admit, there is still the possibility she was in a trance. She does some bizarre things when she goes into one of them."

"All right, maybe there is a miniscule possibility," I admit begrudgingly, "but I don't think so. I am sure the investigation will prove what I said. Hopefully, I can talk with her soon and get some answers."

No one says anything. For the first time, a tiny shred of doubt creeps into my mind. What if I am wrong? What if Niobe does pose a threat to the king? With all my training, I should know not to discount any possibility, no matter how remote.

"Did you at least settle things with Liam?" Puck asks. "Or are you still throwing things at his head today?"

"Not that it's any of your business, but yes, we did talk. Things are fine now. And how did you know I threw something at him anyway?"

"Anne told us last night when she came back to the ball."

"Thanks for giving me up, Puck." Anne says, casting him a sour look. He winks at her.

"And you missed him too," my old friend teases. "The Olivia I know wouldn't have missed."

"Maybe I missed on purpose," I counter.

"All right, you two. Enough. I have some news myself," my sister says.

"I hope it's good news," I mutter, tired of the entire life-at-the-palace experience and all its drama.

"Yes, actually, it is." She leans in close and we all bend toward her in anticipation. "Montgomery plans to ask Father for my hand in marriage over the Christmas holiday."

It takes a split second for the news to register, then we all mob Anne with hugs. After, we explode into a pile of contentment and giggles on the floor. Today, unlike yesterday, looks to end much nicer than it started. My sister's happiness is so vibrant, it is contagious. Matters for her heart are settled. Now it is time to secure mine.

Christmas Day dawns chilly, a fresh blanket of snow lies across the land. Tree boughs sparkle as if covered with diamonds in the early morning light when Anne and I cut through a courtyard headed for the holiday breakfast. The glint off the snow is almost blinding in its whiteness, especially to my tired eyes. Midnight Mass ended in the wee hours. Sadie seemed to wake us only moments after my head hit the pillow.

The Great Hall is still decorated in all the holiday trappings, though the atmosphere is not as festive. Whether from everyone being too tired or the threatening message on the wall, I do not know, but there are more than a few sagging shoulders and drooping eyelids among the courtiers when we take our seats.

Except for Jocelyn. She positively glows in a gown of winter-white velvet, crystals catching the light like stars at her neck and wrists. Her hair is woven with tiny seed pearls in tresses that cascade around her like a luxurious, golden waterfall. My rival sits next to Liam, pressing her body as close to his as she can without actually climbing into his lap. Emily, who is seated with Prince Harold on the other side of the king and queen, mirrors her sister's position. While Harold seems not to mind, or perhaps not notice, Liam's scowl grows with each touch of Jocelyn's hand, each giggle, and each ostentatious whisper. King William is oblivious to his son's discomfort, but Queen Helen watches him sidelong, an unreadable expression on her face.

My fingers absently run along my sword necklace. How I wish it were real so I could hurl it across the room into Jocelyn's throat. She glances my way every few seconds. I keep my eyes averted, not wanting to give her the satisfaction of knowing how much it hurts to watch her act as if she has a claim on Liam. Anne covers my hand with hers and gives me a small nod of support. This gives me enough motivation to act carefree and unbothered. Chatting with some gentlemen who join us, I talk and laugh as though I am thoroughly enjoying myself. All the while, my insides are in a knot of anger.

When the meal is finished, the king toasts the court before exiting with the rest of the royal family. Just like that, Liam is gone. Courtiers mill about extending holiday greetings. Most of them, Anne and I included, will return home now until New Year's Day when another Mass and feast will be held. Happily, my parents accepted my request to bring Kat home to join us. Though she wants to see her family, she decided the trip would be too long and too cold to endure.

We are jostled out of the Hall with the flowing crowd, then turn down a hallway that leads in the direction of our room. Kat and Anne walk ahead, chatting about what to pack for the short few days we will be gone. My feet drag along behind, uninterested in keeping up, and they are soon quite a bit ahead of me. It is only a few days, but it is time apart from Liam while Jocelyn will still be around to throw herself at him.

On the left-hand side of the corridor, a small door opens slightly. When I pass, an arm reaches out and yanks me in. In my surprise, instincts take over and my elbow rises to connect with the face of my assailant.

"Wait!" Liam cries, ducking out of the blow's path.

"You scared me to death!" I exclaim. "A broken nose would have served you right! What on earth are you doing?"

"Hiding. Here. So we can have a few minutes alone before you leave." His grin is too mischievous not to smile back.

The room is little more than a storage closet. Mugs, dishes, and bowls stack in orderly formation on shelves along one wall. Several barrels of unknown content line the other side, leaving only a narrow space for one to maneuver. Brooms and mops lean in the corner like naughty school children. Piles of table linens sit in haphazard stacks where someone left them hastily on the floor near our feet. A feeble amount of light shines through a window on the back wall, leaving the room in soft shadows.

"And if someone comes in?" I question.

"Then I will order them out. Being a prince has its advantages, you know."

"And just what exactly do you propose we do here?" I gesture at the tight confines while trying to suppress my smile.

"Something that does not require a lot of space," he answers, drawing an arm around my waist. "We will have to be quite close together, you see."

"Is that so?" I reply, in the breathless moment before his lips caress mine.

My hands wrap around his head, fingers twining through his curls, pulling him closer. His hands push against my back with urgency, as if he can make our bodies meld into one. The element of danger, of knowing someone could open the door at any moment, only adds to the intensity of the experience. His kisses become firmer, more insistent, and my grip on reality melts with each heavenly second. If the door flew open now and the entire kingdom stood outside, I am not sure either of us would notice. Time elapses with neither of us showing any inclination to stop.

"Prince Liam?" Jocelyn's acerbic voice cuts through the fog in my brain. "Are you out here?"

Her voice sounds in the hallway outside. She passes the room, her shadow darkening the floor along the bottom of the door. Liam and I hold each other, frozen like statues while we wait for her to continue down the corridor. A few seconds later we hear her call out farther away.

"You better go. I am sure she will not give up until she finds you. And I have to pack for my trip home," I say, my heart aching at the thought of leaving this closet.

Begrudgingly, he agrees. We creep to the door and listen closely for any sounds outside. When there is only silence, he cracks it and sticks his head out, then steps into the hall. After a quick look around, he motions for me to follow. He graces me with another kiss.

"Enjoy your trip home. I will miss you."

"I will miss you too," I whisper, our foreheads pressed together, our hands clasped.

"Oh, there you are. I was looking all..." The voice behind us trails off. Jocelyn's mouth hangs agape at the sight she encounters.

Good.

Our rumpled clothes and tousled hair announce exactly what we have been doing louder than any words would have. She looks from us to the storage room door, which stands ajar. While she adds things up, I simply cross my arms over my chest.

"Take care, my love," Liam says and bestows one last kiss. "Jocelyn." He nods at her, then strolls away. His footsteps recede to nothing.

My nemesis and I stare each other down. Her hatred is a tangible force when she sneers. "Kissing him in closets will be the most you can ever hope to get from him. I hope you enjoy being his plaything."

In all my life—and I have run around with outlaws for goodness' sake—I have never been spoken to in such a manner. I want to lunge at her, mostly because her words hold just enough truth in them to scare me. But I maintain my composure and walk up to her until we are nose to nose. Our faces are so close I feel her breath on my face.

"I assure you, I will enjoy it far more than you will enjoy being his untouched wife."

Pushing her out of my path, she staggers back into the stone wall and watches me stalk away. I get a small modicum of satisfaction from the fear in her wide eyes.

By the time I return to my room, Anne is ready to leave. Sadie bustles about putting some last-minute items in my trunk. My sister says nothing as I slump in a chair and stare into the fire. The flames cast dancing shadows on the floor at my feet. I watch their flickering leaps, so much less substantial than their fiery counterparts. Maybe this is what I am destined to become—a secret lover in Liam's life while Jocelyn plays out the public role of his wife. Perhaps I should let King William ship me to Prescott. At least I wouldn't have to watch her charade from there.

When Sadie firmly pats my trunk closed, the hasp clicks loudly. She drags it outside the door where my sister's own stands waiting to be transported to our carriage. Once back inside, she makes sure all the vanity drawers are shut and the wardrobe secured.

"If that will be all, ladies, I will be on my way," her voice breaks the heavy silence.

"Yes, Sadie. Thank you. And may you and your family have a wonderful Christmas," Anne replies. She gives our maid a warm hug, then hands her the gift we bought for her; a new pair of gloves and matching scarf.

"Thank you so much, Miss Anne, and you too, Miss Olivia."

I rouse from my stupor and embrace Sadie. "Enjoy your time home with your family and with Franklin."

"Oh! My heavens, I almost forgot," she replies, then points over to the desk. "That came for you while you were out, Miss Olivia. Now if you will excuse me, I will be on my way."

We bid her good-bye and she practically skips down the hall in excitement. I look at the large rectangular package wrapped in red paper, then at my sister, who shrugs. It is heavier and more solid than I expect when I move it to the bed. There is no card on the outside to indicate where it came from. My fingers run over the finely embossed wrappings, savoring the moment.

"Well? Aren't you going to open it?" Anne chides, never one to wait.

Carefully, I remove the thick paper to find a long, smooth mahogany box. A beautiful work in its own right, its rich surface gleams in the firelight. The hinged lid bends back to reveal a shining silver sword, more beautiful than any I have seen, lying atop a cushion of black velvet. Its blade shines like a polished mirror, sparkling in the late morning sun when I hold it up. But the hilt is the true piece of art. Intricate scrollwork etched all around the surface meets in the middle to form a heart in which sits two crossed keys. After admiring the craftsmanship for a moment, I take a few practice swings. The weapon slices crisply through the air with precision, perfectly balanced for me.

"All right, all right!" Anne yelps. "Put that down before you take my head off. Besides, he put a note with it."

Indeed, a small envelope is tucked in the lid of the box, Liam's initials flourished across it. I pull out the enclosed note:

Olivia dearest,

Please accept a sword worthy of the fighter you are. I can only hope to be as worthy of you every day until the end of time. When you hold it, remember only we hold the keys to each other's hearts.

With love,
Liam

It is the most perfect gift, one that captures the essence of who I am. Liam does not want me to be anyone other than myself. He not only accepts me, but loves me. His faith in us buoys my troubled spirit.

"I hope you got him something good," Anne teases.

"A few days ago, I snuck a cologne Niobe helped me make especially for Liam to Adam, so he could give it to the prince for me today." Somehow my gift seems much less special in comparison.

There is a rap at the door and Madame le Clare's harsh voice calls, "Ladies, your carriage is ready for you."

"Come on. Let's go get Kat. You better hide that before Madame sees it. She may keel right over from the impropriety of it—on so many levels. It would be a shame to kill her on Christmas," my sister jokes.

"I guess so," I laugh, placing the sword back in the box then slipping it under the bed.

Anne hands me my cloak and I tuck Liam's note into its pocket. When we descend the stairs to our waiting ride, I run my fingers over the smooth paper. It will serve as a physical reminder of our relationship while I am home. We settle in the cab, burying ourselves under blankets like newborn kittens hunkering under their mother's warm belly. The horses trot off at a lively clip and the palace recedes into the distance behind us. Each second takes me farther from Liam, yet between his gift and our morning's interlude, I have never felt closer to him. A warm contentment fills my heart as we pass through the city gate and turn for home.

My days home add to my contentment. With Kat here, Puck spends most of his time with us. For the first time in months, everyone I love is under the same roof—well, almost everyone.

Lydia is beside herself with excitement, clamoring for my attention nearly every waking moment. She spends hour upon hour asking details about the palace. Ellen livens as well, her interest in the royal libraries a frequent topic. Lucy stuffs me with my favorite treats, while I regale her with tales of castle life. Even the stoic Grace embraces me warmly each morning when I enter the kitchen for breakfast. It is heartwarming to know I am missed.

The weather becomes milder than it has been in weeks. In the absence of the chill wind, the weak sunshine provides enough warmth to venture outdoors if we bundle up. Days are spent sparring with Puck, playing with my sisters, and showing Kat around. When evening falls, we retreat inside for delicious meals around a full table. After, my father and I withdraw into his study just like old times, the perfect ending to these special days.

"So as soon as you are able to speak with Niobe, I want a full report," my father instructs on one such evening. He tips back in his chair, chewing on the stem of his pipe. A wisp of smoke curls above him before dissipating into nothingness.

"All right. She had still not woken when I left to come home," I reply, snuggled in my favorite chair by the warm hearth, "but it will be on the top of my list when I get back."

"You should know Brother Alastair is ramping up pressure on King William. He wants Niobe tried on charges of treason."

"But she didn't write the message on the wall. Your own investigators agree with me," I exclaim.

"Well, they agree there is enough evidence to prove someone else was in the garden with her and likely caused her injuries, but what actually happened remains unclear. Any information you can get from Niobe could help clear her name, especially if we can find a woman to tie to this. That would help explain the 'she' in the conversation you overheard by the maze."

He lifts up his legs and crosses one ankle over the other on the desktop. His posture, the smell of his pipe, the haphazard stacks of papers all bring me back to a simpler time when my greatest worry was how to prolong my training. How did things become so complicated? I shake my head in despair.

"Don't worry just yet," Father says. "The king has been briefed on the whole situation. He has known Niobe since childhood. I don't think he has any inclination to listen to the friar. Just be warned, your association with Niobe and defense of her may not put you in good standing with Brother Alastair."

A harrumph is my only answer. I couldn't care a lick what such a vile man thinks of me. Any clergyman who sits in posh palace quarters stuffing his face half the day, while his charges toil in the bitter cold without proper clothing, does not understand one word of the Scriptures. The less he wants to do with me, the better.

"And how are things with you and Prince Liam?"

The change in subject startles me, especially since the question comes from my father. Mother has been noticeably mum on the topic, though I find it hard to believe she does not long to know the story. Or perhaps she is just too preoccupied with the rumor of Anne's pending engagement to give me a thought.

"Umm…we are all right…" I shift nervously in my chair. "The king is pressuring him to consider Jocelyn Crawford, but…he has no interest in her…." I decide it is best to not blurt out my entire list of grievances I have on this matter.

"Livy," he starts, his tone serious and guarded, "you understand if King William does not approve of a marriage between you and Prince Liam, then you are going to have to find a way to accept it."

"Yes, I understand," I choke out the words I forbid myself to consider. A hollow forms in my chest. What if the king flat-out refuses Liam's wishes? He may not be able to force Liam to marry Jocelyn, but he could certainly keep him from marrying me. The surety I felt about our relationship when I left the palace spirals down the drain like rainwater.

Father sets his pipe down on the rim of an ashtray. "Please promise me you will maintain your composure in the event this doesn't work out in your favor. I know you love the prince, but you risk punishment if you insult the king in any manner."

"Well, I am so glad I saved him in Lindenwood. Some thanks I get," I grumble, my anger getting the better of me. But then a horrifying thought springs to my mind. "Father, do you know something I don't?" My voice is so constricted by terror, it is barely a whisper.

"No." He rises and walks around the desk to my chair. "I am just worried about you, my sweet Livy."

He pulls me into a giant bear hug. His arms were always a place I found comfort when I was young. Now my problems are so much bigger, so much more out of my control. I wait, but the old feelings of security and reassurance no longer find me as they once did. Another of the many constants lost to me over the past few months.

"I should go to bed," I murmur, worried sadness will overwhelm me.

My father takes my face in his hands. "Olivia, King William is a fool if he disapproves of you. Please remember that."

I force a smile, before standing on tiptoe to kiss his cheek. Then I head down the hall. The house is quiet; everyone else has retired. Shadowy outlines guide me to my old bedroom. I pass Anne's old room, where she and Kat sleep. Stopping briefly outside the door, I have the urge to climb in bed with Anne, having grown accustomed to her comforting presence at night. My old door eases open with a soft protest of the hinges, which once greeted me at the end of each day. Now the noise seems to mock me, reminding me the sanctuary of my childhood is gone.

My father thinks I am worthy of Liam. This should bring me some measure of solace about the situation. Yet I lie in bed listening to my sisters' sleeping breaths and I ache for Liam. He is only a mile away, at best, tucked in the stately bed I felt with my own hands, but a chasm stands between us— one I am unsure we will be able to bridge.

Midnight hops over from the other bed to mine. He rubs his head against my cheek, then lays down beside me. Absently, I stroke his black fur until I fall into a restless sleep.

The next night is New Year's Eve, our last at home. Lord Montgomery arrives. He quickly greets everyone upon his entrance, before my sister whisks him away for a tour of the property. Kat, Puck, and I trail along like ducklings, supposedly to act as their chaperones. We wind up having a snowball fight instead. Lydia hears us and drags Ellen outside to join the fun. Anne and her beau disappear into the empty armory for a stolen moment. Wistfully, I think of the tiny servant's closet where Liam and I found some alone time.

An hour later we return to the house, Montgomery and my sister dreamily holding hands. I dump some snow on their heads just before the door. "So you will look as if you were with us," I explain at their startled faces. *And to cool you two off,* I think to myself.

My mother nearly faints when seven dripping bodies burst through the back door into her kitchen. But even she can't help but laugh at our merriment while Grace and Lucy sort out our hats, mittens, and coats. Some part of her must miss having her family together.

Once we are dried off, we settle by the fire in the sitting room. My father strides out and orders Montgomery into his office, then firmly shuts the door behind them. Kat and I attempt to distract Anne, who paces and looks longingly at the closed room. Lydia sneaks over to peer through the keyhole, but Lucy shoos her away. The seconds tick by loudly, our clock on the mantle seeming to increase in volume whenever tension is in the air. Finally, the door reopens and the two men emerge smiling, Father's arm over the young man's shoulders.

"Congratulations, you two," he says. Anne gasps, then runs into her newly minted fiancé's embrace. The rest of us explode into cheers.

Later that evening, my eldest sister Jayne joins us with her husband, Lord Davis, and their young son. Grace outdoes herself with a bountiful feast. Fresh roasted venison, turkey, and all the trimmings spill over the sides of platters too numerous to fit on our table. Candles are lit all around the room, wax trickling into lumpy pools at their bases. Voices rise and fall with the various conversations happening simultaneously. The mood is cozy and secure, so unlike our meals in the palace dining hall. I wish Liam could be here to soak it all in.

Mother takes a bottle of champagne brought in by Grace and pries it open. The cork pops loudly and flies all the way into the sitting room, which elicits raucous laughter around the table.

"Oh, all right, laugh," she chides, filling a glass for each of us. "I want to propose a toast. To my dearest Anne and our soon-to-be son, Montgomery. May your lives be as full of love and joy as we are lucky to have here tonight."

"Here, here," we chorus and glasses clink all around.

Anne positively glows from the inside out, her face even more lovely when lit with the radiance of genuine happiness. Her betrothed stares at her as if she is the most precious treasure on earth. When I watch them, and notice Puck and Kat's hands clasped clandestinely under the table, I cannot wait to get back to the palace, back to Liam. Tonight is for these lovers. Tomorrow I will be with mine again.

At the stroke of midnight, we ring in the New Year with my family, then, after a few hours sleep, return to the palace in the early morning hours of New Year's Day. Kat, Anne, and I snuggle together under a thick blanket in the carriage while it bumps along the frozen, rutted road. Puck left just after the year turned to man the stables for the imminent return of all the courtiers. My sister lets out an unladylike yawn, echoed by my friend and me. There is to be a midday Mass followed by a feast, but the three of us look more ready for a nap. Kat's eyelids droop, but fly open on a particularly sharp bump. Anne's head lolls on my shoulder, the excitement of last night finally catching up with her.

At length, we pass through the city gates, then the arches that lead to the main palace staircase, where the carriage finally draws to a halt. Unlike our initial arrival, there is no Bartholomew or Madame le Clare to greet us, only a lone footman, who extends his frigid hand on our descent from the vehicle. My feelings are unlike the first time as well. Then, I was scared about not fitting in, leaving home, and managing a life with Liam. Now, I am determined to make myself belong.

Servants scurry away with our trunks like ants dragging a morsel back to the nest. We mount the steps to the main entrance, wind whipping our hair and biting our sleepy faces. Frigid air returned with the New Year. The vast atrium is already abuzz with lords and ladies greeting each other. Though they would never admit it, from the stifled yawns and heavy eyes, I can tell the bulk of courtiers are just as tired as we are. No one wants to miss the first Mass of the New Year. King William likes to see the church full on this day in particular, to set the tone for the remaining eleven months.

Madame le Clare spots us and strides briskly over. "I trust you ladies will be ready for Mass by eleven thirty?"

"Of course, Madame," Anne says. "Happy New Year to you and I hope you had a wonderful holiday break." Our mistress only deigns a perplexed glance at my sister before finding some other ladies to admonish. We snicker when she hurries away.

"Does she *ever* smile?" Kat asks rhetorically.

"We better get to our rooms and get ready before she suffers an apoplexy," Anne muses.

"You two go. I'm going to see if I can visit Niobe." I have been worried about the healer since they carried her to the infirmary last week. Hopefully, by now, I will find her alert and awake.

"All right," my sister murmurs warily, "but make sure you are back in time for Mass."

We part at an intersection of staircases. They head up to our rooms, but my path takes me down several levels to a long windowless corridor. The infirmary sits at the end of this forsaken hall, tucked well away from the notice of the healthy, who do not want to be reminded of its existence.

A young girl, no more than fourteen by the looks of her, mans a desk at the entry, her slight body dwarfed by the large piece of furniture. Behind her, rows of beds line each wall in an orderly sequence. The few that are occupied have curtains drawn around them. The foul smell of sickness looms beneath the scent of herbs and cleansers, like a predator ready to strike, despite the effort to eradicate it.

"Can I help you?" the girl asks. She tries to sound authoritative, but fails miserably.

"Yes, I am here to see Niobe."

"I'm sorry, but she is not supposed to have any visitors," she replies, with a valiant attempt to make her voice sound sure of itself.

"Oh, I am sure it is all right if I visit her. I am her assistant, you see. It will only be for a moment." She opens her mouth to protest, so I add, "Unless you want to go bother someone preparing for Mass about it."

The girl weighs her options. Clearly, she is here alone because she was deemed unimportant enough to miss the service. She could get in trouble for breaking the rule, but her higher-ups will be annoyed if they have to miss any of the Mass or the feast. After a hesitant moment, she points to a bed on the back right. "She is in there. Please don't be long."

My footsteps echo on the floor, magnified by the deathly silence of the room. I walk to the far side of the bed and slip behind the curtain. Niobe lies asleep, a scabbed-over gash on her cheek. Her long white hair fans out around her head like a diffuse cloud. What kind of person would attack an old defenseless woman?

She must sense my presence because her eyes flitter open and her face slowly breaks into a warm smile. A frail hand reaches for mine, enfolding it in a grip that belies its insubstantial appearance.

"How are you feeling, Niobe?"

"Tired, child…very tired." Her soft, slow words require effort to speak. She shifts up a bit and I put another pillow behind her back.

"Do you remember anything from that night?" I ask. If I only have a few moments with her, it is vital I get this information.

"Only that—" She wheezes before she is able to continue, "—I went…to pick…the last of the mint…then I saw…the blur of a dark figure. I wasn't…fast enough to stop it."

"Nothing else?" I hate to press, but know even the smallest detail she recalls could be important.

"No. I'm sorry. I wish…I could be more help." She collapses back against the pillows, already tiring from this small interaction.

"The investigators are looking into every detail. Hopefully they can ascertain who attacked you." I hope to reassure her, but she smiles sadly to herself. "What?"

"I thought the investigators…concluded it was all my doing."

"What? No. Not as far as I know. Who told you that?"

"Brother Alastair. He was here to …question me. He was at it for hours, convinced he could crack me. Imagine his frustration when…I had no information for him." There is a slight pride in her tone at having irritated the friar.

"They let that self-righteous fool interrogate you? For hours?" This is a troubling thought. Why would anyone put him in charge of this matter?

"Yes. He says he will not rest until…I am charged and tried as the witch I am."

Ah, that explains it. He is merely pushing his own agenda.

"Niobe, I am so sorry. I will get the bottom of this."

"Thank you, child," she mumbles, squeezing my hand.

"Now let me get you some warm milk with bread. Then I will comb your hair and give you a fresh nightgown."

Niobe smiles at me. How lonely she must have been, especially if the friar was her only visitor these past few days. The clock on the wall chimes. It is eleven. Madame le Clare must be in a tizzy over my absence, knowing I will not have time to get ready. This probably pales in comparison to the fit she will have when she realizes I am skipping Mass entirely. But right now, I am exactly where I need to be—at my friend's side.

With Niobe in the infirmary, the next morning is unfortunately spent in the queen's room. Kat and I work together inscribing the prayer cards at a small table on the side. Madame le Clare sits a few yards away, staring at me with contempt. To say she was most unpleased when I missed Mass yesterday is an understatement. Her expression right now could cut glass. Likely, she would want to use that same glass to slice my throat. My friend and I have to avoid eye contact because every time we look at each other, it sets off a round of suppressed giggles.

At the feast yesterday, the news of Anne's engagement was met with squeals and shrieks. Emily and the rest of the Wolf Pack surrounded her to examine the ring and ask all about the wedding details. In truth, it will be difficult for my sister to set a date until Prince Harold and Emily announce one. There are several couples who find themselves in this predicament. Father told me the king has been too consumed with the prophecy to give the matter the attention it deserves.

Today, the talk is not about my sister and Montgomery. The conversation is monopolized by Jocelyn, who brags nonstop about the gift Liam gave her for Christmas when she was with the royal family. Her telling would actually be rather comical if every word of it were not like a tiny dagger to my heart. It's hard to sit and keep an unfazed expression on my face, to act as if her story means nothing to me. But I know this is my only choice at the moment, so I keep my eyes trained on the scripture I copy.

"Trust me, ladies, you have never in your life seen such a luxurious cloak—brocaded scarlet velvet lined with rich, dark sable. It is so soft—the sable, like a downy chick. And warm. So warm. And the sable—did I mention it was sable?—contrasts so beautifully with the red fabric.

"It was so romantic when we exchanged gifts Christmas night. There was a box under the tree—the largest box, may I add. And it turned out to be for me! Imagine my surprise." She puts a hand on her heart as if this will convince everyone of her sincerity. Kat kicks my foot and rolls her eyes when I look up at her.

"Then I opened it. And of course, it was so overwhelming. I mean little, unimportant me receiving such an expensive gift. I mean, sable for goodness' sake."

Please. Does she think anyone buys this act?

But the Wolf Pack *oohs* and *aahs* at every juncture of her story, Emily leading the chorus. I sneak a glance at Anne, who reacts with all the other ladies. This, I know is an act, at least. We still need her to be in good with them in case I need information.

Emily and her sister launch into an exhaustive description of the private time they spent with the king and his family. According to them, their parents had arrived the day after Christmas and the families had spent the rest of the week together. There had been private dinners, carriage rides in the snow, long afternoons spent around the fire. They paint a picture of contentedness and togetherness that is enviable.

"It will be so special to have my sister be my sister-in-law as well," Emily beams.

The younger girl manages to produce a blush. "Oh, now, let's hope this is how things turn out." She looks pointedly in my direction.

If they want a reaction from me, they will be sorely disappointed. I arrange my face into the picture of calm indifference and continue with my transcription. It takes every ounce of strength in me, but I manage. Strength, to me, has always been in terms of the physical, but since meeting Liam, I have found facets of emotional strength can prove to be the most difficult of all…especially in matters of the heart.

A page hurries into the room, the same pimple-faced boy from earlier days. He hands a message to Queen Helen, who quickly scans it. The room becomes silent, all heads waiting to see what the communication may say.

"Olivia, your father is meeting with people in the palace and asks that you join him."

Once again, I find myself trailing the page through a labyrinth of corridors, any attempt to make conversation rebuffed with a condescending glare. The outer hallways are bitter, the flames in the wall sconces quivering against the eternal draft even the stones cannot fully keep at bay. My cloak does little to protect me from the biting grip of cold. We hasten down a final hallway lined with conference rooms and finally reach our destination. Pimple Face motions toward a door, then takes off faster than if I had been infected with the plague.

Father sits alone on one side of a long table. He rises when I enter. After a quick hug, I settle into the chair next to him. His tired face indicates he has been here some time already. Papers are scattered about the space in front of him, haphazard notes scrawled in his writing. A nearly empty mug of warm mead stands forgotten by their side. The room is only slightly warmer than the hall and I keep my cloak fastened tight.

"So have you been able to visit with Niobe yet?" he queries.

"Yes, briefly yesterday when I returned. The only thing she remembers is seeing someone out of the corner of her eye before she was attacked. But no specific details."

"Well, perhaps more memories will return as time passes. Remember, even the smallest detail could be important, so don't discount anything," Father instructs.

"I won't," I say, doubtful the healer will be able to provide anything useful.

"I have to station a guard with her from now on. She will be free to go about her business, but he will be with her." Although this doesn't surprise me, I still feel somewhat indignant about it.

"For her protection or to monitor her movements?" I huff.

My father collects the papers in front of him into a neat pile and I am unsure he plans to answer. Finally he says, "For both, Olivia. Look, Brother Alastair is all worked up about her, insisting she be banished…or worse. This measure at least allows her to remain here."

"But she didn't do anything!" I insist. Why on earth is anyone listening to the advice of that pompous clergyman?

"Livy, I know this is our best assumption, but honestly, we have to figure out who the 'she' is from the conversation you overheard in the maze. Brother Alastair has managed to upset Prince Harold enough that he requested the guard for her. As much as I trust your instincts, I still have a job to do. Besides, if it was not her, then someone tried to harm her. Maybe next time they will not be satisfied with simply knocking her out. Better all the way around for her to have protection."

It is not worth arguing. I know he is right. The fact that Brother Alastair holds such sway with Prince Harold does not sit well with me, especially after the elder prince had spoken in my favor. But at least Niobe will be protected from any future attacks and cannot be blamed for anything she does not do going forward.

Two men enter to meet with my father, who bids me good-bye as I leave. A new page stands outside in the hallway and comes to my side. He leans a little too far into my personal space so I back up a step, but am stopped by the wall.

"I am perfectly capable of returning to the queen's rooms myself. I am sure you have more pressing matters to attend to." Hopefully, he will get the hint and leave. No such luck.

"I am here to escort you elsewhere now, miss." He takes my elbow and steers me down the hall. I attempt to yank it away, but his grip is firm. After a moment of debating, I decide the satisfaction I would get for punching him would not be worth the hassle to follow. Pity. I could take this boy out with one swing.

We wend through a salon crowded with courtiers. Some lounge on long chaises and plump armchairs, some stand by the fire casually chatting with drinks in hand. All look profoundly bored with life in general. No one notices us while we skirt along the room's edge. Then we exit to cut across an outer courtyard. The day is overcast, a white sky boding snow hangs above our heads. A lone bird soars across it, a black splotch on a colorless canvass. Mercifully, the page releases his grasp, so I merely have to follow behind him. If he touches me again, he will lose some teeth.

Our path leads to a more deserted part of the palace. Finally, we stop at our destination. Standing right on top of me, he motions me to enter a door, bows, then hurries away. I have no idea where he brought me or why, but at least I am rid of him. The heavy door pushes open with a protesting creak and I cross the threshold into a large, drafty room. It is completely devoid of furniture, except for a few mismatched wood chairs scattered about the perimeter like wallflowers at a dance. A huge fireplace at the far end burns brightly but not with enough vigor to warm the whole space. Sconces line the wall filled with chunky candles, which already dance with flames.

Liam and Adam stand by the hearth, soft words passing between them. They look up at the sound of the door. Liam's face breaks into a smile, his footsteps echoing across the bare stone floor when he strides to my side. After an embrace and my greeting to Adam, I ask, "Where are we?"

"This was a planning room during wartime. It had a large table for meetings, plus tables with maps laid out on them. It hasn't been used in a long, long time."

"Well, that explains the musty smell and the cobwebs six inches deep in the corners," I reply, my nose crinkling before sweeping my hand across the vast open space. "And what are we going to do here?"

Mischief fills his grin. "We are going to spar." He gestures to some gear lying on the floor. Right on top is the box with my new sword in it.

"How did you get that?" I am both astounded and excited.

"Adam got it from your maid this morning." A hint of triumph flickers in his eyes.

I walk over to the box to retrieve my weapon. The sword lifts out into my hand, the hilt glowing in the firelight.

It feels even more perfect than I remember, completely balanced and weighted ideally for me, as though it were an extension of my arm. My practice swings slice through the air with a crisp whoosh.

"Maybe I will run you through with this for buying Jocelyn a fur-lined cloak." I say, only half joking.

He chuckles. "That was arranged by my father. I didn't pick it out or even know what it was until she opened it. Though he tried to make it seem as though I did. How many times did she use the word *sable* when describing it?"

Even Adam chortles at this remark.

"More than I could count."

"Figures. She and her sister certainly enjoy the luxuries our life provides. I can't imagine why my father pushes for a match with her. She is a spoiled brat."

"Hopefully, the king will recognize this soon." My voice holds more hope in it than my heart feels.

"I am certain he will. Besides, I would much rather have a wife I can spar with." He bends to pick up his own weapon and we move to the center of the room to assume an opening stance. "Don't go easy on me, my love."

"I never do," I counter, and the clang of sword blades rings through the room.

❧❧❧

The next morning, Anne sits at her vanity while Sadie pins her hair. My sister quietly compares some fabric swatches for her eventual wedding gown. Others lie about the room like little white patches of snow. I lounge on the bed, lazily fingering a square of ivory satin, not happy about the prospect of returning to the queen's rooms again. Maybe I can just pretend to not feel well and stay here instead.

A sharp rap on the door interrupts my sulking. I crack it to find Madame le Clare, who thrusts a note into my hand and leaves without saying a word. The missive bears Queen Helen's seal, which I crack, then scan its contents.

"Niobe has been released from the infirmary. I am to report to her quarters this morning," I inform Anne.

"Too bad," my sister replies snidely. She rises and reaches for her wrap. "You will get to miss today's boasting by the Crawford girls." Even she has tired of the constant self-important chatter of these two.

"My bad luck, I guess," I tease, settling into the chair she vacates. Sadie deftly pins my hair into a low bun.

A few moments later, we stroll down the hallway, then part to go our separate ways. The cold air hits my face with the harsh bite of January. After shivering the whole way over, the sight of Niobe's door is a welcome one. A lone guard stands outside, only his eyes visible beneath numerous, bulky layers. He merely nods at me when I pull the door open, caressed by the wave of heat that flows from inside.

Niobe sits at her workbench, an open book in her hands. I put my arms around her shoulders, surprised at how much more frail she has become. The fire is large, and a woolen blanket wraps around her small frame, but she is still cold to the touch. It is a wonder she did not catch a lung sickness after her attack. But her delicate body houses a strong spirit.

"Welcome back, child," she greets in a weak voice and pats my hand.

"How are you feeling, Niobe?" I toss another log onto the fire, hoping to warm her some more. It crackles and spits against the flames.

"Tired. And I get headaches now and again, but I dare say I will live."

The bump on her head has faded to a yellowish bruise nestled among a bed of wild gray hair. On her face, a dark red line races down her cheekbone, the scabbed-over remains of the gash. But what strikes me most is her eyes, which usually twinkle like a green-and-blue gem, have lost all their sparkle. She looks old in a way she hadn't before. Yet her grip is strong when she gives my hand a friendly squeeze.

"I am working on a salve for chapped skin. Would you mind going down to the cellar?" she asks, while I take my apron off a peg and tie it around my waist. "There is some calendula down there I need. You will see the jar labeled on the third shelf against the left-hand wall."

Folding back the rug from the trapdoor, I lift the door open. Cold air rushes up like a torrent from the darkness. A lantern dangles on a hook by the fireplace. I light it before carefully descending the few rungs to the dirt floor. An earthy, herb-laden smell envelops the space. The shelves are to my left-hand side, wide wooden planks dotted with a riot of bottles, small pots, and other containers, each carefully labeled. Sure enough, the jar is right where Niobe said it would be. I marvel at the products she has in her stores, herbs and plants from the other side of the globe acquired from traveling merchants and gypsies.

"I also need a book from the shelf down there. *A Guide to Burns and Rashes*. It should be on the fourth shelf toward the right-hand side with a blue spine," she calls.

On my right, against the darkest wall in the cellar, stands the bookcase. Volumes line the shelves like mismatched soldiers, hastily rolled scrolls peek out from them at intervals. She has them more organized than their jumbled appearance would indicate. Indeed the book is exactly where she describes as well. Whatever harm was done from the attack, it has not affected her memory in the least. I place the lantern on the floor and kneel to pull the book out from between its companions. The flame flickers backwards as if pushed by an invisible draft. A stray thought begins to form in my mind, but is cut short when Niobe tells me to hurry.

With the book and herb deposited in my apron's pocket, I ascend the ladder, lantern hooked on my wrist. Once the trapdoor is shut, I replace the rug and hang the light source back in its spot. It's a routine that has become commonplace for me.

"Thank you, child." She takes the items from me and places them on the workbench in front of her.

"Niobe, why don't we move the bookshelf up here? That way the books would be more accessible. There is space on that wall over there." I gesture to the other side of the room, but she already shakes her head. We have had this conversation several times before. Even when I offer to move it all by myself under her careful supervision, she is adamant about keeping it banished in the cellar.

Already she thumbs through the volume I retrieved, all thoughts of the bookcase's location forgotten. When she finds the page she wants, she says, "Here, come help me get the ingredients together for this salve."

We work in tandem, an easy silence filling the gaps between her instructions. It feels so natural to be by her side again. Her spindly fingers, crooked with age, work with a surprising deftness. Soon, we have a jar of a thick ointment used to protect skin from the bitter weather. She roots through a box of various sized lids until she finds the right size, then she closes the container and the book.

"How about some tea, dear?" She rises. Her crooked form shuffles to swing the kettle over the fire.

After hanging up my apron, I pick up two tea balls from a cupboard and fill each with some fragrant leaves before placing each of them in a mug. Then I join her in the chairs by the hearth and set the cups down on the small table between them, the tea balls clanging softly against their porcelain insides. A thin trail of vapor wafts out of the kettle's neck, the water almost ready. As much as I hate to bring it up, I know the time has come to ask.

"Niobe, did you remember anything new about the night you were attacked?" I cannot even meet her eyes, lest she see the guilt in them.

"Only that I went out the gardens about four-thirty in the morning. My stomach was aching all night. I thought perhaps some mint might help it calm down. Besides, I wanted to get those last few bundles picked. They were almost useless from the cold. I remember taking a basket and going outside. When I was going to put the clippings in my basket, I saw a shadow out of the corner of my eye. I thought it was odd someone else was out and about so early. The next thing I remember is waking up in the infirmary." Her words sound sure, but not rehearsed. There is nothing to make me think she does not tell the truth.

The kettle whistles, its shrill pitch slicing through me like a knife. I grab a potholder and swing it off the flames. While I pour some in each mug, I press, "So you don't remember hearing footsteps? Or seeing someone specific? Anything?"

"No, Olivia," she answers wistfully. "I am sorry I cannot be more help."

"Are you certain you didn't, um, enter a trance or anything?"

We have never spoken about the incident in the dining hall, or her spells in general for that matter. Uncomfortable with this line of questioning, I move my foot around, digging my toe into the floor, still unable to meet her eyes. She picks up her tea and takes a long sip and motions for me to drink mine. It slides down my throat like nails. Half-burned logs crackle briskly, but are not the reason why sweat breaks on my brow. The last thing I want is for her to think I am accusing her. In my mind, her innocence is obvious.

Finally, after an uncomfortable silence, she says, "My fingers and toes tingle and I feel light-headed before and after the enchantment takes me. I always remember that part when I come out of it. I don't remember having this feeling at all on the night in question, so I am confident in saying no trance occurred." This is all said matter-of-factly, as though we have discussed it many times in the past. "If I remember anything at all, I will tell you at once."

"I'm sorry to have to pry." I set my mug down on the table, unable to swallow another drop.

"Don't be, dear. The sooner we get to the bottom of this, the better. Now, why don't you take the salve we just made over to Brother Alastair's men?"

"You aren't coming?" I am surprised. She has never sent me anywhere alone before.

"No. I don't want to work my new friend out there too hard." She nods toward the door and I think of the bundled-up guard outside.

"It's for protection." There is more defensiveness in my voice than I intend.

"Indeed? Mine or the king's?"

I don't answer. She knows everyone else considers her a suspect. We both know. There isn't anything I can say. Sighing, I put the ointment in a basket and grab my cloak. Niobe walks me to the door, gently rubbing my back before I step out into the cold. Hopefully, she understands I am on her side. A nearly imperceptible nod is all I receive from the guard when I say good-bye.

My steps are careful on the frozen ground, poor footing slowing the journey to where the penitents labor in the cold. Now that the new latrines have been constructed, they work on repairing parts of the castle wall, a job long in need of attention in my opinion. I think longingly back to the warm day last fall when my sister had breached the broken structure. Lydia earned a new pet that day. But for me, the day is a dividing point between where I thought my life was going and where it actually went. If you had told me then a few short months later I would be living in the palace, involved with Prince Liam, and worried about a plot against the king, I wouldn't have believed it. Times like now, I wish I could return to the days before, when life seemed to make so much more sense. Part of me yearns to go home, but I know now the comfort I seek can no longer be found there. It is swept away with the rest of my childhood.

About halfway to the workers, three children play in a snowy field, pushing some into a round mound in an attempt to build a snowman, but are thwarted when the snow is too powdery to hold a shape. White flakes spray around them like a cloud when the sphere disintegrates, covering them is a frosty film. This only encourages them to throw more snow on each other, their laughter carrying through the cold air. Then one spots me, gets his cohorts' attention, and points. They tumble over to me, small white-covered masses with bright red cheeks. The village children know I usually carry treats in my basket. These three are not disappointed when I hand each one a peppermint stick. Thanking me, they dust off a low stone wall and hop on to enjoy their sweets.

By the time I arrive, my toes are frozen buds in my boots and all I can think of is warming them by a nicely stoked fire. Unfortunately for me, Brother Alastair is there to address the penitents, who huddle around him in a pathetic clump, stomping their feet and rubbing their hands against the unforgiving wind. Most lack any true winter garment, the rough, brown wool robes their only protection. It gives me true pleasure to see the woolen socks delivered by the healer and me on nearly all of their feet. At least we could give them that much.

"…cold though your bodies may be, you are warm in spirit," the friar preaches, his ermine-lined cloak a stark contrast to the thin rags his flock wears. Upon noticing me, he abruptly stops his sermon, and though he tries to keep his face neutral, the disgust can be heard in his voice. "Yes? Can I be of service, miss?"

"I have an ointment for chapped skin that your men may find helpful." It takes a good deal of self-control to keep the annoyance out of my voice. Some of the men smile, others nod in assent. I see sores on some faces which would benefit from this treatment.

"So kind of you, miss. Is this a gift from Her Majesty, the queen?" A self-important air fills his chest.

"No. It was prepared by Niobe."

"The witch? And you would have us use a substance concocted by her accursed hand?" he spits out like venom.

Us? Really? Who is he kidding?

"I assume you understand, Brother, it will still aid in the healing and comfort of your men. It seems the Christian thing to do," I reply in a voice so cloyingly pleasant, it would be amusing if I weren't so infuriated with him.

"Of course," he defers, but hatred fills his eyes. "By all means, let them have it."

He steps to the side, a scowl on his face. I remove the jar from the basket. Once the lid is removed, I say, "Anyone who needs some salve, please come forward."

At first no one moves, afraid of their master no doubt, but then one brave old man steps forward. Most of the men fall into a line behind him and I set to work. There are plenty of raw lips, cheeks, and fingers. Some spread a thin coat over their entire face or their hands. Though none of the wounds are a serious threat to anyone's health, they are most certainly painful and unpleasant to deal with. Thinking about the Brother's unscathed skin makes me fume.

Finally, the last man in line places a red hand in front of me. I help its owner rub the ointment into the swollen fingertips and knuckles. Unlike the others, who have whispered words of thanks, this man pins me with a forceful stare. The moment I am finished he snatches his hand away as if my touch itself burned. It is the same person who snatched the socks so rudely last month; the one with the long, jagged scar. His eyes do not leave mine and the hair on the back of my neck stands on end at the challenging, predatory gaze he fixes on me.

"All right. Enough," Brother Alistair's voice commands the men. "Back to work."

With one last narrowing of his eyes, the man backs away from me and moves off toward where the others resume their work.

Gathering my belongings, I prepare to go. A vicelike grip seizes my arm. "Let me escort you back, miss," the friar croons, belying the pain he inflicts. Sharp stings radiate from where his fingers dig into my skin.

"No need," I reply through clenched teeth, but he steers me away from the men, back toward the palace. His hold is too tight for me to extricate myself without making a scene, so I don't fight him. Yet.

"Oh, it is my pleasure. It will give me an opportunity to instruct you, before you jeopardize your very soul." I am too shocked to respond, while he drags me hurriedly down the snowy fields. "Keeping company with that witch is dangerous. She needs to be tried and burned. This court needs to be cleansed of her unholy ways."

Now, out of earshot of his men, I roughly pry his fingers off my arm and push him away. He stumbles a few feet backwards. Adjusting my basket, I march off, but he is not deterred and follows me, unfinished with his lecture.

"Surely you recognize her sinful ways," he yells. I walk faster, but he is able to keep pace. Perhaps his self-righteousness fuels his stamina. "She is a diabolical presence who feeds on the goodness and humanity of all. Do you want to burn in the eternal fires?"

We pass the field where the children play. They stop to watch me stomp past with the friar hot on my heels. Three little mouths hang open, snow clinging to the sticky remnants of candy left on their faces. One makes to wave at me, but the boy next to him grabs his hand and lowers it down.

"Because this is what awaits you, Miss Olivia. You will be punished for the evil you support. A higher power is watching and..."

Thump.

To my utter delight, a snowball nails the good Brother in the back of the head, knocking him down. The children squeal with victory, then high-tail it off to safety. I walk back a few steps to the friar's prostrate form. He glares up at me, sheer malice firing in his eyes.

"You know, Brother, I think you are right about one thing. A higher power *is* watching." I smile devilishly, then skip off in the children's wake.

24

Winter holds the world in her icy grip. There are more snowstorms this year than anyone can remember in recent times. Cold seeps into the palace through every crevice and gap, making it impossible to ever truly be warm. Numb fingers and tingling toes plague us all, despite our best efforts against them. The days pass with an air of defeated tedium, the celebratory mood of the holiday season long forgotten. January drags into February, and though the harsh weather remains, the daylight lasts a bit longer with each passing week.

Liam, Kat, Puck, and I find respite from the boredom in the old planning room, which we have dubbed the War Room. We have to bundle up, the sole fireplace not up to Mother Nature's challenge, but it does not dissuade us from our daily visits. These afternoons together preserve everyone's sanity.

Today, Liam and I are cuddled on a couch near the hearth, one of the many embellishments made to the room we so frequently haunt now. Kat and Puck mirror us on their own across the fireplace. Adam sits in a chair next to the fire. Liam could dismiss his bodyguard to the hallway, but none of us want him to get frostbite. He largely ignores the four of us, embracing his position as the fifth wheel. An open book rests in his lap and his black hair falls around his face like a dark veil while he bends to read, deep into whatever plot the story holds.

"How is Niobe doing?" Liam asks, one arm around my waist. I lounge against him under a large flannel blanket. The fingers on his free hand entwine with mine, while my head rests in the spot between his shoulder and his chest.

"She tires easily. Many days she goes to lie down as soon as I leave," I explain. "She has not recovered the vigor she had prior to the attack, but whether from the trauma or the sheer brutality of this winter, I do not know.

"Usually, she sends me out alone to tend to people, unless it is a matter beyond my skills, then she will join me, but she detests being shadowed by the guard. More often than not, she remains in her chambers. It's a wonder she hasn't gone mad staring at those two tiny rooms, day in and day out."

"And she has said nothing more of interest about the night of her attack?" Though he tries to keep the skepticism from his voice, a faint trace of it breaks through. He wants to believe Niobe as much as I do, but is not completely convinced.

"No. Nothing. I would tell you if she did. You know that, right?" I tilt my head to look in his eyes and he nods. At least he believes this much.

The door opens and a servant enters with a tray full of dried meats and fruit balanced on her hip. How I long for a bite of a fresh berry or apple, to taste the burst of sweet flavor and feel the juice run down my chin. She grabs a pitcher of warm mead and refills all of our cups. Then she hurries from the room.

"How is Jocelyn behaving these days?" Liam asks. We generally try to avoid the topic of my rival.

"The same. Always bragging about her relationship with you," I answer, rolling my eyes.

"Indeed? I only see her at dinner because I have no choice. You would think she would tire of the charade and move on."

"Doubtful," pipes Kat, her head barely visible amongst the pile of blankets. "She has her eyes on becoming a princess and you are her route there. As long as your father gives her hope, she will not let up."

Liam sighs with defeat. We both know it's true. The king has shown no inkling yet of ridding Jocelyn of her aspirations. He and Liam have reached a stalemate in their arguments about her, so now they just never mention it. I am afraid to express my misery over the whole situation because I do not want King William to send me away. Whatever the answer is, neither Liam nor I have it.

"Come on, Puck, let's spar for a bit before our muscles forget how to be useful," I say. Maybe the physical exertion will take my mind off things.

I hop up and grab my sword. Puck crawls out from his warm nest, then quickly tucks the coverings back around Kat. He stretches his arms and legs out and strolls over to where some weapons lie in a jumbled pile. My friend picks up one sword, then discards it and picks up another.

"Any day now," I tease.

When he finally decides on a weapon, we move to the open space in the center of the room. Liam and Kat are an attentive audience; even Adam looks up from his book. We circle each other, two stealthy predators summing up the opponent. Puck has grown so much this past year. His body has filled out with hard, well-defined muscle. Even his face has matured, his stubble thicker and more pronounced than it ever was. With numerous men to practice with here at the palace, his skills have improved quickly as well. It has made me up my game.

Clang. Our swords connect and we are a frenzy of lunges and parries. Liam and Kat cheer from their respective couches. Adam yells out an occasional tip to one of us. The world disappears, my body reacting instinctively with each move. There is only me and Puck and our blades. Nothing else. No prophecy. No Jocelyn. No confusing palace life. And in that brief moment, my troubles melt away and the warmth of passion renews my spirit.

Early the next morning, I stop in the kitchen on the way to Niobe's. She needs some rosemary oil for a chest rub to ease congestion. The cook may have some extra to supplement the healer's depleted stores. When I enter, Mary, one of the helpers, kneads some dough, her cheeks dusted with flour.

"Help yourself to a hot roll," she offers, the same as every morning I pass through. She flattens the dough into an inch-thick rectangle.

I scoop one out of a basket and savor the warm, buttery goodness. Mary picks up a circular cutter and whips it through the dough. She pulls the extra up around the round shapes.

"Actually, I am wondering if you have any extra rosemary oil for Niobe. She is low on her chest rub with all the lung sickness this winter," I mumble through my full mouth.

"I'll have to check with Madame Bouler," she replies, wipes her hands on her apron, and disappears into the pantry.

A moment later she returns with her superior. While most of the servants rely on Niobe's herbs and skills for their health needs, the head cook is not one of them. Her position allows her access to the royal physicians. Normally, she crosses herself whenever the healer is in her presence to ward off any evil. With lumpy arms crossed over her ample bosom, the woman eyes me up and down as if I were a vermin. "You are too late, miss. Your witch came earlier and I gave her what I could spare."

She strides back into the pantry, disdain flowing off her like a river. Mary shrugs at me while placing the cut-out dough on a tray. I pocket an extra roll for my friend and head out. A guard stands outside Niobe's door as straight as a lamppost, despite the bitter wind that whips across the garden.

"Good morning, Derrick." He nods mechanically. This is his duty every day—keeping watch on an old woman who rarely comes out of her rooms. He cannot be more than a year or two older than I am, so this is the type of grunt work he is assigned. The thought of his days makes my life here seem like a bowlful of excitement.

"Care for a hot roll?" I pull it from my pocket. It will likely mean more to him than to my healer friend.

"No thank you," he replies, despite regarding it longingly.

"Well, I hope you were able to have one when you took Niobe to the kitchen earlier this morning." Standing in the cold is awful enough, but with an empty stomach it is almost cruel.

"The subject has not left her rooms yet today," he replies brusquely.

"Are you certain? Madame Bouler said she was there earlier to get some oil."

"I have been here since four o'clock this morning. I can assure you, she has not left on my watch."

Too cold to argue with him, I go inside, the door closing with a rush against the harsh air. The room is pleasantly warm and brings me the sense of comfort my old kitchen at home does. It is the only place in the palace to invoke this sentiment. My friend sits at her worktable blending cream together in a bowl. Sure enough, a half-filled bottle of rosemary oil sits at her fingertips, its woodsy fragrance wafting over to me.

"How did you get the oil?" I blurt. "Derrick said you hadn't left today."

"Did he?" she muses. "He must have forgotten."

Not likely.

Before I can question her further, there is a loud banging on the door. The guard pops his head in, but is elbowed aside. One of the penitents pushes his way in, stark panic in his eyes. "I am Gerard. Please, ma'am, come quickly. It's Samuel. He won't wake up."

Faster than I have seen her move since the attack, Niobe grabs a basket of supplies and her cloak, and hurries out the door after Gerard. Derrick and I rush after them. We hasten to the back fields where the lodging of the penitents stand, several rudimentary structures that are a hybrid of a hut and a tent. Outside one of them, a number of laborers stand huddled together murmuring. A few more wander over and join them.

Our guide lifts the doorflap and we file in. It is barely any warmer inside, our puffs of breath still visible. Gerard frantically motions to a prone form whose face is partially concealed by a blanket. Niobe kneels down and lowers the covering. Samuel, the elderly man who graced me with such a sweet smile when I gave him socks, is dead. There is no question. His lips are blue, his skin has a grayish cast, and there is something almost expressionless about his face, a look no living person holds in sleep. The healer pulls the blanket up over his head and sighs. Gerard sinks to his knees, silent sobs wracking his shoulders.

The flap rustles and Brother Alastair enters. He surveys the scene with a merciless eye. In one swift motion, he yanks up Gerard, then slaps the man so hard, he immediately crumples back to the ground. "How dare you involve this witch in our affairs?"

I rush to the injured man's side, where he spits blood pooling from a split lip onto the floor. My arms enfold his trembling body and rub his back reassuringly. Rage sparks to life in me. The friar glares at Niobe.

"And you, witch, have you killed one of my men?"

"This man was dead long before my arrival. From lack of nutrition, clothing, and accommodations you never saw fit to provide." She has risen, and though she barely comes up to Brother Alastair's chest, holds a commanding presence in the room.

"How dare you, witch! How dare you judge me, you filthy heretic! King William will hear of your murderous ways. You will hang this time." His face is purple with fury, eyes bulging, sweat on his brow.

I am on my feet, about to confront him, when Niobe starts to shake violently. She curls in on herself, hands on her abdomen, head down. When she looks up, her eyes are unseeing and her voice otherworldly. "You are blind." She points to the friar. "Blind. The boar's downfall is at hand."

There is a horrifying moment of silence before she collapses like a stone onto the floor.

25

Niobe's latest trance is the talk of the court for the remainder of February. She winds up in the infirmary for a few days after the episode. Then she is released to her rooms, where she stays inside for the next few weeks. I spend my mornings blending tinctures and ointments while she instructs from her chair by the fire. This is where she sits the entire day, wrapped in a cocoon of blankets, no urge to go anywhere.

The time with her is pleasant and easy. I can lose myself in the actions of creating a remedy, the tasks of measuring precisely and mixing correctly has a meditative rhythm to them. Niobe does not talk much; there is mostly companionable silence between us. We even manage to write a log of the inventory in the cellar. But, once again, she refuses my advice to move the bookcase upstairs. Still, my time here feels far more productive than the rest of my days.

Father has made me quote Niobe's words an unending number of times. I have repeated them to the princes and the king. Poor Gerard, the only other witness, was dragged in several times as well to recount his version of the story. He looked frightened to death when he stammered out his account. Everyone has pressed me for information, convinced there must be more, some detail I overlooked, which would help explain the meaning of the healer's words. At night, I lie in bed racking my brain for any clue, but nothing materializes. Our afternoon sessions in the War Room are filled with speculation, but even the five of us together can make little sense of anything new her words could mean.

Brother Alastair, of course, had his own explanation for what happened. Naturally, it entailed Niobe casting a spell on poor old Samuel, leading to his demise. Then, to deflect suspicion from herself, she faked the trance in order to throw blame on the good Brother. I have the comfort of knowing neither Liam nor Prince Harold put any stock in this story. King William has been strangely quiet on the matter, but did not have the healer arrested, despite the friar's staunch campaign for it. The guard at her chamber remains, though. Security is tightened around the monarch with extra sentinels posted, and another taster appointed. My father spends every waking hour in the palace, diligently seeing to King William's protection.

With March's arrival, winter finally decides it is time to diminish. Longer days and warmer air awaken not only the earth, but its inhabitants. My outings in the village are met with smiles and chatter, which have been missing the past few months. The promise of the season cheers people, but all remember the words spoken by Niobe last fall. Everyone holds their breath in anticipation of spring—when the prophecy predicts William's doom will unfold.

The first three weeks of the month pass so uneventfully, it is hard not to drop my guard and enjoy the promise of the earth's renewal. King William, in an effort to put any worry at ease, appears in public often, projecting a strong and untroubled air. Were it not for my daily interactions with members of the tight royal circle, I would believe he felt no concern. Each evening at dinner, the monarch sits on the dais with various family members, laughing and socializing. Liam, however, has shared both the king and queen have difficulty sleeping, his father spending large portions of the night pacing the floor.

One morning in late March, I take my usual shortcut through the kitchen. The aroma of warm bread wafts like a spell to greet my growling belly. Mary hums a lively tune with her work. She rolls out small piecrusts, then sets them in the bottom of pans. Her rolling pin rotates in time with the cadence of her song. A lone dark curl escapes from her cap and bounces along with the rhythm. Birds peck at a pile of crumbs outside the open back door, their chirps a welcome sound after the harsh winter.

"Good morning, Miss Davenport. Help yourself." She nods at a freshly baked batch of sweet rolls.

"Have a good day, Mary," I bid when I head out into the courtyard, a roll grasped in my hand.

Lingering snow has all but melted, only tiny patches of white linger in the corners where the sun's rays never reach. The herb garden shows signs of life. Tiny buds appear on the early bloomers, small green nubs in a sea of brown. Niobe and I have been discussing where to fit in some additional herbs this year. One moment I contemplate whether we would get more use out of elderberry or chicory, the next, I stop dead in my tracks.

Derrick lies on the ground outside the healer's door, which hangs open on its hinges. In an instant, I rush to the guard and kneel at his side. Thankfully, he is breathing. A good, hard shake set his eyes aflutter.

"Are you all right, Derrick?"

"What happened?" he asks groggily. He sits up, his head wobbly, his eyes unfocused. I prop him against the wall, then rush inside. My sight needs a second to adjust to the dimness. Nothing looks amiss. There is no sign of a struggle or a ransacking. There is also no sign of Niobe.

Stepping back out, I blink against the dazzling sunlight. The young guard sits, knees pulled into his chest, his forehead resting on top. A few servants stroll by and give us a second glance, but continue on their way. My mind reels. Where is my friend? Was she abducted? Has someone harmed her?

"Do you remember anything at all?" I ask.

"She gave me hot tea when I got here." He lifts his head and points to a cup lying sideways on the ground. "She has been giving me hot tea every morning for a while now. But I think this time there was something in it that knocked me out."

Hesitantly, I retrieve the cup, run my finger along the inside, then sniff. Sure enough, the acrid smell of valerian, a potent sleeping herb, faintly seeps into my nostrils. Niobe drugged this guard. It was no abduction, no intent to harm her. She escaped. But why? There are too many pieces missing from this puzzle to know. Not sure what to do, I stand mutely.

"Is she gone?" Derrick asks, panic rising in his voice. When I nod, he moans, "I will be in so much trouble." He drops his head back down in despair.

As much as I would like to lie for the young man, I know my father needs to hear the truth. There is simply too much at stake. Perhaps he will go easy on the young guard. Though somehow, I doubt it.

Before I can decide what to do, hurried footsteps round the corner. Franklin, Sadie's beau, grabs my arm. "Miss Olivia, you must come quickly to the villager's gate. There is a man who needs you."

"It's not a good time…" I begin, but he interrupts.

"He said it was urgent, to tell you his name was Luke and that Athos needs your help—it is a matter of life or death."

At the mention of the notorious outlaw's name, I forget everything else. Athos befriended me last fall and helped save the lives of my father and my king. My allegiance to him is absolute. Instantly, I race off, Derrick's bewildered yells fading away behind me.

Luke, a cohort of Athos who had planned the attack on the Lindenwood castle, paces nervously outside the village gate. He is just as large and imposing as I remember him. Matted hair frames the mangy beard clinging to his jaw. His ripped clothes are covered with dirt and dried blood. Relief floods across his face at the sight of me.

"Olivia. Thank goodness!" he rushes to my side.

"Luke, where is Athos? What are you doing here?" My brain still stumbles to process the Niobe situation. And now this.

"We fought off a band of outlaws from the Mainland who sought to dethrone Athos. They lost, of course," he explains proudly, though fatigue shadows his eyes, "but Athos took a nasty wound to his leg. He needs medicine. I have traveled two days straight to get to you, hoping you could help me. We heard you were working with the healer here at the palace."

How they know this, I cannot even guess. But given my interactions with these bandits, it comes as no surprise.

"Where on his leg is the wound?" I ask, my months of training with Niobe kicking in.

"Upper right thigh. About five inches long and two knuckles deep. It is inflamed and oozing pus. Do you have something that can help him?" Desperation fills his voice.

"Yes. Wait here. There has been an incident that requires my attention, but I will bring a remedy to you later today. Franklin," I say, turning to the boy who observes us like a wide-eyed doe, "could someone find my friend here some food?"

"Of course," he stammers. "I will take him to my house. My mother will feed him and help clean him up."

"Thank you," I say, hugging him spontaneously. Not everyone would be so welcoming to an intimidating figure like Luke. "I'll be back as soon as I can."

Franklin, who is still confused by my hug, nods. While I speed back to Niobe's, the boy leads the outlaw down the street to his mother's.

When I round the corner by the herb garden, guards spring into my path. "No one is allowed here now, miss," one states.

My father stands in front of the healer's door with Derrick and Sir Michael. The former looks terrified, which, given the latter's penchant for punishment, is understandable. Father notices me and waves to the guards to let me pass. A slight breeze crosses my face, accentuating the sweat on my forehead, the product of running all over this morning. I try to focus my attention on the matter at hand, but it is hard to not think of Athos suffering from his injury somewhere out in the woods.

"Derrick was just detailing his account of what happened and how you found him. Where on earth did you run off to?" my father queries. Sir Michael glares at me and the young guard will not meet my eyes.

"Nowhere. Just, um, an urgent matter in the servant's village." He looks at me skeptically, but I decide it is not the time to bring up an outlaw waiting at Franklin's mother's house. "All taken care of now, though."

"All right. And do you have any ideas where Niobe may have gone?" His tone holds an edge to it. He is not happy. Not. At. All.

"No, Father. Honestly, I don't know where she could have gone."

Though it is the truth, I shift uncomfortably. I have been the biggest advocate of my friend's innocence, and now this. For all I know, everyone will think I helped her. Father pins me with his eyes in a way that made me squirm when I was young. He knew then, if I wasn't telling the truth, I would spill my guts like a boned fish. But today, there is no lie to tell. After a long moment, his expression eases and I know he believes me.

"Very well." He motions toward the two other men. "Time for us to go report all this to the king. Sir Michael, would you please go find the princes so they can join us?"

Sir Michael nods, then hurries off. Derrick looks about to pass out. It's not even nine o'clock in the morning and more has happened than has happened in a month. While we march off in the direction of the royal chambers, I glance back over my shoulder toward the servants' village where Luke waits for the medicine. Hopefully, the meeting with the king will be brief. With each passing second he remains untreated, the danger grows for Athos.

It takes a good half hour to locate King William, who is in his primary receiving hall near the main entrance of the castle. Once a month, citizens are allowed to bring petitions and requests to the monarch for consideration. The room is packed today, the milder weather luring people from their homes. Peasants line the walls in their Sunday best, hair combed and faces scrubbed. Our entourage elbows past them toward the front. This is met with some angry muttering at first, until the offended realize who we are.

At the head of the room, a man dressed in simple woolen clothes stands before the king. He clutches his hat in front of him, fingers anxiously playing with the brim while he states his case for needing additional field acreage for his cows. Though his body language displays his nerves, his voice is confident and calm. I remember how intimidated I once felt in the presence of King William and I give this man credit for his bravery. When he notices us, the peasant stops speaking and bows his head in deferment. Father approaches the throne, steps up quietly to the monarch's side, and whispers in his ear. They confer quietly, then the ruler rises. Immediately, we all drop to one knee.

"An urgent matter requires my attention. I shall return soon," he announces.

Father waves Derrick and me over to the door off a small antechamber into which the king has disappeared. There is a collective sigh from the crowd, who waited all month to be heard only to have to postpone their concerns even longer. The peasant, who was speaking, looks particularly distressed. Poor man. I hope he gets his extra fields.

King William, who had left the room the picture of calm, now stands with one hand on his hip and the other rubbing his jaw. The room is a tiny box tiled in marble with windows set high in the far wall. Besides a small table and chair, it is bare.

"What happened now?" he demands. His voice echoes off the hard walls.

"Niobe managed to escape. I have my men searching for her as we speak," Father replies.

Before anyone can add more, there is a sharp rap on the door. The princes enter with Sir Michael in tow. The small chamber can barely contain all of us comfortably. Prince

Harold goes right to his father's side and puts a hand on his arm. Liam stands by his side. We link eyes and I see the unspoken question in his gaze. I shrug imperceptibly.

"How on earth did she manage that?" the king huffs.

"That guard," Sir Michael booms, a finger in Derrick's direction, "accepted some tea from her. It was laced with a sleeping herb."

If the young man looked upset before, he now looks utterly terrified at the scowl on his superior's face. Likely, he imagines all sorts of punishments that await him. But King William smiles and shakes his head. "That sounds just like something Niobe would do."

"Your Majesty, this is serious," Prince Harold admonishes. "If she is involved in a plot against you—and truly, we cannot be sure she isn't since there is some mysterious 'she' out there—then her escape puts you in grave danger."

So, the elder prince has his doubts about my friend. I cannot blame him. Though I have tried to think of a plausible reason why Niobe would want to escape, one eludes me. For the first time, more than a tiny particle of doubt enters my mind. I push it firmly aside, unwilling to abandon the woman who has been so kind to me, who has taught me so much. There must be an explanation for her actions. My mind is so jumbled from all of this, plus Luke's unexpected appearance. Thoughts of Athos wounded and in pain plague me. All I want is for this meeting to end so I can get the outlaw his medicine and start looking for Niobe myself.

Suddenly, a commotion is heard out in the receiving room. The door to the antechamber bursts open and Brother Alastair rushes in, his face red with exertion. Everyone stares at him, dumfounded, while he wedges past our crowded bodies to the king.

"Your Majesty," he pants, "I must...report...a terrible event."

What else could happen this morning?

"Please, Brother, take a moment to regain your breath," Father says, and the chair is pulled among us so he can sit down. We stand in awkward silence until he is ready.

"I was on my way to your chambers for our usual midmorning prayers. I had forgotten you would be down here today. When I arrived, there was not even one guard stationed outside your rooms."

We all gasp—a sentry is supposed to be in that position at all hours.

"Moreover, your door was standing ajar. When I pushed it open, I saw her." A note of triumph cannot be hidden in his tone.

"Who?" multiple voices shout as one.

"The witch, of course. She was examining a carafe of wine on the table. I called to her to stop and come with me at once. That is when she used her magic to escape me."

"Her *magic*?" I retort, my disbelief evident.

"Yes, she was able to rush past me, turned a corner down a long hallway, and simply vanished by some trick of devilry. She is threat to you, Sire. She must be hunted down and executed."

King William is silent, his eyes staring off into the distance. My father takes charge. "Sir Michael, stay here and guard the king. The rest of you, please accompany me to the king's chambers at once."

We file out into the receiving room. Although it is packed, there is less of a claustrophobic feel than in the antechamber. Every head turns to watch our steps toward the door. A loud communal whisper rises when we exit, the group no doubt gossiping about the turn of events in an already unusual morning for them. They will have stories to tell their families tonight.

Once at the king's chambers, the wine is whisked away for testing and the room examined for clues by additional men summoned by my father. Nothing is found except for the sentry, who emerges from a nearby closet with a large welt on the back of his head. I examine the wound, a knot the size of an apricot, and send him to the infirmary. There are no items missing, according to a royal valet, who checks the room as thoroughly as the inspectors. Everything seems in perfect order.

My father stands staring out a window in contemplation. It is a look I know well from my years of instruction with him. I stand by his side and lean my head on his arm. The gardens below are just beginning to show signs of life. A faint green hue breaks through the tired, yellow grass of last fall. White, fuzzy heads of pussy willow peek out from the hard brown buds lining the branches. Small wrens flit happily among the trees and peck between the garden stone path, looking for insects.

"Well, Livy, what do you think?" he asks softly enough, only I can hear him.

"Honestly?" At his nod, I point out the one fact nagging at me. "I'm wondering how Niobe could possibly hit a young man on the head with such force and then drag him all the way to the closet. She is simply too frail, Father."

"Yes," he says, fingers drumming on the stone sill. "However, there were those men you heard speaking in the maze. Perhaps Niobe is the 'she' they referred to and she elicited their help in the matter."

True. We have never been able to figure out who or what that conversation was about. Two men approach my father. He asks for their full report on the matter by day's end and dismisses them. My mind works over the whole situation, as it has so many times these last few months. One question has bothered me the most.

"But why? Why would she want to kill the king? After all these years? In all my time with the healer, she has never mentioned the king or any grievance she had with either him or the kingdom in general. I cannot imagine a motive."

"Nor I. But given the circumstances, once she is found I will have to arrest her."

"I understand, Father. Please just let me know when it happens."

He gives my arm a comforting squeeze. "I will. You may go now if you are needed elsewhere."

The morning has already been so chaotic and now I have to figure out what to give Luke for Athos. While I rush back to Niobe's, I pray she has some wound cream left. A remedy made by her experienced hand would give me more reassurance than any I throw together under such stress. His leg injury should also have a poultice; a mental list of those ingredients run through my head. Those I assemble quite often. Speed is of the essence, since every moment I lose is a risk to Athos' life.

The healer's door is barred shut when I arrive. Francis, an old training companion of mine, stands a few doors down whispering with a kitchen maid. She pats his arm flirtatiously, while laughing coyly at his words. They are the only people in sight.

"Hey, Francis," I greet him, much to the annoyance of the young lady, "are you guarding Niobe's? I need to go inside."

"Yes, Olivia, I am. Her chambers have been searched and sealed. I'm not supposed to let anyone in." Kitchen Girl's face relaxes when she perceives I am no threat to her territory. She leans her head on his arm while he speaks to me.

"I just need to go in for a few minutes. There is a wounded person's life at stake. I need to make a salve and a poultice." I try to sound authoritative. The last thing I need is a showdown with Francis.

"All right. Go in and shut the door behind you. I'll watch from here until you come out." Kitchen Girl's eyes light up when she hears he is staying by her.

"Thanks, Francis."

Two bars form an X across the door, but it is not hard to open the door and squeeze under them. Probably not what the commander had in mind when he ordered them sealed. I expect the room to be rather dim, but to my surprise, a small lantern burns faintly on the workbench. Odd that they left it lit after the search was completed. When I lengthen the wick so it will shine brighter, I almost yell out in shock.

On the table sit a jar of salve and a poultice. A note lies next to them atop a book. With trembling hands, I move it into the ring of light and read:

Olivia,
Here are the things your friend will need for his injury.
As for your other question, this book will give you the answers you seek.

The message is unsigned, but the spidery scrawl clearly belongs to Niobe. Sure enough, the preparations are exactly what Athos will need to fight a leg infection. How the healer knew what I needed and how she got in here to make them, I cannot even fathom.

With lantern in hand, I search her entire chambers, cellar included, but they are empty. Back at the table, I finger the book, *A Guide to Burns and Rashes*. What answers would I need if she has already made the remedies? Besides, my outlaw friend did not have a burn or a rash; he had a sword wound. My fingers drum the wood surface of the workbench while I try to assemble the puzzle in my head.

"Almost done, Olivia?" Francis' voice calls from outside.

"Yes."

Whatever is going on, I cannot stand in here indefinitely to figure it out. I place the note inside the pages of the book, which I shove into a pocket in my cloak. Then, with the ointment and poultice in hand, I exit into the courtyard. The sun shines brightly behind Francis, his body just a black silhouette against its rays. Kitchen Girl lingers back against the wall where I found them, a complacent smile on her lips.

"Thanks, Francis," I say, hoping I look composed.

"Sure. Just don't tell anyone I let you in."

"My lips are sealed," I call over my shoulder, already on the way to Franklin's. Clearly, my old colleague is unaware the owner herself was inside the chambers. Until I get a better handle on what is going on, I will keep this information to myself as well.

Luke's stern face melts with relief when I hand him the remedies. I give him instructions on how best to care for the wound. He nods understanding at each directive, worry etched in deep lines on his face. My stomach drops at the thought of a wounded Athos, who had such an air of invincibility in my brief time with him. The fact that Luke traveled all the way here is an indication of just how sick he must be.

"Promise me if he takes a turn for the worse, you will bring him here. Even if it is against his will. I will personally speak with the king on his behalf," I plead.

We now stand just outside the village gate. Out of the tree line a man appears with two horses. Luke waves him over and the man walks the animals in our direction. A brisk breeze flows across my face, but unlike the icy burn of winter, this wind has an edge of warmth to it. At least they do not have the weather working against them and can make it quickly back to their leader.

"I will do everything I can to convince him," he assures me, "even if it means knocking him on the head and dragging him here."

When his companion reaches us, Luke places the salve and the poultice in his saddlebag. Then he hands his friend two large bags of supplies that were given to him by Franklin's mother. It always strikes me that those with the least to share are usually the most generous. They are stowed in his own saddlebags. The horses stomp their hooves on the softening ground, anxious to get the journey underway.

"Tell him I wish him a speedy recovery," I say. "And tell him I hope to see him again someday."

"I am sure he would love that, Miss Olivia. Thank you so much for this. From the bottom of my heart. We would be lost without him." He folds me into a strong embrace, then steps over to his mount. His comrade gives me a grateful nod and swings into his saddle. They gallop off quickly, not wanting another second's delay. Soon, they are two small specks on the horizon. The horses round a corner and disappear from sight.

For a long while, I stand in the cold staring at the empty horizon. A large part of me longs to saddle up Pepper and follow the men back to their band. Everything made sense in the time I was lucky to spend with them. There was no pointless drama, petty gossip, and trifling with people's hearts, just honest conversation and genuine excitement. I certainly fit in better with the outlaws than I ever hope to here at the palace. But a future with my bandit friends is not meant to be. I send a fervent prayer out for Athos' recovery, then turn wistfully back towards where my real future lies.

On my way back to the palace, I stop in at the cottage of Franklin's mother to thank her for her hospitality. When she opens the door and invites me in, the smell of a baking pie wafts out. The home is small, but cozily decorated. Sadie's needlepoint house hangs framed on the wall and I realize it is a miniature of the one I now stand in. Mismatched furniture pieces are squeezed into every nook and cranny. A large table takes up more than its share of space in the center of it all, a great floating ship in an ocean of chaos.

"Thank you, ma'am, for hosting my friend this afternoon."

"The name is Mae and it was my pleasure, miss. All my babies are grown and doing their own thing all day. I loved having the company." Her dark face beams with a bright smile. Never once does she intimate Luke is an outlaw. Perhaps she did not know, or perhaps she did not care.

She pulls the fresh pie out of the brick oven and sets it on the counter. After a once-over, she nods at its outcome, the stiff white bun at the top of her head bouncing up and down in time. Although my list of worries is long, I sit and have a cup of tea with her. The time spent in her company is a much-needed escape from the concern of missing healers, prophecies, and romantic rivals. It reminds me of afternoons at home with our housekeeper Lucy. Mae might be the only person I have ever met who matches Lucy's eternal optimism. A weight seems lifted off my shoulders in the short visit, and when she asks me to stop in again as she sees me to the door, I earnestly promise to do so.

Slowly, my feet drag me back, where I find my way into one of the inner corridors. There, I wander aimlessly. Courtiers bustle past, an air of importance in their step. They would likely scoff at the comfort I just found in the humble dwelling of Mae. A servant moves down the hallway with a long taper in his hand, lighting the wall sconces. The day has gotten away from me entirely. I never even made it to the War Room and wonder if Liam was there or if he remained by his father for the rest of the day.

"There you are," Kat calls from behind me.

She and Anne catch up to me and flank my sides. They usher me around a few turns to a warmer hallway, each remarking how cold I feel. The chatter of the dining hall fills my ear, the noise and brightness of the room disorienting me momentarily. We are in our usual seats before I realize I didn't have time to change. I loosen my cloak to expose my simple day dress, its plain black fabric a dark stain against the other ladies' colorful array of gowns. Embarrassed, I cower down between my sister and my friend.

"Did Niobe really escape?" Kat whispers to me.

"Yes. I will give you all the details in my room later," I promise. There are too many ears here to listen in.

The sound of a knife clinking on glass rings through the room, the shrill sound rattling my already disjointed thoughts. Silence spreads throughout the hall. Brother Alastair looms in front of the royal dais, a pious expression plastered on his face. He waits until he has the attention of all, then takes another moment to survey the room while we wait, clearly enjoying the spotlight.

"Ladies and Gentlemen, as you know, I arrived some months back with a group of men seeking atonement for their sins." He gestures towards the far wall where they stand in a line. "As one of their final acts, they will help serve the Easter feast and wait on His Majesty and his family, who will grant them each a special blessing of forgiveness. Tonight they are here to practice for this occasion."

The penitents scurry off under the supervision of kitchen staff. They are washed, shaven, and in new robes for the duty. Brother Alastair looks most pleased with himself when he sits to join the king and queen. Liam and Prince Harold are absent, no doubt still discussing matters of the monarch's safety with my father. King William is here because he wishes to appear unfazed by the prophecy, in the hopes this will maintain calm among the courtiers. No trace of concern mars his face or his wife's.

Unfortunately, in the absence of the princes, Emily and Jocelyn have opted to dine at our table. They cluster with the Wolf Pack members at the other end of the table. My sister elects to stay with Kat and me. Her engagement assured, she has cut her time with the other ladies dramatically. She decided the small amount of gossip she heard about Liam was outweighed by their pettiness and shallowness. Anne spent so many years dreaming of being part of the inner court, only to find out it was not what she truly wanted out of life after all. A year ago I never would have thought she would become one of my greatest allies.

The penitents flow back in from the kitchen with trays balanced in hand, bobbing through the room like toy boats on a pond. A bowl of hot stew is placed in front of each diner, steam billowing merrily from the surface. One of them approaches our table. Cleaned up, I almost don't recognize him as the man who has been so unfriendly to me twice now, but his jagged scar gives him away.

"So, do you have any idea where Niobe is?" Kat asks, too anxious to wait for later.

The man sets a bowl down in front of her.

"No." I have decided not to tell anyone about the mysterious appearance of the salve and poultice. For reasons I cannot articulate, my gut still tells me to trust my healer friend.

"Sadie told me you had a visitor," Anne remarks softly.

The man sets the bowl down in front of her a little too hard. Liquid splatters over the side of the bowl onto the table. My sister looks sidelong at the man, but says nothing.

"Yes," I murmur, "it was one of Athos' men. He needed a favor."

"Athos? The out—"

She doesn't get to finish her sentence. The man loses his grip on the last bowl and dumps the entire contents right down the front of me. I screech in pain while Kat and Anne valiantly try to wipe the hot stew off of me with their napkins. Their abridged amounts of cloth are not nearly up for the job.

"All pardons, mi'lady," the man says, a voice full of apology, but when our eyes meet, his gleam with spite. In the confusion, he merely stalks away.

Meanwhile, Jocelyn bursts out laughing, pointing and chuckling like a hyena. The other Wolf Pack members at least attempt to keep their amusement under control. All heads turn in our direction. At the royal table, Brother Alastair merely shakes his head, as if I were the cause of the trouble. Queen Helen looks genuinely distressed, but King William's expression is one of disgust. There sits Jocelyn in all her golden-haired glory, perfectly coiffed and dressed, and I am in my simple dress, now covered in chunky, brown muck. He glances from her to me and I can almost sense his thoughts about my lack of suitability for his son emanating from the room.

"Don't bother," I say, pushing the blotting napkins away. "I'm going back to our room."

When I step over the bench to leave, Jocelyn croons, "Olivia, maybe you should just stay. I mean, the stew actually improves the look of that ugly dress anyway." Stifled laughs fill my ears as I wordlessly stride out.

A half hour later, I sit in a warm, clean robe beside a crackling fire. Sadie sets a tray of food beside me and my mouth waters at its smell. I set to work on a new bowl of stew with some hard bread and tangy cheese.

"I'll take this dress down to the laundry. They will be able to fix it up good as new," she promises. For her, it will be a matter of pride to restore the garment to its original state. "Here, drink this." She offers me a warm mug of mead. "It's been a long day for you, Miss Olivia."

"It certainly has, Sadie." I sigh. A log cracks and sparks in the fire before diminishing back into the flames.

"Franklin told me about your friend. Were you able to help him out?" she asks, while she lays out my bedclothes.

"Yes. I gave him what he needed. Please thank Franklin's family again for me."

"Of course. Now, I will be off with these." She gathers up all my soiled clothes. "I will be back in a little while."

Finally alone, I pick up the book and note that lie on the table beside me. Over and over again, I study the cryptic message. Why would Niobe leave me this book when it did not contain the remedy I needed? What other question needs answering? One which involves burns or rashes? It doesn't make sense. What I truly want to know is how she got in her chambers undetected to help me.

I run my fingers over the title on the spine. It's a book we use quite often, though she insists on keeping it in that abysmal bookcase in the cellar.

The cellar!

In my mind, I see the flickering flame of the lantern when I placed it on the floor in front of the bookcase, the cruet of rosemary oil on the workbench when there was supposedly no trip to the kitchen. Niobe's clue is suddenly crystal clear. In seconds, I don a fresh dress, wrap my cloak around me and run out the door, ready to find the answers I seek.

The guard who stands outside Niobe's is unfamiliar to me. I hide in the shadows of a nearby hallway weighing the merits of different ideas to get past him. One seems to hold the most chance of working, so I head into the kitchen. Most of the people are busy with the cleanup from dinner. No one seems to notice when I help myself to a large mug of ale and a stew-soaked hunk of bread. Back outside, I saunter over to the guard, who turns a bored eye in my direction.

"My friends and I in the kitchen thought you might enjoy this." I try to adopt the sultry pose I saw Kitchen Girl use on Francis earlier.

He greedily eyes the food, then nods. The bread is devoured in two monstrous bites and washed down with a generous gulp of ale. After a brief moment's pause, he drains the rest of the mug before handing it back to me with the plate. "Thank you, miss."

"My pleasure," I drawl and sashay back to the kitchen.

Once inside, I deposit the dirty dishes on a large pile of unwashed items. A heavyset woman, who scrubs them, does not even glance my way. Water sloshes over the edge of the sink, creating small lakes on the floor that I navigate on my way out. The evening air is cold on my face after the warm embrace of the kitchen.

I resume my post in the cover of the hallway and wait for the ale to do its work. Almost an hour passes before the guard begins to shift from foot to foot. A few more moments has him looking around. Confident all is secure, he walks to the back wall of the herb garden and steps behind a tiny shed to relieve himself.

Quick and quiet as a cat, I slink to Niobe's door, duck down under the nailed crossbars, and open the door a crack. I am in, and the door shut behind me in the blink of an eye. The chamber is dark and I sit on the floor while I let my vision adjust. Not much moonlight enters the one small window. Shadows, though barely visible, start to take shape, darker forms spread throughout the room. Coming up onto my hands and knees, I crawl slowly across the floor until my fingers touch the edge of the area rug, which covers the trapdoor. Bit by bit, I ease it off the spot.

The door lifts easily, only a soft creak to be heard. My groping hands find the lantern and I loop it over my arm. In my pocket are the flint and tinder to light it. Carefully, my feet descend the rungs until I feel the soft, earth floor under my feet. A spark ignites the lantern wick, but I make sure to keep the flame low. Stealthily, I ascend the ladder and pull the trapdoor shut. Back on the ground, I walk over to the bookcase.

There it stands, shelves full, but for the one volume sitting back in my room. In all my trips down here, I have never thought to examine the bookcase itself, only noted the draftiness around it. This fact makes sense now. I shine the light down one side, then move to the other. The draft is stronger here, so I put my fingers behind the wood back and pull. Sure enough, the shelves open back like a door, exposing a secret tunnel behind it.

An hour or so later, I climb the staircase back to my chambers. Exploration of the tunnel led me to various points in the castle. The kitchen, several unused salons, and a little used corridor off the Main Hall all exited off of it, the latter behind a statue of Hermes, where I emerged for the night. There were no clues as to Niobe's whereabouts, but working with the light of the meager lantern, I had not expected any.

Tomorrow, I will return with a proper torch to investigate more fully.

Anne lies in bed, but sits up when I enter. "Where were you?" she demands. "Sadie had no idea."

"Oh, I, um, just went for a walk to, you know…clear my head." Keeping the tunnel entrance a secret will likely come back to haunt me, but I just cannot bring myself to disclose it yet.

"I'm sorry about what happened at dinner," my sister says softly.

Dinner seems so long ago, I had forgotten all about my "stew bath." Now it actually strikes me a bit funny. "What? You didn't care for the new fashion trend of wearing your meal? I think it may really catch on."

"Let's hope not," Anne replies with an exaggerated shudder, then adds in a more serious tone, "Jocelyn and her crew were way out of line laughing at you like they did."

"Well, I wouldn't expect anything less from them. If nothing else, they are consistent in their cruelty. But enough about the Wolf Pack. Let's talk about your wedding plans. Anything new? Did you decide on a fabric yet?"

While I don my bedclothes and slip under the covers, Anne catches me up on plans for her big day. We talk, laugh, and whisper as only sisters can, years of common experiences and emotions bonding us uniquely with each other. What would I have done without Anne by my side these last few months? She dozes before me, her back pressed against mine like when we shared a bed as children. Her steady breathing anchors me, and I drift slowly to sleep.

The next day, Prince Stephan arrives from Prescott. He wants to be on hand to show his uncle, the king, moral support at the advent of spring. After the nephew receives a briefing on the Niobe situation, he expresses concern, sharing the same feelings as the friar he sent to court. Father reassures him extra safety measures are in place.

My search of the tunnels has turned up no clue as to where the healer may be hiding. Further inspection showed them to be little used passageways full of cobwebs and rat droppings. Their layout suggests they used to be shortcuts used by servants to move items quickly throughout the castle. Somehow over time they fell into disuse. I did see footprints in the familiar pattern of guard's boots in a few of the main tunnels, which means my father thought to check them out in part at least. Yet so far, nobody has discovered the remote outlet in Niobe's cellar.

Several weeks pass, the first day of spring elapsing without incident. Though a modicum of relief fills the court, the diligent watch on the king's safety remains. There is a permanent furrow in Father's brow. He stays at the palace day and night, unwilling to be more than a few strides away from His Majesty, a circumstance I am sure upsets my mother. Liam acts as though the prophecy is the foolish talk of an old lady, but worry clouds his clear blue eyes when he thinks I do not notice.

One morning, I stroll over to Niobe's through the gardens paths, the warm weather abolishing the need to cut through the kitchen. There was a bit of an uproar in the servants' village when the healer vanished. People worried about the void her lack of services would leave. Queen Helen intervened and allowed me to continue what duties I could perform in Niobe's absence. The king's physician and midwife are available for serious crises and births, but the day-to-day administering to colds, cuts, toothaches, and such are left to me.

This morning I am happily surprised to see Derrick standing outside the healer's door. A sentry remains stationed there at all times in the event Niobe suddenly reappears. Little do they know she sneaks into her cellar nightly to prepare salves and tinctures for me. Wherever she hides, Niobe knows what goes on in the village and makes sure I have the medicines I need to help them. One evening, I left some notes on a chest in the cellar detailing the items I would make the next day. When I returned in the morning, the notes were gone, replaced with the remedies I needed. It is now our unspoken system and our only connection with each other.

"Good morning, Derrick," I say when I reach the door. The crossbar has been removed in favor of a sturdy lock.

"Good morning, miss," he replies, unlocking the door, then slipping the key back in his pocket. The poor young man was punished for his role in Niobe's escape with some harsh labor over the last few weeks. His face is gaunter with deep bags under his eyes.

"It's nice to see you back."

He only nods curtly before I enter. The front door stays open while I work, part of the agreement to let me be in here. Sir Michael, who is ultimately in charge of this operation, did not want me to "compromise any evidence," whatever that means. But Derrick stays outside while I put on my apron and gather items from the workbench, humming to myself.

After a few minutes of mixing and grinding, I place some items in a basket, then move the rug back from the trapdoor and climb down into the cellar. Every day I go down and pretend to finish the remedies. So far, none of the guards have paid my trips below any mind. The bookcase is back in place, blocking its secret. I make sure to keep it closed at all times when I am here during the day. On a small table next to it lie two poultices and a tincture for headaches, each labeled accordingly. Two men in the village cut their legs on a barbed wire fence while trying to dig out a post. My original poultices did little to help; these new ones must contain ingredients I am yet unfamiliar with. A tincture is for old Lettie, the widow of a farmer. She gets headaches when the pipe she smokes is too strong. Niobe has a special concoction to alleviate them.

I scoop up the items and put them in the basket, then loiter a few moments before returning upstairs. Derrick only glances inside while I rearrange the rug over the door. Tossing some supplies into the basket, I head out to the village.

"I'll be back in a bit," I call to the sentry, who stands at stiff attention outside the empty chamber.

The air is so mild, I wear no cloak. Trees are laden with bright green buds ready to burst into leaf. Daffodils and tulips bloom in random clusters by walkways and buildings. Fluffy white clouds dot the sky like fat dollops of whipped cream. A soft breeze caresses my cheek as gentle as a mother's stroke. Winter was so harsh, it almost made one forget the world could be so alive, so embracing.

Villagers greet me with smiles and waves. Children run up to me for the expected peppermint, while appreciative mothers sneak sweet cakes into my basket. The three patients from yesterday are grateful for the new aid I bring. Lettie even asks me to stay for a smoke. I politely decline her offer of the pipe, but do sit for a spell and eat a scone before returning to my duties.

Finally back at Niobe's, I unpack my supplies at the workbench. While munching on a sweet cake, I pull a notepad in front of me. Today the only cases beyond my skill are a baby's stubborn diaper rash and an old man's leaky eye. I jot these down on a piece of paper, admiring the carefully painted roses that adorn the side of the square sheet. Climbing down into the cellar, I leave the note on the small table where I found this morning's remedies. Back upstairs, I take several empty jars out to the garden pump to wash. Water sloshes into an oaken bucket and I place the containers inside. One is caked with a dried, hard film. It likely needs to soak overnight. Kneeling, I plunge my hands into the cool water to grab one of the others.

"Olivia." My father's voice startles me. "Come here, please. We have something to discuss."

I rise and see him next to an equally flustered Derrick, a serious look on his face. My stomach sinks like the jars in the bucket. Could he have figured out about the tunnel leading to Niobe's?

Wiping my hand on my apron, I walk over, my legs alternately hitting one of the two wet spots on the front of my skirt. From years of practice, I am able to turn my face into an expression of innocence. "Father, what can I help you with?"

"Come with me. I need to show you something."

"Of course," I say sweetly, "let me just put things in order."

Inside, I double-check the rug is over the door, neaten the workbench and hang my apron back on its peg. The entire time I expect him to expose the secret in the cellar, but he remains outside. Apparently he is none the wiser to it. I relax a bit and rejoin him. Derrick stands as erect as a marble column, hands at his side, eyes straight ahead—the picture of the perfect solider for his Master-of-Arms. Inwardly, I am sure he is relieved I am the one being led away by his master right now.

"As you were, lad," Father says when we start to walk away. His only movement though is a slight exhale.

It is challenging to keep pace with my father's brisk strides. People jump out of his way as though he carried a lighted brand in front of him. We head through several corridors, then up a flight of stairs toward the royal chambers. The sense of ease I convinced myself to feel in Niobe's innocence thus far slowly melts away. At length, we stop in front of a door and Father knocks.

"Enter," King William's voice booms from the other side.

This can't be good.

In the center of a small room, the monarch sits at a table with Queen Helen, the three princes and Sir Michael. The latter holds a piece of paper in his hands. Father pulls a chair out for me across from the queen and I slide down into it, wishing it would swallow me whole. Everyone looks at me expectantly, but I don't know what to say.

"Sir Michael, if you will," my father directs.

"Miss Davenport—" My name drips off his tongue as though it contains a foul taste, "—I, we are wondering if this looks familiar to you."

He slides the paper across the table and my heart sinks. In front of me, a square sheet with hand-painted roses comes to rest. On it, in my own handwriting, it says:

Tom Flint and Gregory Sanders – leg wound from barbed wire

Lettie Frey – tobacco headaches

A suspenseful hush in the room hangs like a suffocating fog. Father, who stands behind me, places his hands on my shoulders. I need to say something, but I cannot lie, not to the king. This is a charge punishable by imprisonment. "Yes, it does look familiar. I wrote it yesterday. It's my notes after visiting the village."

"And what did you do with it after you wrote it?" Sir Michael asks, eyes narrowed like a cat waiting to pounce.

"I'm not sure… If I remember correctly, I left it on a table in Niobe's."

Not a lie.

"Then perhaps you would find it interesting that it was found in King William's bedchamber."

Uh-oh.

"Yes…that is, um, interesting." My father's hands dig into my shoulders.

"But…it also contained this message on it." He flips the paper with a dramatic flourish of his hand.

There in Niobe's slanted scrawl, it reads:

Beware of Easter – it is the day you await

Silence fills the room again, seeps into every corner. The weight of all eyes press on me like hands shoving me underwater. All I can do is stare at the paper. Why would Niobe risk entering the king's chambers to leave him this? One thing is certain, though. If she had wanted access to hurt him, she had it. This further cements her innocence in my mind.

"Have you seen Niobe?" Sir Michael booms.

"No."

Not a lie.

"Is that her handwriting?"

"It appears to be."

Still not a lie.

"Did you give her this paper?"

"No."

Technically not a lie. I did not hand it to her.

"Olivia," my father interjects, "do you know anything that could be useful in discovering who threatens the king?"

"No."

Not a total lie, since I believe Niobe is not the threat.

"I sincerely hope that is true, girl." Sir Michael slams his hand on the table and drops of wine fly out of the queen's goblet. "Because this message is a direct threat against the king's life."

"Or a warning," I counter, finally fed up with this whole meeting. At his bewilderment, I continue, "Perhaps she warns him to beware of Easter. She has been known to predict events before. Maybe she had a premonition."

Sir Michael boils so red with anger, he looks about to burst. Father's fingers have surely left bruises on my shoulders by now. King William remains silent, his fingers steepled by his lips.

"I am not sure we have the luxury of looking at it that way," Prince Harold says. "After all, she did manage to get into the king's chambers twice now."

"Exactly. And she did not harm him either time." Why is this not as clear to everyone else?

"As of now, Your Majesty," my father begins, finally removing his vicelike grip, "we will double our protection guard. Specific plans will be drawn up to deal with the Easter ceremonies, and I will order another search of the secret passageways. Clearly, this is the only way she can be getting around."

He casts me a sideways glance and I try not to flinch. A fleeting thought of leaving Niobe a warning note in the cellar crosses my mind, but I will likely be watched too closely from now on. Hopefully, she can manage to stay one step ahead of them as she has so far.

King William rises, thanks everyone, and takes his leave with the princes on his heels. Sir Michael and my father confer quietly. The commander still eyes me with fury until he rushes out to complete some task. My father then pulls me over to the side. "Olivia, if you know anything I implore you to let me know immediately. I understand you are fond of Niobe, but don't let it cloud your judgment."

"The way Sir Michael's hatred of her clouds his?" I retort.

Father merely shakes his head, then heads out the door. Only Queen Helen remains, wiping the drops of spilled wine with a handkerchief. Tiny red spots bleed into the pristine white material, growing wider and wider. Though she says nothing, I sense something is on her mind, so I wait.

"I agree with you, Olivia. I think her message was a warning," she says.

"Do you? Then why didn't you say this when the men were here?" I blurt before I can stop myself. "Apologies, Your Highness," I whisper contritely.

"No. It is a fair question," she admits. "The answer is because I have no proof of it. Like you, I am going by my gut. Niobe has been with William since he was a young boy. She has done nothing but try to protect and nurture him. I cannot fathom anything that would alter the bond they share." She smiles wistfully. "Men though, they prefer proof. They prefer all things to be logical. Perhaps in their positions they must, while we are more at liberty to consult our feelings."

I nod, glad Queen Helen is an ally in my theory. She folds up the soiled handkerchief and leaves it on the table, then rises. "And I will trust if you discover—or remember—anything that will aid in the investigation, you will tell us immediately."

"Of course, Your Highness," I say, avoiding her keen eyes.

"You may go. I know you want to spend the afternoon with my son."

I nod, then curtsey. When I reach the door, she says, "Olivia, like my gut feeling about Niobe, I also have a gut feeling about Jocelyn Crawford. She is not the right match for Liam. My husband will eventually come to this logical conclusion himself. Be patient."

With a final nod, I take my leave and head for the War Room. The queen sounded so confident in her proclamation about Jocelyn. I wish I could share her sense of certainty. But the king does not appear to be swayed by matters of emotion too easily. Though I try to take comfort in Queen Helen's words, my heart simply aches at the uncertainty of it all.

"It's strange how your note wound up in the king's bedchamber," Puck muses. He lounges with his back on the seat of a chair, his long legs hanging over the arm like awkward tree limbs.

"Yes, I suppose it is," I murmur from the sofa Kat and I sprawl on.

The War Room is a much more pleasant space in the spring. Gone are the frigid corners and unforgiving drafts. Now the widows are thrown open along with two doors at opposite ends of the side wall. A cross breeze filters across the space, carrying in the fresh smells of the new season. The hearth stands empty and Adam has moved his chair under one of the windows where he can read in the sunlight. At the moment a book sits open, spine up on the sill, waiting for the guard to return from an errand.

"What do you make of it, Prince Liam?" Kat asks. My friend is far more at ease with him than she was the first day in the archery yard.

"I sincerely hope Olivia is correct and the note is meant for a warning. But I would feel better if Niobe was found so we could be certain." He looks at me pointedly from where he stands by the unlit fireplace.

Liam has been understandably on edge these past few weeks. He is worried about his father's safety. It is a hard decision not to share with him my knowledge Niobe uses the tunnels, but all my intuition warns me against it. She vanished because this is her best chance to protect the king. I need to trust my instinct on that.

In the meantime, I try to be as supportive as possible to Liam. Besides having the prophecy hanging over us, we also have Jocelyn trying to work her charms on the king. Our relationship is stalled, stuck at a standstill, and the frustration eats me alive. In the recesses of my mind, what might be the most insidious force on the planet worms its way in…doubt, an emotion able to drive out all reason and taint all interactions. The question of whether Liam loves me enough to fight for me echoes in all his statements, all his glances, all his kisses, where previously his affections were always so evident to me. Today he comes across as even more distant than usual, or is it just the sinister qualms of my imagination?

Adam enters the room, a small, brown ball of fluff peeking out from the crook of his arm. "I wanted to show you all the newest addition to my family," he beams.

We all surround him to get a look at the puppy he holds. The animal shakes and shies away from all the attention, hiding his head under the guard's elbow. One of the hounds in the royal stable recently birthed a litter and Adam asked for one of the pups to give to his son. Kat and I have pestered him all week to see it after he could not stop gushing about the creature. A little head peeks back up and lets out a small bark.

"He's so tiny," Kat croons, stroking the silky fur between the floppy ears.

"Have you decided on a name yet?" I ask, while Adam sets him down on the floor.

"Achilles."

The dog sits immobile for a second, unsure how to handle his newfound freedom. Then he scrambles off on clumsy canine legs. His paws are too big, too out of proportion with his body, and he stumbles, landing chest first before popping back up and trotting to the other end of the room.

"Well, hopefully he will grow into the name as he grows into his feet," I quip, picturing his namesake, the mighty Greek warrior.

Adam trails off after him with Kat and Puck following behind. Before I can take a step in their direction, Liam takes my elbow and steers me into one of the shadowy corners at our end of the room. Instead of the stolen kisses I expect, his face is somber.

"I have something to tell you and you are not going to like it," he warns.

"Great, I love when a conversation starts that way," I attempt to joke, but he remains serious. "What is it?"

Fear creeps in like frost on a windowpane, steadily growing from edge to middle. My stomach constricts in its merciless grip.

"The Crawfords have invited Harold and me to stay at their home for two weeks at the end of April as a retreat for us and their daughters. My father insists I go."

"And you would go with the danger that lies over the king's head right now?" I ask. Though far from my only complaint it is the first one I verbalize. Nervously, I finger the fabric on the edge of my sleeve.

"I suppose he hopes the matter will be resolved by then. The Crawfords want to discuss wedding plans in the hopes of setting a June date. My father wants to give the kingdom something celebratory to focus on."

"Why do you have to go?" I ask, trying hard to keep the petulance from my voice. This is my more pressing complaint. Outside, two birds squawk shrilly, at odds over something.

"Because the king feels it is a good show of support for their family, who will be our in-laws in the near future," he replies grimly.

"And it gets you alone time with Jocelyn, away from me. I am sure he hopes your feelings toward her will soften." I cannot keep the sourness from my tone.

"You know it won't help her cause." He sighs, holding the bridge of his nose between pinched fingers. "You know I can't stand her."

"Yes, I know. But does it matter? How can we continue to maintain our relationship when it is constantly being sabotaged? And by the king, no less."

The sheer desperation I feel must be evident, because he takes my hand from where it pulls on my sleeves into his and looks me in the eyes. "We just have to ignore it and rise above. Our love will win out in the end."

There is a burst of laughter from the other end of the room where Achilles bounds playfully among our friends. They have a stick and attempt to show him how to fetch, but he is more interested in trying to eat their toy. He scampers toward the open door where he hesitates only a moment before leaping into the unknown. Three bodies hurry out after him.

"Ignoring won't solve the problem. The king does not seem inclined to change his mind," I spit out. The words Queen Helen spoke to me earlier rise to mind, but they feel hollow. While she may consider love a factor in marrying off sons, her husband does not.

"I told you, if I am ordered to marry her, I will refuse."

"Which will likely earn me a trip to Prescott where I will be given to the highest bidder," I snap. What he sees as an easy refusal, I see as a line in the sand where the king is concerned.

Liam shuts his eyes and takes a few deep breaths. "Come on," he says, "let's have a nice stroll in the gardens and enjoy our afternoon together. Fighting will not solve anything."

He kisses me softly, making it hard to argue with him. We walk out the door of the War Room hand in hand. Adam spots us and scoops up the puppy to trail his prince. After a winding route though newly budding courtyards, we wind up in the archery yard, though there are no targets or bows on hand. Now that the weather is warmer, we will be able to return here. I cannot wait to pretend one of the bull's-eyes is Jocelyn's face.

On a backless, curved bench, we whisper and kiss as though everything were normal, as though our future together were assured. But inside, my emotions churn. When I met Liam, he was the missing puzzle piece. He slipped into place and completed my heart. Now it feels more like when you think two pieces fit together, but they are just slightly off. No matter how much you force them together, you can't make them seamlessly join. There is always a space where light shines through. And a little voice in me wonders how long I should waste in the effort before I realize it is useless and give up.

These thoughts still plague me when Sadie helps me dress for dinner. Anne dines at Montgomery's parents' estate this evening, so I knock on Kat's door when I am ready to go down. There is no answer. Perhaps she couldn't wait to get back to Puck's side and went down early.

The walk to the dining hall is lonely. A random servant passes me, but for the most part the halls are quiet. I am late, my depressed state not conducive to speed. Rounding a corner, I find myself in front of the door to the storage closet where Liam and I kissed all those days ago. Usually the sight of it elicits a mischievous grin, as though the closet and I share a special secret. Today, I merely stand there, my fingertips pressed against the door, wishing the room could conjure up the confidence I felt in our relationship back then.

It doesn't. Emptiness is the only emotion I feel.

"It's a shame, isn't it?" a voice behind me says. "That this closet will likely be the best memory you have of Prince Liam. Fitting though. An inconsequential, forgotten room, much like yourself."

Straightening my shoulders, I turn to look at the speaker. The sympathetic pout on Jocelyn's face is rendered counterfeit by the smug gleam in her eyes. "Funny that you thought someone like *you* would make an acceptable princess."

Every sensible fiber in my body urges me to walk away, to not engage with her. But sensibility was never my strong suit, especially after months of living in this castle surrounded by phoniness and malice. I stride right up to her and stand nose to nose. A servant scuttles out of the dining hall, stopping at the sight of us.

"Jocelyn, I know you will not believe this or even understand it, but I have no desire to be princess in a court where my every principle and value must be compromised to fit in."

She tosses her head back and laughs. It physically hurts me to restrain from punching her in the throat. The servant skitters past us, head down, obviously hoping to avoid any involvement in a disagreement between two ladies of the court. When he reaches the corner, he bolts away like a startled rabbit.

"Pretty words from someone who knows she has lost," she sneers. "You would be the most disgraceful princess this court has ever known. Disguising yourself as a boy, conspiring with outlaws, befriending a witch. Is there no end to your scandalous behavior? Princesses need beauty, grace, and decorum. They need to understand they are more important than everyone else and act accordingly. When I have Liam alone at my parent's house, he will realize once and for all what an embarrassment you truly are. What a blemish your presence would be on his family's reputation."

There is a rustle and King William rounds the corner, two guards flanking his side. He stops in front of us and my rival and I step away from each other. We each drop into a curtsey.

"Is everything all right here, ladies?" he asks, his eyes scrutinizing each of our faces.

"Of course, Your Majesty," Jocelyn coos out, all the spite in her voice drained away. "Please, let me accompany you to the Hall."

King William looks to me, but I cast my eyes to the floor. I am not sure how long he stood around the corner listening, but he at least heard Jocelyn's last remark about me being an embarrassment. A statement I gather he agrees with. After a moment, he offers his arm to her and they glide past me down the rest of the hallway. I seriously consider sticking my foot out to trip her, but know this will only exacerbate my situation.

There is no reason for me to follow them. I have lost my appetite.

Easter morning dawns gray with steely clouds racing across the sky. By the time we file into Mass, fat raindrops splash on the cobblestones. The unsettled weather echoes the collective worry that ripples through the court today. Although it was to be kept secret, the contents of Niobe's note spread like wildfire throughout the citizens of Stewartsland. Puck even told me of some less than ethical courtiers gambling on whether or not the prophecy would be fulfilled.

Security is high in the chapel. Guards surround the king and his family, while more stand in strategic positions around the building. Wine is brought up from the royal cellar and kept in the presence of two of my father's most trusted men until the moment Brother Alastair pours it on the altar. A taster takes a hearty sip before it is given to the king, lest the "vessel of the faith" proved to be the holy drink.

The Mass is uneventful. Brother Alastair's harsh sermon somehow manages to put a damper on what is normally one of the most glorious of church holidays. I sit in the balcony box reserved for the ladies-in-waiting, inwardly groaning at his fire and brimstone message. Kat is by my side and spends a large part of the service mooning at Puck, who stares up at her like a lovesick puppy. From my vantage point, I can also see Anne, who is seated with the Montgomerys. Her hand is clasped in her fiancé's discreetly by their sides. In the front with the royal family, Emily Crawford sits glued to Prince Harold as though her life depended on maintaining physical contact with him. Jocelyn is beside Liam, whose posture is rigid as a statue. She finds numerous excuses to whisper to him, rub his arm or bat her eyes. Though his body language clearly shows his revulsion, the sight still gnaws at my core.

When I was forced to move to the palace, my only consolation was I would be with Liam. I hoped our relationship would have a chance to blossom. Instead, love bloomed all around me—for Anne, for Kat, even for Puck, while I have been left behind. Like the lone weed in a field of beautiful flowers, my stark forlornness is magnified by their coupling. I note Prince Stephan, the only unpaired member in the royal box. With my luck, the king will find me a suitable match for him.

Mass ends and courtiers jostle out of the chapel, hoping for some interaction with the royal family, who lead the procession on the way to the feast. Guards maintain a tight circle around them. A sea of bright colored hats and wraps, at odds with the colorless sky, drift in their wake. Kat and I move slowly down the stairs from the balcony, a bottleneck at the door impeding our progress. When we reach the main floor, Puck elbows his way through the crowd and offers us both an arm. He and Kat whisper and giggle, some inside joke passing between them. Anne, who looks resplendent in a peacock-green ensemble, smiles at me over the crowd. Montgomery waves before they murmur to each other. Even my father and my mother walk arm in arm, talking quietly to each other.

Once outside, the thought of attending the feast suddenly nauseates me. I am in no mood to watch Jocelyn hang all over Liam. Perhaps I should say I feel ill and return to my room, but staring at those four walls will make me lose my mind. Better to find an occupation that will keep me busy.

It has stopped raining, so maybe I could go for a good long horse ride and clear my head. But no, if anyone saw me doing this in lieu of the feast, it would be considered highly disrespectful. My steps slow to a stop while I contemplate my options. Puck and Kat look at me questioningly.

"I feel a bit…dizzy. I think I will go back to my room and lie down. Please apologize to my parents for me."

Kat immediately rushes to my side, feeling my cheek, whispering soft words of comfort. But Puck, well, he has known me too long. He can tell when I am being dishonest. His eyes bore into mine seeking the truth. To his credit though, he says nothing.

"Do you want us to walk you back to your room?" Kat asks, the picture of concern.

"No, I'll be all right," I assure her, avoiding Puck's gaze.

Reluctantly, Kat allows him to pull her away. He wraps his arm around her shoulder and they melt into the receding crowd. Soon, I am the only one left in the chapel's courtyard. A few mourning doves peck among the stones, their feathers as gray as the sky overhead. The leaden atmosphere sinks into my being, leaving it as raw and chilled as the breeze, which hits my cheeks. Easter is a day of hope's renewal, yet little hope is left in my heart.

Nothing makes sense here at the palace…except my work with Niobe. Helping her in the servants' village and learning to formulate remedies brought me a level of satisfaction I would not have thought possible. As if my feet already reached this conclusion on their own, I find myself standing in front of Niobe's door. Today there is no guard. Every possible man they could spare protects the king.

I want to go inside and get to work, lose myself in the rhythmic work of grinding and measuring herbs, but the door is locked. Frustrated, I jiggle the handle, but to no avail. With a sigh, I place my forehead against the wood. The one place where I could find comfort today is shut tight against me. Then, to my astonishment, there is a click and the door slowly opens from the inside. Niobe's head appears in the space, her hair a wild shock of gray.

"Come in, child. I have something for you."

A moment later, I sit bewildered in one of the armchairs by her fire. So many questions hurtle through my mind; I don't know what to ask first. The healer places a lantern on the table, its wick low to keep the flame dim. It is the only extra light we dare to supplement the weak light filtering through her window. If we are found, it means her immediate arrest. She shuffles over to her workbench and gropes around the surface.

"Here it is," she declares and returns to my side. "I was returning to the grounds this morning while everyone was occupied at Mass. A young man carried this. He said it was for you."

She holds out a sealed letter. Even more baffled, I take it from her hand. The mark on the seal makes me gasp:

It is the mark of Athos. Hurriedly, I rip it open and read:

Miss Olivia,

First and foremost, thank you for the remedies for my leg. They worked wonders and I am back to my ornery self much to my men's delight and chagrin.

Luke filled me in on the rumors at the palace. I want you to know I heard from a reliable man in the south that Lord Otto landed down there some months ago. My contact's band tracked him to the small hamlet of Bethel just outside of Prescott. Then they lost him. To my knowledge, no one has seen him again, but he must still be somewhere in Stewartsland. If I find out any further information, I will let you know.

Until then, may blessings be upon you. I owe you a great debt, which I one day hope to repay.

Athos

Relief floods through me like a gentle stream. Athos is healed. The worry of him suffering, which had clung to the recesses of my mind, floats away. "My friend is healed, Niobe. Thanks to you."

"I am glad to hear it, child." She pats my hand, a pleased grin on her face, while she settles in the chair across from me. Nothing makes her as happy as helping a person get better.

"Do you know anything about a hamlet down south named Bethel?" The name does not ring a bell with me, but Niobe knows Stewartsland well.

"Nothing noteworthy. Only that there is a rather large monastery there," she replies.

I will have to show the note from Athos to my father. Hopefully, I can find him after the feast. For now, my main concern is protecting Niobe.

"If you are found here, you will be arrested," I warn. "Where have you been staying anyway? I found the tunnel in the cellar, but never found any sign of you."

"Mostly I stayed in the woods. There is a cave there where I sometimes hang herbs to dry during the summer. Then I would use the tunnels at night to check back in with you. I knew you would figure it out, you clever girl." She appears unfazed by any of this, as if living out of caves was a normal occurrence. "Some of the villagers helped me as well." This does not surprise me; many of them owe her their lives.

"But why didn't you just stay here and use the tunnels to sneak out?"

"I kept having premonitions William was in danger and I had to try to help him. If the guards discovered me missing, they would have found the tunnel and my freedom would have been lost. To keep the secret safe, I gave that poor boy some valerian." She smiles sadly.

"So your premonition is why you were in the king's chamber the first time? And why you subsequently left him the note?"

"The first day, I was going to slip out of the village, when I saw one of the penitents skulking about. Imagine my surprise when he slipped into one of the tunnels. I followed him to the king's chambers where he disposed of the guard, then snuck into the room. He was holding up the decanter of wine on the king's table. When I confronted him, he knocked me to the ground and fled. I attempted to check the wine, but that annoying friar interrupted. I slipped into one of the tunnels to escape him."

This explains the *magic* the Brother was so sure she'd used. It also explains how the guard wound up unconscious in the closet. I knew it could not have been Niobe.

"Why didn't you tell anyone?"

"What good is my word with no proof? Brother Alastair has already turned so many against me. The note I left was meant to be a warning. I hoped the king would understand." The sadness in her voice communicates how hurt she is King William may not trust her. It is heartbreaking to hear, but I am pleased to know my instincts were correct.

"I decided to keep a close eye on this man. For days, nothing happened, then one night, he started lurking around the back of the maze garden. Another man joined him, but I could not see them. It was dark and I needed to stay concealed. They appeared to argue over something, but I am not sure what. The other man left. When the penitent passed my hiding spot, he was whispering wildly to himself. He kept saying, 'On Easter, I will finish the matter myself. I will end this now. King William will not live past Easter.' So I left the note in the king's chamber."

At the mention of the maze garden, my hair stands on end. The second conversation held in that place. I contemplate this along with the strange fact that a penitent may be involved. A thought floats on the outskirts of my mind, like the loose string of an errant kite just out of reach.

"Were you ever able to get a good look at which of the friar's men it was?" I ask.

"The sour-faced man, who has a scar on his face."

Images of him snatching the socks from my hand and dumping stew on my lap rise up in my mind, the sheer malice in his eyes still vivid. I glance down at the message from Athos. And then, the elusive thought from a moment ago becomes clear. "Niobe, did you say Bethel was the site of a monastery? Could Brother Alastair be associated with it? Would people have known in advance his intention of bringing penitents to the king?"

"He sees to all of the abbeys around Prescott," she replies. "I would guess the Brothers there knew of his plan, as did the general populace."

Icy claws grip my heart. Terror paralyzes me. But then, my training kicks in and I hear my father's voice in my head. "*Focus.*" Time is of the essence right now. I leap from my chair and head for the door.

"Stay here," I order Niobe, who rises with me. "I think Lord Otto infiltrated the penitents. They are at the feast right now where the king is to bless each of them individually. I must warn him."

Her startled face it the last thing I see before I hurtle out the door.

29

The world becomes a blur. Hallways whip past me, shocked servants leaping out of the way. My heeled shoes, which I begrudgingly wore to Mass, slow me down, so I discard them halfway down a corridor, much to the astonishment of two well-dressed ladies who stand to one side conversing.

"Miss, your shoes…" one calls to my fleeting back.

"Well, I never," the other gasps.

At last, I turn the corner to the dining hall. Francis guards the outer door with Seth, another old training companion of mine. The former steps out to block my path.

"Halt right there, miss."

"*Miss*? It's me, Olivia, you fool!" I blurt, skidding to a stop in my stocking feet.

"Olivia? What on earth are you doing?" Seth asks. "Running at us as if death is on your heels. The king is about to address the room. Show some respect. You look like a banshee, for goodness' sake."

Wayward strands of hair, loosened during my dash, cling to the sides of my face. I brush them away impatiently and get right in Seth's face. "I need to get to my father. It is urgent. The king is in danger."

Thankfully, these two men know me well. They know when I am serious. With a mutual glance, they quickly step aside.

"Can we help?" Francis asks, his voice soft but keen, like when we used to train patrols. I look down at the dagger in his belt and he slips it quietly into my hand with a firm press.

"Just guard this door and make sure none of the penitents are able to slip out."

They nod in unison, then step back into the doorway after I pass through. Their faces scan the room intently. At least one exit is now watched.

No one notices my entrance except for a few guards, but it raises no alarm since Francis and Seth allowed me access. All heads face the front of the room where King William stands in front of the royal dais, his hands on the top of the bowed, gray head of a penitent. Brother Alastair is at the monarch's side, a few steps behind in deference, his self-righteous expression on full display. Behind them, Queen Helen sits flanked by her sons. On one side, Prince Harold sits with Emily and Jocelyn; on the other, Prince Stephan sits beside Liam. My father and Sir Michael stand on either end of the table, only a few arms' lengths from His Majesty.

In front of the dais, the Brother's men stand, a cluster of brown robes. My eyes hunt through them, seeking one face in particular, but most have their hoods up and their heads down. I inch my way down the side of the room toward where my father stands, the dagger concealed in my sleeve.

The king confers a blessing on the elderly man, who rises and nods gratefully, before shuffling away. Brother Alastair motions the next man forward. A rotund man wobbles up and kneels before the king. Halfway down the room, my father looks my way. He trained me for so many years, there is almost a sixth sense between us. When our eyes lock, he can tell there is danger. I quicken my steps.

"And may the blessings and forgiveness of this kingdom be upon you," the monarch's voice booms.

The plump man totters up to his feet, still bowing his head in homage. Brother Alastair nods to the next man. A man strides forward and removes the hood of his robe, revealing the long scar now etched in my brain. An expression of pure evil fills his face when he approaches the king. Desperately, I break towards the dais, but freeze at a shrill howl.

"*William, beware!*"

Every head whips in the direction of the scream. Gasps at the use of the king's Christian name can be heard. Then Niobe rounds the dais, her hair flying behind her in wild tangles as she discards a server's hat. She used the tunnels to get to the kitchens so she could gain entry without the guards catching her.

In the moment of distraction, Otto makes his move. He pulls a large knife from the folds of his sleeve, grabs the king, and holds the point of the weapon to his throat. All heads fly back to the endangered monarch. The room is a succession of screams, then slowly recedes to dead silence. Across the space, the metallic scrape of swords pulled from their sheaths rings out like a shout of its own. Queen Helen and the princes jump from their seats in alarm. Brother Alastair backs away, abject fear on his face. Father and Sir Michael stand with blades drawn, but make no move.

Only King William remains calm. He does not struggle or shout, merely stands in as regal a pose as he can manage. In the deafening quiet, he booms out, "Who are you who dares enter my kingdom with such treacherous intents?"

Lord Otto laughs, an eerie mirthless cackle, which rebounds off the stone walls. "Dear brother, has it been so long you don't even recognize me?"

Realization flickers in the eyes of the king, his family, even my father. Niobe steps forward, causing Otto to press the knife harder into his captive's flesh.

"It is as I predicted," she proclaims. "He came with a vessel of the Lord."

She glares at Brother Alastair, who blanches. "I assure you, Your Majesty, I had no knowledge of who this man was or his intentions"

"Silence, you fat fool," Otto yells. "Your ignorance and arrogance allowed this moment to occur. And you, witch, you may have stopped me from lacing his wine with poison, but you cannot help him now!"

I edge behind my father, concealed by his large frame. Lord Otto is only about ten feet from me. Slowly, I ease the dagger out of my sleeve. Father motions me to step on to the dais. On silent feet, I slip up. Liam notices me. We share a long look and I look down at my weapon. He motions something. It takes me a second, but I realize he points to his calf. Two times on our Lindenwood adventure, a knife placed here changed the course of a battle. While I nod, he reaches for the dagger on his belt.

"Now, Otto," King William says, his voice restricted by the tight grip, "it's been so long. Let's not argue about the hows and the whys that brought you here. I missed having a chance to visit with you at Lindenwood last year. You left in such a hurry thanks to my sons who were there to defeat you, as they will always be. Now what is it you want this time?"

How the king keeps his composure, I can only guess. It is not only commendable, but it buys valuable time.

"Only to see your blood spilled and my mother and brother avenged." Lord Otto and his brother, the deceased King John of Lindenwood, were illegitimate children of

William's father by a long-time mistress. They both felt entitled to a stake in Stewartsland.

"And you think this will bring you peace? The only thing it ensures is your own swift execution."

"Then I will die happy," he snarls. He pulls the king's head back tighter, the point driving into the skin hard enough to draw blood. A fine, red line trickles down his neck onto his bright white collar.

We are out of time. I lunge forward and sink my blade in his calf. To my shock, without losing his grip on the king, he kicks my hand with amazing strength, the puncture wound not even a bother to him. "Stupid girl," he spits in my face, "you think you can thwart me a second time? You may have rescued him in Lindenwood, but I am in charge now." His foot drives me back into my father, his grip on the king redoubling.

"Men," King William addresses his guards, "I want him alive. I want to interrogate him thoroughly."

Again the haunting cackle from Otto. "What makes you think you will be around long enough to interrogate anyone?"

"Even if I am not, my sons will rule in my place. You will never have a claim to this land." For the first time, anger laces the king's voice.

"And your claim is over," Otto snarls. He pulls the king's head back hard, then positions the knife to slit his throat.

Instead of stiffening, King William slings himself backwards with all his might, knocking Otto off-balance. He is able to wrestle out of his grip and shove the would-be murderer away. But Otto recovers quickly, his hatred fueling his movements. The assailant raises the knife over his head ready to strike a death blow.

Time slows, seconds elapsing in thick, dreamlike drops. The blade descends towards the monarch's exposed chest until a black figure appears in front of the King's breast. Frail arms extend to shield him. When the knife connects the figure crumples, gray hair floating down around her head like luminous spider's silk. My father advances on Lord Otto, who shouts, "That foul witch—I should have killed her in the gardens the night of the ball. But she cannot protect you forever. You have no idea what evil lurks within…"

The sentence is never finished. Another blade hurtles from behind the royal table and embeds itself deeply into Lord Otto's heart. He drops like a stone to the floor, blood erupting from the wound in pulsing gurgles.

And then there are screams. The room explodes with them—courtiers', guards', the royal family's and my own. I thrust my way toward the fallen body, which rests now in the king's arms. Blood pours from her chest just below her right shoulder, the dagger still lodged in place. King William holds one of her hands, while the other strokes hair from her face.

"Remain calm," Sir Michael shouts over the chaos of the room. A gradual silence falls, like thunder receding into the distance. "Please evacuate the room in an orderly fashion and return to your chambers or your home."

Guards form a tight circle around the royal dais, closing in everyone on the platform. With nothing to see, the crowd slowly filters from the room. The queen walks to William's side and kneels down next to him, her arm on his shoulder. Prince Liam and Prince Harold stand behind her while Prince Stephan pours some water for a nearly hyperventilating Brother Alastair. Emily and Jocelyn remain behind the table, arms crossed over their chests.

"Quickly," my father commands one of the guards, "run and get the royal physician."

"Niobe, can you hear me?" I plead, grabbing her other hand.

She murmurs unintelligibly and weakly squeezes my hand. Even as tears fill my eyes, all the lessons this healer taught me surface. Assessing her wound, I know the bleeding needs to be stopped. I claw at my dress trying to rip off a piece of cloth, but the fabric is too thick.

"Please," I beg to Jocelyn and Emily, "give me one of your scarves to staunch the bleeding."

Neither of them moves. Jocelyn only wrinkles her nose in distaste.

"*Now!*" I yell. "I need something now!"

There is the sound of tearing material and a bright blue cloth dangles in front of me. Queen Helen holds out a piece of her own skirt. I push it down around the upright blade's hilt, applying as much pressure as I can.

"It's all right," I croon to my friend. "You will be all right."

Tears run down my face, but I cannot release my hold to wipe them. A hand rises to my cheek and brushes one away. I raise my eyes and meet King William's gaze, his eyes moist with emotion. Then Liam kneels next to me, rubbing my back and offering words of comfort. Niobe's head lolls to one side. All I can do whisper for her to hold on.

The physician arrives with two assistants. They hoist the healer onto a stretcher and carry her out, one of the aides holding the cloth, now a putrid purple, firmly against the wound. Slumped on the floor, I force myself to take several breaths, but my lungs are constricted with the fear of losing Niobe this way.

"How long do we have to stand here?" Jocelyn whispers to her sister. "The blood of that witch is seeping over here. These shoes cost a fortune."

"Hush," Emily wisely scolds.

The urge to leap up and force Jocelyn face down onto the floor, wet from my friend's grave injury, almost gets the best of me. But then, a hand extends down in front of me. King William helps me to my feet and pats my shoulder in a fatherly way. For a brief moment, I see the face of a man instead of the face of a king. He is as distressed as I am about Niobe.

"Well, Sire," Prince Harold sighs, "I don't suppose there will be any interrogation."

All eyes fall to the corpse on the ground. No more blood spews from Otto's wound, but a large red pool flows over the dais step onto the main floor where it breaks into haphazard rivulets. His eyes are wide open, mouth hanging slack. Whatever tale he had to tell died with him.

"That is my fault, Sire," Prince Stephan nervously admits. "It is my dagger in his chest. I feared for your life."

"You did what you had to do, nephew," the king says, placing a hand on his shoulder.

Brother Alastair, who has remained remarkably quiet until now, adds, "Yes, Prince Stephan, you should feel no guilt for taking this man's life, liar and thief that he was. To think, disguising himself as a man seeking atonement. His road in the afterlife will be difficult, but you have the comfort of knowing you may have spared him from the eternal fires."

"How so?" Prince Stephan stammers, wiping his brow with a handkerchief.

"That is the punishment when one murders one's king, one's sovereign, one ordained by the heavens to rule," the friar preaches, though his bluster is toned down by the shocking course of events.

The king's nephew blanches and staggers back. Prince Harold offers a steadying arm. Prince Stephan must be unused to such gore unfolding right in front of him. I hope I never have to follow him into battle. He would not command the authority of either his uncle or his cousins. King William, a natural born leader, takes control of the situation.

"I think we all need to recover from this shock. Let us escort the ladies back to their quarters. Sir Jack, please dispose of my…this man—" He nudges Otto with his toe, "—then put an intelligence report together. We will meet first thing tomorrow morning to discuss the matter in full. I will need to make an announcement to the entire court. Schedule that for noon. Until then," he says and we all bow.

"As you wish, Your Majesty," my father replies.

While Father gives orders to his men, the royal family clusters together and walks toward the door. My eyes follow Liam's retreating form with despair. Then, the king leans in and whispers something to him. They both turn, look at me, and Liam nods. He strides back over and offers me his arm.

"Come," he says softly. "My father insists I escort you back to your room."

Anne leaps up from her chair in surprise when Liam and I enter the room, almost knocking poor Sadie over. The handmaid was in the middle of brushing out my sister's hair. She drops the brush onto the vanity, where it clangs against a perfume bottle. A fire burns low on the hearth, combating the slight chill in the room.

"Are you all right?" Anne gasps, taking in my bloodstained dress.

"Yes…I…mean I'm not hurt…" I burst into tears.

The two women flank me, each taking a hand while I stammer about the graveness of Niobe's injury. They escort me to a chair and Sadie rushes out to get me some hot tea. My sister sits on the arm of my chair, gently stroking my hair. Liam walks over and sits down across from me. He takes my hand in his large, steady one and says, "I must return to my father, but I will leave word with the royal physician that you are to receive all updates on Niobe's condition."

I nod, squeezing a handkerchief balled up in my other hand. He leans in and kisses me, a soft caress of his lips on mine, then presses his cheek against my tearstained face.

"Take good care of her," he instructs Anne on his way out the door.

"I will," she replies and wraps an arm around my shoulder.

An hour passes, then another and another. Time stacks like stone blocks on my heart. Sadie and Anne help me change into a warm robe, then coax down some tea and broth the maid brought up from the kitchen. My mind fully understands everything that took place, but emotionally I need to catch up. All I keep picturing is Niobe's fragile little body with the knife protruding from her chest.

Still no word arrives.

Later in the day, Sadie brings up some food and warm mead for my sister and me. The sun finally makes an appearance at day's end, casting its rays in long slants to create chunks of light on the floor. Though I have barely eaten all day, the bread feels like ash in my mouth.

Still no word arrives.

"Have some cheese." Anne offers me a slab off a tangy block. She has been amazingly restrained for someone who must have a million questions. Instead of pelting me with a barrage of inquiries, she just sits quietly by my side, the solid presence she has been for me since we first set foot in the palace. I think back to how we had almost become strangers in those last few years at home. Now we are sisters again, in the best possible way.

By sunset, her eyelids droop heavily and she fights the urge to nod off. Eventually, Sadie helps us get ready for bed, then departs for the evening.

And still, no word arrives.

Finally, just as Anne and I are ready to retire, the sound of boots echoes on the staircase down the hall, low at first, then louder with each successive step. They stop in front of our door, followed by a loud rap. I am across the room in a heartbeat and open the door for one of the physician's assistants.

Without fanfare, he launches into his explanation. "Niobe survived. She has a severe puncture wound in her upper right chest, which has been tended to. Her breathing sounds clear. Now all we can do is keep it clean and pray her body can recover from the trauma."

"Can I see her?"

"She is not awake and may not be for some time now. There was a significant loss of blood, which in a person half her age could prove fatal. She will not be aware of any visits, if you would prefer to wait until morning."

"Thank you," I say. He nods and strides away while I click the door shut.

"Well, she survived," says Anne, embracing me. "That is good news."

"She was already so frail after the garden attack. I pray she has the strength to recover," I murmur. All my own strength has suddenly drained away.

"Come and rest," my sister says, leading me to the bed. "You will need all your energy to help her."

To my surprise, I fall asleep almost immediately, exhaustion finally overcoming worry. When I wake, there is only the stillness permeated by Anne's breathing, so peaceful. It takes a moment for it all to come crashing back. After tossing and turning for over an hour, I slip out of the warm cover of the bed. My bare feet land on the cold stone floor and a gasp almost escapes my lips. But I know where I must go.

Quietly, I don a plain day dress, then wrap my cloak around my shoulders. When I cross outside, the moon hangs halfway down the sky, a muted semicircle amid some passing clouds. Barely anyone stirs. Dawn is yet a few hours off. The few people I do pass cast me curious glances, but keep to themselves. One woman, too scantily clad for her well-endowed figure, eyes me skeptically. She must think, like her, I have just left the company of some adulterous lord.

At last I arrive at the infirmary. The grisly smell of sickness hovers in the outside hallway. I expect to encounter only whatever nurse is on watch but there by the door stands a guard. He blocks the way with his large frame.

Really? Are they still keeping watch on her? Even now?

A heavyset woman looks up from the desk behind him. "Can I help you?" she asks in a tone that indicates she would rather do anything but.

"I came to see Niobe."

"She already has a visitor, miss." The nurse gestures to a bed where Niobe lies like a frail baby bird who fell from her nest. At her bedside sits King William. Well, that explains the guard at least.

"It is all right, Agatha," the king says. "She can join me."

"As you wish, Your Majesty." Agatha bows her head and the guard steps aside.

On nervous legs, I approach the bed and curtsey. King William sits on the far side and motions for me to take the chair on the near one. I sink down across from him, then look at my friend. Her face is pale, transparent almost, her crepe-like skin less wrinkled in slumber. A large bandage wraps around her one shoulder, secured at her waist. The rise and fall of her chest is steady and her pulse is strong when I check it. Our monarch remains silent during my assessment.

"What do you think?" he asks when I sit back, Niobe's hand clasped in mine.

"Overall she looks better than I expected, but she is not out of the woods. We must make sure the wound doesn't become infected. I will make a poultice to help with the healing."

"I am glad to hear that. She has taught you well," the monarch says. He wears only a long red robe over a simple tunic and pants—no crown, no jewels, just a man in a chair by the bedside of a friend.

We sit in silence for a while. For my part, I am not supposed to say anything unless addressed by him. And to be honest, I don't know what I would say. Half of me sympathizes with him and his grief over Niobe, but the other half is angry about Jocelyn, about keeping Liam and I apart. The patient stirs a bit, a restless tremor, then she quiets.

"You knew it was Otto before he revealed himself, didn't you? How?" King William says.

"Niobe had been following him, not knowing who he was, only that he meant you harm. He snuck into your rooms on the day Brother Alastair discovered her there. I put this together with information I received that Lord Otto had been seen in Bethel."

"Where did this information come from?" he asks, an eyebrow raised.

"Athos." The word is barely a whisper. Consternation crosses the monarch's face, but he doesn't question how I had contact with Athos. Though the outlaw was instrumental in the king's rescue last fall, he is still regarded warily by the monarch.

"Well, it seems I owe that man again," he muses.

"If only I had reached my father before Otto had a chance to act," I complain. An hour's more time might have changed the entire outcome of events.

"You acted both smartly and bravely," he proclaims. "Not that I would expect anything less of you. Still, I wish it had not come to this."

He waves his hand at Niobe's prone form, then stares off into the distance. I try to not relive the moment when the knife struck my friend's chest, the sickening thud. Closing my eyes only brings it back more fully, so I focus on her face instead. Her fitful starts have passed; now she sleeps serenely.

"This is the second time she saved my life," the king says. "The first time I was twelve." His eyes do not look at me, but gaze over my head, unseeing, while he recounts the tale. "I was recently orphaned and set to be crowned king. But I was angry. Angry at life, at the burden of the mantle that awaited me. There were well-meaning elders who wanted to guide me, but I felt so…restricted by all the rules.

"One night, in the dead of winter, I got it into my head to run away. To where? Who knows." He chuckles to himself while I sit mesmerized. "A foolish boy—that is what I was. In any case, I wound up trying to cross Miller's Pond to hide in the woods. I thought the ice was thick enough to hold me. It wasn't. Next thing I know I had fallen through.

"I struggled a terrifying moment or two, cursing my rashness. Suddenly, an arm grabbed me and fished me out. It was her. She woke with a bad feeling and had them check my bed. Two guards followed her as she ran screaming to the pond. They thought she was crazy until they saw me. As I lay shivering from cold and fear in her arms, she promised she would always be there for me." He pauses, tears in his eyes. "I am ashamed to say, I allowed people to let me doubt this these past few weeks. But you and Helen, you never doubted her loyalty to me. Thank you for that, Olivia."

"You are most welcome, Your Majesty," I whisper, still in awe at the story.

He shakes his head a few times as if to dislodge the childhood memory, strokes the side of Niobe's face, and rises. "Now if you will excuse me, I will try to catch a few hours of sleep. It comforts me to know she has you by her side."

I stumble up and curtsey. When he passes me, he places a hand on my cheek, and in his eyes I see the orphaned boy and his love for the healer, faithful to him still.

"And so, it was from Athos' letter I was able to make the connection between Bethel and Lord Otto," I explain to the group at the table.

Birds sing outside the window the next morning. I have just spent the last few minutes detailing my conversation with Niobe on Easter morning to the king, the queen, the three princes, and my father. After King William left the infirmary, I went to the healer's chambers and made a poultice for her wound. With Agatha's help, we applied it and rewrapped Niobe's bandages. Then I sat with her until I was summoned to this meeting. Tiredness creeps into every inch of my body. No one else here looks particularly well-rested either.

"According to Brother Alastair," Father states, "the monastery in Bethel recruited the penitents from various prisons and labor camps. How Otto devised to hide himself among them goes to the grave with him. But the friar insists he knew nothing of his presence in the group."

"You feel confident this is the case?" Prince Harold questions, while Liam tries valiantly to stifle a yawn.

"Yes. Sir Michael and I interrogated him extensively with a fair amount of…pressure, if you will. Let's just say, I can tell you he is not the type of man who withstands such questioning without cracking. He is far too pampered and self-preserving."

My thoughts exactly.

"Besides," adds Liam, "he does not have any clear motive to hurt the king. It was Lord Otto who wished revenge on my father. And he got exactly what he deserved—a dagger in the heart. May his soul rot a thousand times longer than his bones."

Prince Stephan blanches, still queasy about the whole incident yesterday.

"I think the only thing remaining to discover is who his accomplices were. Niobe heard him with a man, as did Olivia, and there was also the mention of a she. He obviously garnered assistance from people inside the palace. Servants who knew about the tunnels."

"Likely some peasants," Prince Stephan states. "They can be easily bought. They lack a moral code and any sense of decency if the price is right."

I think of Mae in her cozy cottage, happily welcoming my outlaw friend into her home, Mary in the kitchen always looking out for me, Sadie and her faithfulness and compassion. It annoys me Prince Stephan would lump all the villagers together with such callousness. My opinion of him grows lower with each encounter.

"While I do not agree all of our hard-working citizens fall into this category," Prince Harold says, and I want to get up and hug him, "there is certainly always a bad element to be found if one looks hard enough. Many of the servants know of those old tunnels, so it would not be terribly difficult information to find out. What troubles me is the woman who was mentioned said she had the king's trust."

"Likely just exaggerated words," Prince Stephan rationalizes, "to earn her more money."

"I will be conducting extensive interviews with the servants and exhausting any leads," my father explains, "but whoever helped him was not the mastermind of the plan, and given the outcome, they may have already fled the kingdom."

"We trust you in this matter entirely, Sir Jack," Prince Harold affirms with a bow of his head.

"Very well," King William says. "I will address the court at noon to give an official account of what happened. The kingdom needs to know the prophecy went unfulfilled and we can move on. I also want my people to know Niobe is a hero. She showed loyalty and courage, as did those who stood by her." He nods at me, then rises. "Now if you all excuse me, I want to speak with Prince Liam and Olivia for a moment."

Liam and I lock eyes, both with the same questioning look. Queen Helen smiles enigmatically. My father takes his leave, talking with Prince Harold about the investigation with Prince Stephan trailing behind. The door shuts behind them and the four of us are alone.

"Please sit, you two," the king orders, indicating the two chairs across from where he and the queen settle back down.

We slide into the chairs and Liam grabs my hand under the table. Neither of us knows what is coming, but we know it will be a defining moment in the future of our relationship. I try to take some slow breaths, but my heart beats like a hammer against my ribcage.

"I have given this matter a lot of thought," he begins. "As you both know, representing Stewartsland as a princess requires certain qualities. Birthright and etiquette are two of these."

I look at my lap, knowing I have neither. A picture of Jocelyn with her golden hair and her perfect grasp of court protocol enters my mind. She looks the part. I don't. Liam squeezes my hand, sensing the impending blow as well. My head starts to pound, utter exhaustion fills my body. I cannot face this news today.

"But," King William continues, "they are not the only important qualities. Kindness and faithfulness are equally vital. And it has come to my attention these past few weeks that Jocelyn possesses neither of these. So this morning, Queen Helen informed her she is no longer considered an appropriate match for Prince Liam. She has chosen to return home to Prescott and packs her belongings as we speak."

The statement is so unexpected, it is met with stunned silence. Liam and I gape at him, then face each other, our hold on each other's hands relaxing. After a moment, Liam asks, "What changed your mind?"

"Her heartless comments and behavior, particularly directed at Olivia, drew my attention more than once. The last straw was yesterday when she was far more concerned with the condition of her shoes than with Niobe."

Queen Helen smiles triumphantly at me, her prediction fulfilled. She not only kept faith in Niobe, she kept in her husband as well. Her green eyes glow with happiness.

"Well," Liam sighs, "I am glad you finally realized she is not the match for me. I am quite confident she would have made us all miserable."

"That she would have," agrees the queen.

"In my speech today, I will announce June fifteenth as the wedding day for Harold and Emily. The kingdom needs something positive to focus on for a while."

I wonder how the elder Crawford sister reacted to her sister's failure. While she is the less caustic of the two, it will be awkward around her from now on.

"Now, as for the two of you," King William says pointedly and Liam tightens his grip on my hand, "I am willing to let a courtship progress. If, at the time of the royal wedding, we all agree it is warranted, I will announce your engagement."

Liam jumps up, circles the table and embraces his parents. "Thank you, Father."

Still stunned, I only manage to stand and smile. It is like a dream and I fear any word from me will break the spell. Queen Helen walks around the table and hugs me. We pull apart and smile broadly at each other.

"Oh, and one more thing, Olivia," King William says. "You will continue to perform Niobe's work. It is a valuable service and an honorable endeavor for a future princess. By the grace of all which is good, Niobe will recover and finish training you in her work. It is time she passed on her extensive knowledge to someone."

"Thank you, Your Majesty. I am truly humbled by all of this."

"Very good. Now if you will excuse me, I must prepare for today's speech."

Liam hugs him again while I drop into a low curtsey. When I rise, the queen folds me into another warm embrace. Then King William steps over, places his hands on my shoulders and kisses my forehead. They open the door, the guards outside springing to attention, and are gone.

For a long moment, Liam and I stare at each other, then we laugh. It starts as a soft giggle, a sound of disbelief, but soon it is a full-hearted chuckle and we fall into each other's arms. He pulls back and takes my face into his hands. Gently, he leans in to kiss me, our mouths together in a long, lingering way. The world reduces to just this room, just the two of us. My heart overflows with joy, a huge burden lifted from it.

"Well, that was unexpected," Liam states when we part.

"It certainly was, in the best possible way," I agree. "Not only do we get each other, but I get to perform work I enjoy that provides a meaningful service to the kingdom. There may be a place where I fit in here after all."

Liam smiles and strokes my cheek. "I'm so happy you have found your niche here. The work comes so naturally to you."

"And there is still so much Niobe has to teach me, if…" The words die on my lips. My happiness dims at the thought of the healer lying in the infirmary, fighting for her life.

The prince embraces me when he sees my face cloud. "Go sit with her for a while. I will pick you up in your room just before noon so we can go to the speech together. I want you up on the dais next to me."

"All right. I will feel better if I can see her for a bit."

He walks me out the door and we share one last parting kiss.

Back down in the infirmary, a new woman mans the desk. When I tell her why I am there, she points towards Niobe's bed. "She is in and out of consciousness, but she has been asking for you."

Eagerly, I stride to the bedside. The healer's eyes are closed, but there is much more color in her cheeks. The poultice is still wrapped in place, its pungent smell not lessened any. A piece of hair lies across her cheek and I softly brush it away with my fingers. Her eyelids flutter, then open. She focuses on my face, then says in barely a whisper, "Hello, child."

Overjoyed, I lean down and kiss her cheek. She manages a weak smile. Her lips try to move again, but the effort is too great.

"Don't talk." I pat her hand soothingly. "What you did was so brave, Niobe."

A satisfied smile crosses her face and I know in her heart, the king is still the little orphaned boy she vowed to protect—protect enough to give up her own life. She shifts slightly, wincing at the pain in her side, and the smile fades.

"I have wonderful news. King William asked me to be your permanent assistant. You will get to teach me all your tricks." Her whole countenance brightens at this. "So you need to rest and recover fully because I plan on being a very pesky student."

"And…a pesky princess too…no doubt," she utters, mischief filling her eyes.

How she already knows my other news, I cannot guess. But that is Niobe for you. Her teasing gives me hope she is on the path of healing. She drifts into a peaceful sleep. For a while, I sit, content to hold her hand. About an hour later, I take my leave with one last glance at her slumbering form. Love fills my heart and I send up a silent prayer for her full recovery.

Sadie waits in my room, a beautiful saffron-colored dress laid out for me. She helps me into my corset, pulling the strings tautly against my back. I will never love dressing formally, but for Liam I will learn to tolerate it. The dress slips over my head and my handmaid painstakingly buttons up the back. When she finally finishes, I sit at the vanity and she fixes my hair. Now all grown in, the handmaid has more choices when styling it. Soon she is at work on a complicated updo. Hopefully they will not expect me to dress this way every day when I am a princess.

The door bursts open. Anne rushes in, Kat on her heels, and they both start speaking at once, a cacophony of phrases. We stare at them while they spew unintelligible words. Sadie has stopped mid-brushstroke, a hairpin dangling from her lip.

"We saw-"

"Heard the queen talked to her-"

"Packing up trunks-"

"One at a time, please," I order.

Anne takes a deep breath and straightens her turquoise gown, then shuts the door. Her hair sits atop her head in an intricate bun. I cannot help but admire how beautiful she is, even in this excited state. Kat looks radiant in a dress of lavender, her golden hair pinned up in loose curls.

"We just saw Madame le Clare and she was supervising the moving of trunks out of the Crawfords' room. Camille told us Jocelyn is leaving."

"Yes," Kat bursts in, unable to stay quiet another second. "Rumor has it the queen told her to leave."

"Well, that is not exactly what happened," I say.

Their faces change from the excitement of revealing a secret to confusion. Sadie's eyes are round as saucers.

"Wait…you know what's going on?" Anne demands.

"According to the queen, Jocelyn was informed this morning she was no longer considered an appropriate match for Liam. She decided to go home when she found out." Their chins hang open, so I add, "Then King William told Liam he could publically court me."

A few seconds of silence pass while they process this information. Suddenly, both of them rush to me, squealing and shouting. We all embrace, even Sadie, in one big tangle of arms. When we finish our celebration, I blurt out the whole tale for them. Anne and Kat jump with excitement, while my handmaid tries to salvage my hair, which fell out during the hug. Just as she sticks in the last pin, there is a knock on the door.

My sister opens it and Liam enters. To say he looks handsome is an understatement. He wears his military uniform, a black jacket trimmed with red sashes. His silky, ebony hair is combed off his face, falling in loose waves around his collar. And those eyes, the bluest I have ever seen, sparkle like water in the sun. All four of us curtsey, though we giggle like schoolgirls. Liam merely smiles and holds out his hand to me.

"We will see you ladies down at the speech." He inclines his head to them and we stroll out of the room.

Passing down the staircase, he guides me toward the Main Hall. At an intersection of corridors, we find ourselves face to face with the Crawford sisters. Jocelyn's face is tearstained, eyes red and swollen, but Emily's is etched with anger. She glares at us, an incensed snake waiting to strike.

"Jocelyn," Liam says, "I wish you well back in Prescott."

She does not even look at him. There are no words, not even a curtsey, before she storms off. Her sister folds her arms across her chest, her eyes flicking between the two of us. "You think you have won, but we will see what the future holds." She drops into an exaggerated curtsey, then slithers away.

"What is that supposed to mean?" I ask, once she is out of earshot.

"Nothing. She is just angry right now. Believe me, once she starts planning her wedding, her sister's woes will be forgotten."

"True. It will give her an opportunity to focus on her favorite subject—herself. That should be loads of fun," I reply. "But we still have to deal with her today."

He takes my hand again and we continue on our way. Courtiers pass us, bowing at the prince. I notice a few lingering stares at our clasped hands. Of course, the court all knows about our desire to be a couple and about the possibility of Liam winding up with Jocelyn instead. Gossip such as this moves with lightning speed through the court, people always looking for a new tidbit to share.

"Today is supposed to be a happy occasion," Liam states. "A wedding date announcement, Niobe being lauded a hero, the threat to the king is over."

"Is it though?" I question. It bothers me that Lord Otto had inside help. The accomplices are still out there and we never found out the identity of the mysterious 'she.' "We still don't understand what Otto's motive was or who helped him."

"I don't know if we ever will. Likely he bribed the right people, but whoever helped him knows the game is up," Liam says. "Besides, if you are going to be part of the royal family, you have to accept threats to our lives as an unpleasant, but not unexpected occurrence. It's all part of the fun." He winks in an effort to allay my concerns.

"I can't wait," I mutter.

"Well, I can't wait to have you by my side forever."

He stops and turns me to him, then kisses me firmly. Several courtiers stop to gawk, some even point, whispering to each other behind their hands. I can hear the rumor mill begin to churn. But I suppose this is just one more thing I need to accept if I am to be Liam's bride.

We reach the doors the royal family use to enter the Main Hall at the head of the room. Guards stand ready to pull them open.

"One second," I say, and pull Liam aside to straighten the lapel on his jacket. When I pat it into place, I say, "You look so handsome. I've not seen you in this uniform since the day of the Lindenwood ceremony last fall."

A day I had my dreams of becoming a knight shattered. Instead, I was sent to live here at the palace, a place I had no desire to be. Now it is the only place I can imagine for my future. The old picture of how I thought my life would be is like a child's dream, one I have outgrown. This most unexpected path has led me exactly where I was meant to be.

"A lot has happened since that day, hasn't it?" Liam smiles and leans closer to me.

"Yes, though it was a rough start."

"Well, my love," he says, "we made it through together, just as we will for the rest of our lives."

"Together," I echo, our cheeks pressed close. Wrapped in his embrace, I finally know I am home.

We part and clasp hands. Liam nods at the guards, who bow, then open the doors for us. The Main Hall stands before us, filled to capacity, the royal family already assembling on the dais. With the eyes of the court upon us, we walk as one into our future.

About the Author

Jane McGarry cannot remember a time she did not love reading and this progressed into a passion for writing. She lives in New Jersey in a house full of boys including one over-indulged cat. In her rare quiet moments, she can be found curled up with said cat and a good book. You can visit her online at janemcgarrybooks.com.

Clean Reads
GREAT STORIES. NO GUILT.
www.cleanreads.com

www.ingramcontent.com/pod-product-compliance
Lightning Source LLC
Chambersburg PA
CBHW061640190726
48289CB00006B/1687